Forever Home

WHERE FAMILY
COMES FIRST

ANGELA HARTLEY

This book is a work of fiction. Names, places, characters and events are all based on the author's imagination or are used fictitiously. Any resemblance to actual persons, living or dead, or actual events is purely coincidental.

ISBN: 9798352286197

Cover design by Aubrey Labitigan Jai Design

Forever Home

WHERE FAMILY
COMES FIRST

By the Author of Finding Home

Thanks again go to my family and friends who have helped me along the way and encouraged me to write this sequel to Finding Home.
It was great to revisit the characters, as well as developing some new ones, who I hope you will enjoy getting to know.
I also hope you love this story as much as you did the first.

For Barry, my own Forever Home.

Chapter 1

June 2021

It was Friday morning and already nearly eleven o'clock, the sun was high in the sky, temperatures were set to soar and the day promised to be glorious, but already Amanda was starting to get a bit heated under the collar, even though her long blonde hair had been neatly tied up in a clip to keep it off her neck. For a mid-June day, it was too warm for her liking and although technically she was off work, she had a busy day scheduled. Unless she got the girls moving quickly, it was all going to get very difficult; no doubt made worse because the roads would be heaving with increased holiday traffic, people trying to escape early for their long weekends away, motorhomes trailing motorhomes, congesting the narrow country lanes and creating no end of tailbacks. One of the joys of living in the prettiest parts of England, Amanda thought to herself sardonically.

'Come on Maisie, Alice – I can't wait all day for you two to get ready,' she shouted from the foot of the stairs waiting for her daughters to appear. Their overnight bags were already packed at her feet, ready to be thrown into the back of the car, along with an assortment of coats, shoes, wellies and toys that were travelling with them 'just in case'. 'Grandma and Rob have a fun afternoon planned, and unless you both get your skates on, they'll be going without you!' she added in exasperation, gently tapping her foot whilst she waited, noticing that perhaps the bright red nail varnish on her toes peeping out of her sandals needed touching up when she got a minute.

They had only gone up to their bedroom to collect a teddy bear each, one they apparently could not do without for their sleepover, but by the sounds of the commotion they were creating upstairs, every cupboard and drawer was being opened and slammed shut in search of whatever it was they needed.

'Mummy, we're coming – stop fretting!' said Maisie as they emerged from their bedroom door, displaying an attitude that belied the fact she was not yet seven years old, and speaking with the confidence of a teenager twice her age. Having nearly completed her second year at primary school, she now acted like she had the answers to all of life's questions at her fingertips, and with Alice starting school in September, Amanda was beginning to wonder what life would be like with two little divas in the house. Heaven forbid!

Eventually, the two came down the stairs, each dressed in a matching pretty summer dress and cardigan, with co-ordinating frilly socks, teamed with in Maisie's case pink sandals and in Alice's blue sandals. Both wore their hair in pony tails with sparkly ribbons tied in a neat bow. Whilst they were definitely individuals, they loved to dress in similar clothes, with Maisie often taking the lead when deciding each morning what to wear, and Alice falling in agreeing to anything her big sister said.

'Finally, I thought I was going without you! Come on now, pick up your bags and we'll get off,' said Amanda more sternly than she intended as she ushered them out of the door, picking her water bottle up as she slammed the door behind her and led them towards her car, parked on the double-width driveway alongside the house. Parking in the village had recently become a premium following the ever-increasing number of new houses that were being built, bringing with them extra shops and amenities, all seeming to have sprung up from nowhere. Having private parking was a godsend.

She had recently treated herself to a new five-door Audi A3 Sportback; leaving Damian to enjoy their trusty, reliable Volkswagen estate for his regular commutes into his office in Cirencester. He had stopped using the train as often, claiming the car gave him more freedom to come and go as he pleased, leaving Amanda to need a new car after her old one had finally given up the ghost. She loved the feeling of fun the Audi gave her whilst she cruised down the country roads nipping around doing her errands, with the added ability to just put her foot down if she needed to pass the occasional tractor or caravan that stood in her way. The Volkswagen was a good family car that had served them well, but it just did not have the same umph, or if she was honest, glamour. Sitting now behind the wheel, in her cut-off denims, a stripy cropped top and Ray-Bans she felt pretty cool!

'Right, seat belts on and we'll get going,' she checked behind her as she carefully reversed the car out of the drive and headed towards her mum and Rob's house. The drive should only take around ten minutes, but Amanda expected it could take much longer today given the weather; thankful she had built a bit of contingency into her planning.

Her mum, Monica, and Rob had bought an apartment in an old converted property on the main dual carriageway just outside the village, heading towards Bristol. They had moved into it a couple of years ago shortly after their marriage, and had spent both time and money getting it to a standard that they could each feel comfortable living with. Monica had been brought up with a very traditional British sense of fashion and décor, surrounded by antiques and family heirlooms handed down through Ken, her late husband's family, whereas Rob's tastes were much more contemporary and American in design, leaning heavily on the New England and nautical trends and colours from his home state. They had tried to marry the two extremes, with perhaps not the best outcome as yet, but it was early days and they were still very much in the honeymoon period of finding out more about each other's tastes and preferences. Amanda was aware a lot of compromise had been required from both of them, but that was surely part of what they had both signed up to, wasn't it?

At first it had felt a little uncomfortable for Amanda, and if she was honest perhaps a touch disloyal to her dad Ken, when she was around her mum and Rob. She witnessed their obvious joy at being together, with her mum, perhaps laughing and having fun in a way she had never witnessed with her dad when he was alive, even though she knew they had enjoyed a long and happy marriage. Being with Rob had definitely brought a different aspect of Monica's personality out; a much younger, vibrant side of her that had perhaps laid dormant for many years.

Ken, her dad had now been dead for just over three years, and although Amanda knew he would be happy for her mum to be getting on with her life, she often wondered whether he could have ever foretold that by leaving Amanda with the secret on his death bed that he was not her biological father, even asking her to seek him out, that by doing so his widow Monica, would fall in love with her one-time fling and his daughter's biological father, get married and live happily ever after. It all sounded a bit farfetched and surreal, with possibly a touch of karma thrown in, but with each passing day it began to feel more 'normal' to everyone.

As she pulled up outside the converted property within which Monica and Rob's luxury apartment was situated, she was pleased to see them already sitting at one of the wooden tables on the lawned area to the side of the property, enjoying what looked like a pot of tea and a plate of sandwiches with another couple, all chatting away under an umbrella protecting them from the sunshine. As Amanda smiled and waved over to them, she recognised them as neighbours of Rob and Monica's, their apartment being on the floor below, but could not for the life of her put a name to them. It would come to her no doubt later when she was least expecting it.

One of the advantages of the type of living Monica and Rob had bought into, was that they were never alone if they needed company, but equally they had as much privacy as they wanted. Their apartment was fully self-contained, but with all the benefits of beautiful and private communal areas, managed and maintained by someone else. No grass to cut or gardening to be done, unless you wanted to volunteer to do some that is, and best of all no maintenance required if the gutters started to overflow, or worse still the toilets got blocked. There was a resident odd job man on site, plus a maintenance company employed to deal with all the more technical or demanding tasks, which was invaluable to Rob and Monica given they spent long periods away from the property. Having the ability to simply leave it secured and managed was essential for them.

'Hi there, you all look like you're enjoying the sunshine,' smiled Amanda to the group as she went over to kiss both Rob and Monica, just moments before the girls launched themselves at them, desperate not to miss out on kisses and cuddles from their grandparents. Both Maisie and Alice had accepted Rob unconditionally as their grandad, and Rob in return continually looked like the cat that had got the cream whenever his 'girls' were around, Amanda included in that.

'Are you sure you're still okay to have them stay over? It's just I hadn't realised that today was an inset day at school, or that Damian would be away again, but if it's a problem I can change my plans for this evening and come back for them before bedtime,' said Amanda as she unloaded the car and put enough bags down to suggest they were staying a fortnight, not just a couple of nights.

'No, we're fine to have them. We've been really looking forward to seeing them again. In fact, we've got a surprise in store for later, and we might even order in some pizza for tea tonight,' said Monica, smiling down at her granddaughters as they attached themselves to both her and Rob like a pair of limpets, adding 'and tomorrow if they are good, then I think we'll head to the seaside if this weather holds, and get an ice-cream or some chips.' As the girls jumped up and down at the suggestion, it was clear to see that there was an awful lot of mutual love going on, and if anything, they were both anxious for their mum to leave so their fun could start.

'You go, Mum, we'll be fine, won't we Alice?' said Maisie turning to Rob, 'Grandad, can we go fishing again, please, please?' she added. Rob had taken them to the old pond in the grounds of the house last time they had visited, buying them each a net and a bucket to catch some of the wildlife; small fishes and tadpoles that inhabited the murky water. Becoming not just a dad, but a grandad too when he discovered Amanda was his biological daughter, was a dream come true for him, and he now played both roles with relish. Added to that, the happiness he felt after marrying Monica was beyond words. His health was also in a much better place after he had received his kidney transplant, so with all things considered he could not imagine a happier or luckier man on God's earth than himself.

'And Grandma can make us some eggy sandwiches again' added Alice, remembering the picnic Monica had made last time, not wanting to be outdone by her sister.

'I'm sure we can,' laughed Monica at the memory of the picnic, 'but now give your mum a big kiss so she can get off, and then we can go and get ourselves sorted. You'll see her again on Sunday,' she added, taking each girl by the hand and leaving Rob to pick up their bags.

'We'll bring them back in time for lunch, and we can either eat at yours or I'll treat us all to lunch at the pub – whichever's easier for you. I do like the Sunday lunch at the King's Head though,' Rob added. Although not yet considered a regular at the pub where Ken and Grandad Tom had spent many a night playing dominoes or darts in their youth, he did enjoy the atmosphere of a traditional British pub. It was not something he was used to living in America. The locals had taken a little time to adjust to seeing him with Monica after so many years of seeing her with 'their old mate Ken', but they had at least made him welcome, although so far Rob had not been invited onto the dominoes team, so there was obviously still some way to go to win them over!

'Thanks, that's perfect. You're both a godsend. I don't know what I'd do without either of you,' said Amanda, adding before she forgot, 'I'll let you know about lunch on Sunday, either way suits me,' whilst blowing kisses in their general direction as she carefully reversed the car, desperate to make a quick exit before anyone changed their minds.

Chapter 2

Five minutes after dropping the girls off with her mum, Amanda indicated right and drove into the Willow Tree retirement village, less than a mile from where Monica and Rob now lived. She parked in her usual spot, thankfully in the shade of one of the old willow trees that gave the village its name, meaning the vehicle would be cool when she returned. She took the box of provisions she had bought for her grandad out of the boot of the car and headed towards the old house.

Willow Tree was one of those modern, purpose-built communities for the elderly, with all the facilities they would need, either on-site or close at hand. The village comprised a series of linked bungalows for independent living, plus a larger property where residents had their own bedrooms, bathrooms and sitting rooms, but opted to eat in the communal dining room. There was also a small convenience store, a bar-cum restaurant that served snacks and a hair salon that did both men's and women's hair, with pensioner rates available daily! The village was accessible by public transport, with a bus stop conveniently positioned just outside the gates to make visiting easier, but it also operated its own private mini-bus service that could regularly be seen ferrying residents around town should they need to go further afield, or even out on day trips to see something specific, or perhaps to the seaside for some of the more adventurous residents.

Grandad Tom had moved himself into the village over twelve months ago, opting to go there for several reasons, but principally he said because the bar did a good draught ale and he knew they held a regular dominoes night. More seriously though, at eighty-six he was not getting any younger. He had lived alone in his cottage for nearly twenty years after his wife Jessie's death, managing not only to look after himself, but to enjoy a healthy social life in the village too. Recently though most of his friends had moved away, one way or another, leaving him to realise that he not only needed to move too, but importantly it was time for him to get his affairs in order.

His decision had been cemented shortly after he experienced a minor accident in his car. He had been driving home from the supermarket after doing his weekly shopping, when a small dog darted out in front of him, escaping from a house's driveway, straight into the road and the oncoming traffic. Tom reacted, but not soon enough to avoid hitting the dog, causing it to need to have its leg reset in a splint. Tom was mortified, but just thankful it had not been a child that he had hit, or that he had caused any more serious damage to the dog or anyone's property.

He lost his confidence in driving thereafter, and the more he pondered the accident itself, the more he realised that over the previous months he had struggled to do an increasing number of the things he once loved, that until this point, he had taken for granted. He had noticed his reactions were not as sharp as they had been; his hearing meant he often missed the phone or the doorbell ringing given his television was set on maximum volume, and lifting and carrying hot pans or boiling water was something he avoided doing in case he tripped or scalded himself. Old age was creeping up on him, there was no doubt about that. No, the village was the best of both worlds, providing the safety and security he wanted, but with the independence and companionship he craved, plus a lot more besides, all just on his doorstep.

Amanda climbed the flight of stairs and knocked on Tom's door. He was expecting her, so hopefully he would be in and not out gallivanting. Amanda was a frequent visitor, often bringing the girls to see their great-grandad, ensuring he had regular company and a healthy supply of his home comforts. His meals were all prepared for him, so no need for basic shopping, but she regularly dropped off cakes, biscuits and treats of a more alcoholic nature, for when he was staying in and not venturing down to the bar or lounge area to meet his many friends.

'Hello Grandad, you're looking bright and breezy today,' observed Amanda, smiling and straining to stifle a giggle when Tom opened the door, wearing an old Hawaiian shirt, a pair of navy shorts, with a straw hat that had seen better days, plus open toe sandals teamed with red socks that went almost to his knees. He looked a pretty picture. 'You're all glammed up. Are you off out?' she added as she made her way into the apartment, closing the door behind her with her foot.

'Yes, we're having a BBQ in the gardens this afternoon, so I thought I'd get into the spirit and make a bit of an effort. It's quite warm today, isn't it? When I called into the shop to get my newspaper earlier this morning, it was already getting warm, so out came the shorts. Not bad legs if I say so myself,' he laughed to himself, patting his thighs.

Amanda smiled in return. 'Well, I'll not stay too long then, but I've brought you the whiskey you wanted, plus some of your favourite biscuits – chocolate digestives and of course your custard creams, plus I've even brought you some of the cakes Maisie and Alice baked yesterday. I did supervise them, so they shouldn't kill you, but feel free to bin them when I've gone if they don't look too appetising!'

Tom started to unpack the box Amanda had placed on the table in front of him, pleased to see it contained all the items he had run out of, as well as the extra treats she had added. He was so lucky to have such a thoughtful granddaughter.

'Have you time for a cup of tea before you go, and we can try the cakes together – that way I'll know you're not trying to poison me?' he laughed.

'Sounds perfect, why don't you sit down and I'll put the kettle on,' suggested Amanda, happy to sit for a while and chat with her grandad. She always enjoyed her visits to the village, and particularly over the last couple of years since Monica had been frequently to-ing and fro-ing across the Atlantic with Rob, she had become her grandad's main point of contact. Tom was a great storyteller, and if he was honest loved a bit of gossip, so he regularly recounted tales of what the other 'inmates' as he called his fellow residents got up to, often embellishing their exploits if it added to the overall story, leaving her not only laughing, but happy that he seemed so contented and settled.

Amanda had made an effort to get to know the people who were in charge at the village, ostensibly now 'caring' for her grandad, and had even met a few of the characters he played dominoes or shared a pint with, as these people now played an important part in his life. Such was her involvement, that it was now her the village manager contacted if Tom needed anything specific, or they had any concerns over his health; she who had de-facto become his next of kin, even taking over the management of his finances now he had moved into the village.

As part of putting his affairs in order, Tom had asked Amanda to take over a power of attorney for him in case, in his words, he ever went 'ga-ga' and could not deal with things himself, or make important decisions about his health. He was still relatively spritely, but you never know 'what's going to pack up first' was his mentality. Having seen a few of his friends develop dementia, or have strokes or heart conditions that seemed to come from nowhere and invade the body without warning, he knew that although today he still had his marbles and most of his faculties, that might not always be the case.

He had also updated his will, transferred the cottage into Amanda's name and sold off what remaining shares he had, effectively clearing the decks, ensuring that once he did go, there would be no doubt about his wishes, or more importantly any arguments within the family over his money. Not that there was likely to be any, as he was the last man standing as far as the Moreton name was concerned, and who would want to argue about the small amount he had left anyway?

Amanda was very well-settled financially. She not only had what Ken had left her in terms of money, but also the impressive Georgian townhouse she now lived in with Damian and the girls that she had inherited from the family estate. This would continue to be held in trust for her daughters, plus she now had Tom's cottage and her share of the property that she and Damian had previously lived in, but now rented out to tenants. On top of all that, she had a good career ahead of her that paid a decent salary, so overall she was more than financially independent.

Monica, his daughter-in-law and his son's widow, was equally well provided for. Having remarried to Rob, who was by anyone's standards a very wealthy man, she had no need or desire for anything. Rob had, when they married, put their property in England in Monica's name, thereby ensuring her financial security, and with the lump sum she had received from Ken's pension when he died, whatever happened she would always be provided for. No, he was lucky that none of his nearest and dearest had anything to worry about on that score, and provided they laid him to rest in the family plot with his Jessie whenever the time arrived, they could do whatever they liked with what he was leaving behind.

Chapter 3

After spending a good hour with her grandad, mainly listening to him chattering on, updating her with all his gossip from the previous week, peppered with some of the old tales he repeatedly told each visit, plus the occasional new one, she escorted him downstairs to join the rest of the residents at their summer BBQ. Although there was a lift, he still felt able to take the stairs, which in itself was a blessing, although Amanda did notice he held more tightly onto the rail as he descended, ever mindful of his step.

A few of Tom's closer friends were already assembled in the garden, equally attired in their summer best, waiting for the festivities to commence, along with a couple of older ladies that she did not recognise, also suitably dressed in their best summer frocks and bonnets. Amanda waved over in greeting, before giving Grandad Tom a kiss and a hug, promising to come again soon. She walked over to her car, glad again she had parked it in the shade, put the key in the ignition, checked her mirrors for any wandering pensioners, before starting off on the next leg of her hectic day.

After leaving the relative tranquillity of the Willow Tree village, Amanda turned left to join the mounting traffic that was not unexpected at this time of day. Living in the Cotswolds had many an advantage, but as far as traffic was concerned, it was a nightmare.

Beautiful tourist hotspots such as Oxford, Bristol and Bath, to name but a few, were all within easy commute, as were the roads to Devon, Cornwall and the south coast, which collectively attracted no end of motorhomes, caravans and coaches that collectively snarled up the small country roads throughout the duration of the holiday months.

Looking at her watch, and as a result of her careful planning, she knew she still had enough time to comfortably get to the airport; if she headed east along the M4 Motorway, thereby avoiding the minor roads as much as possible, she should get to Heathrow Airport within ninety minutes or so, which was perfect timing to meet Maria's flight as planned. The plane should be arriving around six o'clock that evening, so there may even be enough time to get a coffee and a spot of something to eat en route if she successfully avoided the caravans and motorhomes.

Tuning the radio into one of the Smooth stations, she relaxed into the journey, happily singing along to tunes she knew and enjoyed. She allowed her mind to wander to the weekend ahead of her, smiling at the thought of having the chance to kick her shoes off and relax, enjoying a glass or two with her friend, without the pressures of work or kids to worry about for two whole days.

Chapter 4

Over the last two years, Amanda and Maria had struck up an unlikely, but exceedingly close friendship. They spent many an hour chatting on the phone, or in person whenever Amanda travelled over to Boston, covering some of the most trivial of things, from children, to schools, to work, to family; but regardless of the topic, their views, and more importantly their values were very much aligned. They both seemed to be on a similar wave length, despite there being perhaps fifteen to twenty years between them. Amanda had never asked Maria directly how old she was, but presumed she was somewhere in her mid-fifties, whereas Amanda was still in her thirties, albeit only just.

They had first met at Monica and Rob's marriage, where Will, as one of Rob's oldest friends and best man for that occasion, had brought Maria along as his 'plus one', taking the risk of introducing her into quite a diverse family gathering in the midst of a wedding celebration. At the time, Will and Maria had only been dating for a matter of months, with Maria admitting later that she had been rather nervous about what she termed her 'baptism of fire', likening it to being thrown to the wolves. But her fears were misplaced as everyone warmed to her immediately, instantly seeing the positive and stabilising effect she was having on Will. Over the last two years, not only had their relationship blossomed, but it had got to the stage where people now wondered what their own lives would be like without Maria in them. She was definitely a force for good, with the future for her and Will looking promising.

Will and Maria had each been divorced long before they met one another, with both suffering the messy consequences a separation brings; going through a series of tough years before finally reaching a point where they felt able to start to rebuild their lives. For each other, their timing had been perfect.

For Will, as a successful local business man, his divorce played out in the public eye, meaning it not only bruised his ego, but it significantly hit his bank balance. Thankfully, his company, that designed and manufactured leisurewear, was strong enough to withstand the storm, so with hard work, dedication and a steely focus, he was able to eventually pull himself through it. At the time it had been at the expense of everything else; his social life became non-existent, and the passion he had once felt for the business sustained a massive blow. It took meeting Maria to fully appreciate he could not continue as he was for much longer; simply existing, not living. Something within his work life dynamic sorely needed to change if he was to find happiness.

For Maria, abandoned in her early thirties with two young children to bring up by herself, the impacts of her divorce, or more specifically her ex-husband's desertion, had been deeply felt on both her financial and physical health. She had been forced to go out to work to earn a living, sufficient to bring up both children and keep her own head above water. Custody of the children had not been contested, which only left her feeling it was not just her that had been abandoned, but her children too. Dating had not been high on her agenda for many years; merely survival and keeping her children fed and out of trouble sapped any energy or enthusiasm she had at the end of the day.

Meeting when and how they did was nothing short of miraculous, almost destiny, with Maria thanking her lucky stars each and every day for venturing down that particular frozen food aisle at the exact same time Will was aimlessly looking for something quick and easy to put in the microwave for own his dinner. Just think where her life would be if that evening, she had fancied a curry rather than a pizza!

From that chance meeting, a friendship soon developed, which with time built into a romance, and then over the last two years had further matured into a relationship that neither Maria nor Will was prepared to risk, agreeing to move in together in Will's apartment over recent months. No, it felt right, and both were experienced enough to know that in matters of the heart, second chances like theirs, particularly at their time of life did not come around too often. This knowledge made everything more precious.

Amanda spotted Maria as soon as she walked into the Arrivals Hall at Heathrow's Terminal 3, but with all the chaos and confusion of bodies scooting around the concourse trying to locate their loved ones, it was clear that her friend had not yet seen her. The flight from Boston had been delayed thirty minutes, resulting in an increased number of people hanging around the Arrivals Hall awaiting the latecomers.

'Maria, Maria, I'm over here,' shouted Amanda, desperately waving to attract her friend's attention. She had considered doing a wolf whistle, as Lisa her best friend had taught her many years ago, but did not think under the circumstances it was either appropriate or particularly dignified. Eventually the crowds thinned and Maria spotted her and waved back.

Maria looked a little flustered, which was most unlike her, but Amanda knew that even though her friend had travelled to England perhaps three or four times in the last couple of years, previously she had always had Will at her side to guide her through the airport and deal with all the formalities. This was her first solo trip, and having spoken to Maria two nights ago, Amanda knew she was a little anxious, hence why she had arranged her day to be here to meet her, and then transport her back to her house. They were planning a girly weekend and a long outstanding catch-up, involving more than the odd glass or two of prosecco, she presumed.

Maria was staying at Amanda's home until Monday, before catching the early morning train into the centre of London to attend an education conference for four days, flying home on Friday evening. Amanda knew her friend had mixed feelings about the conference too; happy to be invited to what was a global initiative, geared towards exchanging and developing strategies for dealing with both gifted children and children with special needs, but also more than a bit anxious as she had been requested to lead one of the syndicate groups, delivering a presentation on the topic. Maria, as principal of one of the major high schools in Boston had received plaudits for the school's approach to dealing with both gifted and special needs children, so she and her colleagues had a wealth of experience to share, but speaking in front of such an audience was something she was neither accustomed nor looking forward to doing. Amanda sensed that once she took the podium, the nerves would evaporate and she would smash it. Having got to know Maria quite closely over the last couple of years, it was clear to see she oozed sincerity, apart from being one of the most inspirational people she knew.

Walking alongside Maria was a young lady who Amanda immediately recognised from her photo as

Rachel, the daughter of one of Maria's oldest friends in Boston. Rachel was a slightly built twenty-three-year-old, wearing black jeans and a faded red hoodie, with what looked like a football logo on the front of the sweatshirt, carrying an oversized rucksack on her back and dragging a suitcase, that not only looked like it had seen better days, but was big enough for her to hide herself in.

As they reached Amanda, Maria immediately gave her friend a hug. 'That was a long flight! Sorry we're delayed, but something to do with a mechanical hiccup before we took off apparently. Thankfully there was an engineer who could sort it, or the flight would have been grounded and we'd have had to catch tomorrow's flight,' she explained, a little out of breath.

'Don't worry. I managed to get a coffee and catch up on a few emails, so no harm done. At least you're here now, that's the main thing,' replied Amanda, reassuring her friend.

'Sorry, let me introduce Rachel. Rachel, this is Amanda,' added Maria, suddenly realising Rachel was standing next to her, probably feeling a bit like a spare part.

'Hello Rachel, welcome to England. It looks like you've come prepared if the size of that suitcase is anything to go by. Do you want me to drag it for you to the car?'

'Thank you, but I'll be okay' whispered Rachel, suddenly feeling quite self-conscious meeting Amanda for the first time. They had spoken over the phone a couple of times, but now meeting her face--to-face in a foreign country, she had no idea what to say or what was happening next. She had never flown before, and it was her first time outside of the States, so everything was not just a big adventure, but a little intimidating also.

'Well, let's get on our way then. The car's just a few minutes' walk away, so if you both want to follow me,' indicated Amanda, feeling a bit like a tour guide as she pointed to the lift that would take them to the short stay car-park, before adding to Rachel, 'I'm so glad you're finally here, and I'm so looking forward to getting to know you. I think we're going to get on famously,' smiling at her, trying to put the young girl at ease.

'I hope so too,' smiled Rachel weakly in return, as she followed in the wake of the two women, who she could hear busily chatting away already as if she was not there.

'I didn't know whether Damian or the girls would have come with you to pick us up; is everyone okay, I can't wait to see Maisie and Alice again?' enquired Maria as they waited for the lift to arrive. The Arrivals Hall was clearing slowly, but there was still a small queue waiting patiently for the lift doors to open, most looking as tired as Maria and Rachel after their own journeys.

'No, I've dropped the girls off with Mum and Rob. They're going to stay there for a couple of nights and we'll see them on Sunday. I don't know who was more desperate to see the back of me,' she laughed, adding 'I'm not sure if you'll see Damian this weekend. He's been staying at the flat a few nights most weeks recently, in fact, I'm not sure to be honest what his plans are at the moment,' before qualifying in an attempt to defend her husband, 'I think with you coming over, he might be planning on giving us some space for a proper catch-up, and he did mention something about one of his friends' fortieth birthday this weekend, perhaps going out for a few beers, so who knows.'

Although she had tried to defend her husband, not wanting to spark questions in front of either Maria or Rachel, if Amanda was truly honest with herself, if no one else, she had to admit she really did not know what his plans were at the moment, on so many different levels!

Chapter 5

3 months earlier

'What do you mean, you're staying at the flat three nights this week? I thought we'd agreed you were managing your work more from home wherever possible, only going into the office on Wednesdays and Thursdays?' reacted Amanda, more than a little surprised, particularly given this was the first she had heard about it. Damian had just put on his jacket, picked up his laptop and was making for the door as he dropped it casually into the conversation, presumably not expecting it to land like the proverbial H-bomb.

It was Monday morning, the first day back to school for Maisie after the Easter holidays, and Alice was being dropped off at Susie's, her childminder as Amanda had some work she needed to concentrate on. Having family time together was a luxury they could not always manage, but over the Easter break they had both organised their diaries to take some well-deserved holiday time while the girls were at home. They had even hired a cottage for a week in Devon, planning to relax and enjoy the change of scenery, encouraging the girls to play on the beach and paddle in the rock pools. Their house was big, but with both of them working from home most of the time, occasionally it felt a little claustrophobic, so a change of atmosphere and routine was long overdue.

Amanda had presumed he was just putting his coat on to drop the girls off, before returning home so they could both concentrate on getting back into the swing of work after their short break. The house renovations the previous year had ensured each had their own space or 'office', meaning that although they were under the same roof, they generally did not get in each other's way. They would occasionally meet up for a coffee in the kitchen, or a sandwich for lunch as a bit of a distraction, but otherwise they kept themselves to themselves. Both were extremely busy, Damian with his IT and Communications business, and Amanda working for Will with her fashion designing. Sometimes it did feel like they were ships that passed in the night, but it did mean they were both on hand to help out with the girls should it be necessary. It seemed to be working well, or at least Amanda thought it did.

'Sorry, I thought I'd mentioned it last week. It's all got a bit chaotic in the office recently. You know I've had a couple of my managers handing in their notice after being headhunted by that new start-up company I was telling you about, and if I don't go in and show a presence, it could be mutiny among the others. I can't afford to lose anyone else, or let them lose focus. It's all getting a bit cut-throat at the moment, with morale at a pretty low level, so I'm sorry, but I need to be there.'

'Okay, if that's the case, but it's not going to be easy with the girls. I've got a deadline approaching too that I really need to focus on, and the time difference doesn't help as most of my team only comes awake as the girls are coming home!' As Amanda's work was predominantly supporting a team based just outside Boston in the States, the time difference had always been a challenge, but one that until now she had managed with Damian's support. He had done the bed and bath routine, leaving Amanda free to handover to her American colleagues before closing down for the evening.

Their relationship over the last couple of years had been on a bit of a roller-coaster ride by anyone's standards, but it had felt to Amanda that whilst they were on holiday in Devon, they had at least started to turn a bit of a corner; almost like it was not only the end of one chapter, but the start of another one and it had felt good. They had felt more relaxed and at ease with each other than they had for a long time.

Since his affair with Chloe had ended two and a half years ago, and Amanda had decided to forgive him and move on, their relationship had taken a while to rebuild, but with patience and trust on both sides, they had achieved it. Whilst Damian was shouldering most of the guilt, she had accepted some of the blame for all the angst that had been going on between them, understanding perhaps she may have pushed Damian away, inadvertently into Chloe's waiting arms. It had not been an easy time following not just her dad's death, but then discovering he was not her biological father, eventually tracking Rob down and getting to know him and her half-brothers, Ben and Lucas. What with that, and then her kidney donation to save Rob's life, it had been a challenging time to say the least. So, perhaps understandable that things had gone off the rails between her and Damian. They had each taken their eye off the ball as far as their relationship had been concerned, and paid a high price into the bargain.

Discovering she was pregnant again two years ago was cathartic, and in a way a visible demonstration of the circle of life; one life lost, another one created. But sadly, seven months into the pregnancy, and so close to the finish line, they lost their baby son; a son they had named Theo. He was stillborn. The image of their perfect baby boy, born asleep, being laid gently in his mother's arms haunted her memories. Although the medical teams did, and said, everything they could to reassure them, both the initial heartbreak and the continued ache over the subsequent seventeen months had been hard to bear. She thought about Theo constantly, the photo of her cradling him framed beside her bedside, with no words anyone expressed making it either right or acceptable; but nevertheless, she had to find the strength from somewhere to face the future and move on for the sake of their family.

Damian, she knew, had struggled equally with the loss of his son, grieving in a way that Amanda found harder still to witness; bottling up his emotions, afraid to voice his true feelings. Her attempts to reach out to him were often thwarted as he went deeper into his shell, on occasion blaming himself that this was perhaps payback for the hurt he had caused. This introversion, at a time when all Amanda wanted was answers and reassurance from those closest to her, was difficult to deal with. For a long while they tiptoed around the subject, each dealing with their grief as only they knew how; neither wanting to add further upset to the other, nor risk their own relationship by confronting the subject, both failing to provide the comfort the other so desperately needed. In those early days, with Damian unreachable, Amanda recalled relying heavily on Lisa and Clara for emotional support; telephone calls late into the evenings, countless tears shed, everyone knowing that nothing they said would change the situation. Eventually, with the support of some counselling, both Damian and Amanda found a way to deal with their loss, and importantly a way to express what it meant to each other. With each day, the pain lessened. It would never go away, but they had to find a way of learning to live with it; Theo would always be part of their family, their story.

Being in Devon, the girls had loved having both their parents around to spoil them, and Damian and Amanda had enjoyed the freedom to wander arm-in-arm along the beach, like any other happy couple, spending quality time with their children, paddling and fishing in the rock pools, building sand castles when the tide was out, even enjoying an ice-cream or two as they walked along the promenade. It had been a relaxed time, with lots of laughter and many happy moments that would undoubtedly create some good memories to help counter, if not completely dispel, the bad ones that would never go away for either of them.

‘So, is this going to be a more regular arrangement, or just a one off, because if it’s going to be regular, we’ll have to give some serious thought to how we’re going to manage, because I for one can’t go back to being the girls’ full-time carer on top of everything else,’ Amanda added with a mix of exasperation for herself, balanced with an element of support for her husband. She did not want Damian’s business to suffer, or worse still watch it go under, but at the same time she was enjoying her time; building a new career for herself, and she was not prepared to give that up at any cost.

When she had taught Art at the sixth-form college and their daughters had been babies, Monica and Ken had helped her out considerably; always being there to provide not just practical support, but more importantly the emotional and trusted support that only one’s parents can provide. Working at the college also meant that the regular school holidays had eased any childcare pressures, providing periods of time that Amanda could plan around; thereby allowing space to concentrate not just on their daughters, but on the many demands of running a household. By taking on the homemaker role, this left Damian the opportunity to focus on growing his business and securing their future. It had worked well, but childcare like everything needed to move with the times, and like it or not the realities were changing.

‘Well, it’s not getting any easier at work. We’re running at the moment to just stand still, so perhaps we might need to give some thought to getting extra help if your career is going to take off too, particularly now you seem to be travelling more than you used to.’ Amanda heard a tone in Damian's reply that she neither recognised, nor liked. It suggested he was not as supportive of her becoming a designer as she had previously assumed; or was it the working for Will, or the frequent travel it involved he objected to, she wondered? Had she taken his support for granted, and just presumed he was happy with her new direction?

Amanda accepted that as she got more experienced the travel demands were increasing, but if she was honest that was one of the elements of the role she relished. Travelling to some of the more remote parts of the world to meet fabric designers, buyers or suppliers, talking to people to understand what was selling and where trends were going all added to the excitement. She was working with professionals and learning so much, which had awakened in her a passion she was not prepared to miss out on. She was carving out a life for herself and becoming someone other than a wife, a mum, a daughter, and it felt good.

'Okay, I'll give it some thought then. I'm off to Boston again next week for three days, I hope you've remembered? Are you still alright having the girls, or shall I see if Mum and Rob are around?'

'It might be worth seeing if they're around if you don't mind. That way I can keep focussed on the business,' he replied effectively drawing a line under the conversation by adding, 'right you two, come on now, hurry up and I'll drop you off on my way,' as he gave Amanda a quick peck on the cheek, before herding the girls towards the car.

Monica and Rob had been in the UK for a few weeks over Easter, and as far as she knew were not planning on returning to the States for another three weeks, so whilst it would probably not be a problem, she could not just assume they would be free to babysit their grandchildren. Although she knew they loved having them, she did not want to take them or their generosity for granted. No, a longer-term solution would need to be found and by the looks of it, she was going to be the one who would need to find it.

Chapter 6

'Right, Maria, just dump your bags down there and follow me. I'll show you up to your room in a minute, but let's get our priorities sorted first,' instructed Amanda, as she closed the front door and led the way through the hallway, directly into the kitchen, making her way straight to the fridge. It was nearly midnight and the journey back from the airport had been more difficult than normal after an accident on the motorway that had seen them sitting in traffic for fifteen minutes without moving. 'Now, how big a glass shall I pour, because I for one need a big one! It's been a long day and I don't seem to have stopped,' sighed Amanda, opening the fridge and retrieving the bottle of Sauvignon Blanc she had mercifully had the foresight to put in to chill before she left home that morning.

Knowing it was a rhetorical question, she poured two glasses almost to the brim, before passing one over to Maria, adding before taking a healthy glug from her own, 'Cheers!'

'Cheers!' replied Maria, 'I think Rachel will sleep tonight. When you dropped her off at the cottage, she looked exhausted. I'm surprised she didn't fall asleep in the car. It was a good job we stopped off for a burger at that service station on the way back, as I don't think I could face anything to eat now.'

'Yes, she did look exhausted, but I'm so glad she's finally here. Thanks for sorting everything out, I really do appreciate it.' Amanda replied, smiling at her friend.

'No problem, but I can't take all the credit. I just hope it works out well for you all.'

When Amanda had visited Boston three months earlier, for one of what was becoming her regular business trips to meet up with the team, she had confided in Maria over dinner one evening how difficult things were becoming at home; not only the pressures of Damian's business, but the knock-on effects it was having with childcare, and the potential impact that could have on her burgeoning career. They had developed a strong friendship and were able to talk candidly, and although Amanda was never indiscrete about her marriage, she knew she could confide in Maria without the risk of anything getting back to the wider family. She would never be disloyal to her husband, and was fully supportive of his desire to build up his company, but at the same time she wanted more for herself. She was not prepared to fall back into the support role in their relationship, the dutiful wife, working nine-to-five around the needs of the family. If nothing else, the last two years had taught her how important it was to live your best life, which for Amanda meant putting herself and her needs first sometimes, however difficult that became for others.

Rachel was the eldest daughter of one of Maria's oldest friends and someone Maria had known from birth, watching her grow-up alongside her own children, all roughly being the same ages. Rachel was one of four siblings and after her father's sudden death, due to an unfortunate accident at work eight years ago, she had been relied upon to help her mum bring up her younger brother and twin sisters. Financially the insurance had paid out after her father's death, so the family managed, but without him around it put an increased pressure on Rachel and her mum to fill the gap his death had created.

Despite being forced to grow up quickly, Rachel had matured from a pretty child into a beautiful young woman; very quiet and unassuming, but at the same time dependable and polite. Maria's children were now adults and had flown the nest, but Maria had continued to keep close to Rachel, with Rachel volunteering at the school where Maria was Principal, helping to run one of the after-school sports clubs that her twin sisters attended.

Rachel herself had just graduated from college, majoring in English, but without a clear idea of what she wanted to do with the rest of her life. She had considered going into teaching at some stage, or perhaps training to become a nurse as she was bright enough, but did not feel ready for settling down, or making any big commitments yet. For now, she simply wanted to look for a job that would give her some spending money, with hopefully a bit of adventure and life experience thrown in for good measure.

Maria knew how good Rachel was around children; a few parents had commented on how well she interacted with the youngsters at the various events the school ran, and could personally vouch for her from a reliability and honesty perspective, so when Amanda had mentioned she needed help with the children, Maria had questioned whether the concept of an 'au pair' was anything she had ever considered.

Over the next couple of weeks, they discussed this, garnering the views of both Damian and Rachel's mother, before suggesting it to Rachel, who when faced with the opportunity of travelling to the UK for a year or so, jumped at the opportunity. Her mum now had a new partner, who had recently moved into the house with them, and although she had nothing against him, perhaps some independence might not be a bad thing. Also, her brother and sisters did not need her anywhere near as much as they had previously, so the timing was perfect for her to spread her wings and have the freedom and opportunity to do something for herself for a change.

She and Amanda chatted on Skype through what would be expected of her. Taking the girls to and from school and their childminder's; helping with their homework; cooking the children's teas and generally mucking in with whatever they needed, seemed to be the key elements. From what Rachel understood, it was all pretty fluid, and basically involved filling in the gaps that Amanda and Damian created due to their work commitments. With neither Amanda nor Rachel having any experience of 'au pairs' before, they just agreed to go with the flow and pray for the best, both assured they would find a routine that suited them before too long. Amanda warmed to Rachel the more they spoke; she seemed easy to get on with, if perhaps a little shy, but she was sure she would fit in perfectly, and certain the girls would love her.

There were practicalities to consider, not least of which were visas and passports, as Rachel had never left the States before, but none of these proved insurmountable. Before too long, plans were in place for Rachel to come over and help Amanda out, and with Maria needing to come over for a conference too, combining the two events seemed perfect timing.

The timing was also perfect from an accommodation perspective, as the tenants that had been in Grandad Tom's cottage had recently given notice that they were looking to move out within the month, thereby allowing Amanda to offer it to Rachel as part of her package, along with Grandad Tom's trusty Volvo that was still in the garage, thought Amanda to herself, after she realised Rachel could drive. Once she got used to driving on the left-hand side of the road, that would certainly come in handy for ferrying the girls around. Also, by being in the cottage, Amanda knew that Rachel would not only be close, but would have her independence. Having grown up in a large family, she was used to always having people around, but if she was looking to spread her wings, then having her own space would be important. At the same time, her being in the cottage ensured Amanda and Damian still had the privacy they needed once their laptops were switched off and the girls tucked up in bed for the night.

They had initially agreed on a twelve to twenty-four months period, but Amanda reassured Rachel and Rachel's mum, that if at any time, or for whatever reason, it did not work out for her, then the arrangements would be flexible and Rachel could go home, but secretly she hoped it would be just what she and Damian needed.

Looking at the clock, Amanda suddenly realised how late it had become. She and Maria had sat for the last hour or so catching-up and finishing off the bottle of wine between them. They both looked exhausted. 'Do you think we should call it a day or else we'll be good for nothing tomorrow?' asked Amanda, conscious that Maria, apart from anything would be feeling jetlagged tomorrow.

'That sounds like a good idea. What have you got planned?' she asked, picking up the dirty glasses and walking them over to the sink, realising how weary her legs had become when she put her weight back on them and how tired she was feeling from the flight.

'Well, I was thinking I'd go over to check Rachel's settled in and take her to get some shopping in the morning, leaving you to have a lie-in because you look whacked. I've done a basic shop, but no doubt there'll be things she likes that I've not thought about. In the afternoon, we can sit in the garden as the weather is promising to be good, and just chill, maybe have a BBQ? I think it's just going to be the two of us, as I've still not heard from Damian, but Rachel might want to join us. I'll ask when I pop round. Mum and Rob are keeping the girls until Sunday, so tomorrow is a day's peace and quiet and a bit of grown-up time!'

'Sounds perfect. I think you'd better show me the way upstairs, as you're right, I'm fit to drop – and I'm already liking the sound of that lie-in,' yawned Maria in response.

Chapter 7

Just before lunchtime the following morning, Amanda was in the kitchen making a much-deserved cup of coffee, whilst waiting for Maria to get up so they could have their brunch together; scrambled eggs, smoked salmon and fresh bagels, when she heard her mobile ringing somewhere in the distance. She went into the hallway to retrieve it, remembering she had dropped it on the side table, along with her car keys, when she had hurried into the house earlier, arms full of the shopping and dry cleaning she had picked up on her morning's errands. She had called into the cottage on her way back from the supermarket, dropping off a couple of essentials Rachel had messaged her about; also assuring herself Rachel was settling in, before leaving her to get acquainted with the WIFI and TV package which Amanda had upgraded to when she started renting the cottage out. Grandad Tom had not been one for the new-fangled internet, and his television set had seen better days, so installing something more state-of-the-art had been a priority if Amanda wanted to rent the cottage out. Living in the countryside has many benefits, but access to good WIFI was unfortunately not one of them.

She had also installed a new kitchen and bathroom, plus arranged for a builder to do some general maintenance on the property. It was fair to say her dad had not inherited his DIY gene from his own father. Ken had been the one everyone turned to when anything needed fixing, so after his death it was easy to see how things had just fallen into disrepair. Sprucing up the furnishings, a fresh coat of emulsion and tidying up the garden had given the cottage a new lease of life, making it not just a better rental prospect, but a much more inviting place to live.

When Grandad Tom had transferred the property into her name the previous year, Amanda had initially considered selling it, but her heart was not in letting it go. Apart from feeling a little disingenuous after being given such a wonderful gift, the cottage held too many happy memories for her, precious memories of both her grandad and grandma when she was growing up, spending time with them in the cottage and feeling the love and comfort they showered on her. She remembered returning from university and sitting at the kitchen table the year her grandma had died, listening to her grandad cry as he recalled the final days of his wife's life. It had been Amanda's first real experience of death, of losing someone close to her, that the memory was forever etched on her mind. It still touched her how fragile her grandad had been at that time and how helpless she had felt, being unable to do anything other than hold him as he wept; those memories like the tears, had seeped into the walls and it just did not seem right to let them go, particularly whilst Grandad Tom was still around.

So, when it was suggested by her mum that she could possibly rent it out for a while, and at least earn a little income from it, that presented the perfect solution. It would also give her some thinking time to decide what was right for the property in the longer-term. It was a long way off, but Maisie or Alice might want to stay in the village when they grew up, and the cottage could provide a great first property for either of them when that time came. Yes, having the property gave her options, and being a landlord might not be too bad for the time being.

The tenants who had taken the cottage, initially on a twelve-month lease, were a recently married middle aged couple from Scotland. They were both specialist doctors who had been appointed on short-term contracts to work at the local teaching hospital undertaking a project, apparently related to the introduction of new practices on behalf of the NHS. They had told Amanda a little about their work, making it sound both exciting and cutting edge, but nothing Amanda could really relate to. They explained why they needed somewhere close by, but not on the hospital's doorstep, with Castle Heighton proving to be the perfect location; a beautiful village in the heart of the Cotswolds, but an easy commute to the hospital.

They had both been very happy with the cottage, but their contracts had come to an early end due to funding cuts, so they were moving back to Scotland. The timing worked perfectly, meaning Amanda had not thought twice about letting Rachel use it once they had left. It seemed senseless to leave it unoccupied, and foregoing any rental income was a small price to pay for the reassurance that Rachel would be settled and close at hand. After all, she was only a young girl who would struggle to find affordable accommodation in the village otherwise, particularly on an au-pair's salary.

'Hello there, I wasn't expecting to hear from you today. I thought you and Clara were away this weekend, going to some concert or other in Birmingham?' said Amanda, surprised to be answering the phone to Lisa, her oldest and dearest friend.

'Yes, we were, but our plans got changed at the last moment, so I wondered if you were around for an hour or so later this afternoon? We were thinking of driving over and calling in to see the parents! My mum was moaning the other night when I spoke to her on the phone that a visit is long overdue, and Clara quite fancies a drive out too, so we thought we'd kill two birds, so to speak and call in on you if you're around. Bristol is packed with tourists this weekend it would seem, and we just need to get away!' replied Lisa, sounding a little exasperated.

Lisa and Clara, who just happened to be Amanda's American cousin, had recently bought and renovated an apartment in Bristol as their first home together. They had been a couple now for just over two years, and although their relationship was relatively new, they both appeared as happy as ever with their decision to not only buy a property and move in together, but more importantly Clara's decision to pack her life and career up as a newspaper editor in Boston and transfer it lock, stock and barrel to Bristol to start anew with Lisa. She had secured a job as a fashion editor with one of the top British magazines, and so far, everything seemed to be working out well for them.

'That'd be great, why don't you both come over after you've finished at your parents', and if you're free tomorrow you can even stay over for the night. That way you can have a glass or two of prosecco, because by the sounds of it you'll need it after your duty visit. Maria and I were planning a BBQ this evening, and I've bought enough food to feed an army, so plenty to go around,' but noting her friend had gone quiet at the other end of the line, she enquired, 'you do remember me telling you I was picking both her and Rachel up from the airport, and that Maria's staying over for a couple of nights before she goes to London for that conference, don't you?'

'Er, yes, I'd forgotten, but now you come to mention it I do. That sounds perfect though. I'd love to meet Rachel too. I'll obviously need to vet her if she's going to be looking after my God-daughters,' she laughed. 'We'll see you in a few hours then; get that prosecco chilled. By the way, are the girls and Damian going to be home?'

'No, and Rachel won't be here until tomorrow either. I invited her, but she's feeling a bit tired and getting herself settled in today; I think her priority this morning when I called round was getting her Netflix account sorted!' responded Amanda, adding 'I think it's all a little overpowering for her, so I'm taking it slowly. Maisie and Alice are at Mum and Rob's at the moment. I dropped them off yesterday morning and Rob was taking them fishing of all things in the little pond on their estate. They're coming home tomorrow in time for lunch. That'll be the first time they'll meet Rachel too. I'm not sure they fully understand what an au pair is, but when they've spoken to her on Skype, they think she's funny. I think they like her accent. And frankly, I'm not sure where Damian is, but I think he's making himself scarce for the weekend to allow Maria and me to have some girly time. He mentioned something about one of his friends having a fortieth birthday celebration in town, so he was going to that and then staying over at the flat. So, tonight, my friend, will be an adults-only zone!'

'Brilliant. Even more reason to sleep over, and if lunch is on offer, we'll stay and see everyone else too. I'm long overdue some cuddles, and I haven't seen Monica and Rob for a while, so it will be lovely to catch-up with them and hear all their news. I'll go and tell Clara now and pack our PJs,' laughed Lisa excitedly.

'Great, see you both soon, and by the way, say hi to your mum and dad for me. Tell them I'll try to pop over myself to say hello if I get the chance,' smiled Amanda to herself before ending the call, knowing how much Lisa would not be looking forward to going home. Over the last couple of years, her parents had not only aged, but had become increasingly cantankerous, always bickering at each other for no good reason, with Lisa as their only child left to play umpire.

No, she would definitely be in need of some calming down when she arrived. It was shaping up to be a fantastic evening though. Her three greatest friends all under one roof, with enough Prosecco to sink a battleship, and not a childcare responsibility between them. She just now needed to concentrate on not burning the sausages. The BBQ was normally Damian's domain, but today she needed to rally herself for the challenge.

Chapter 8

Later that afternoon, but earlier than planned, Lisa and Clara were pulling up outside Amanda's house, after what had been a curtailed visit to Lisa's parents, leaving neither woman particularly at ease. Unbeknown to Lisa, her parents had planned a trip to the local garden centre for afternoon tea, and were not too keen on changing their plans, regardless of the fact she had 'deigned to visit', screamed the look on her mum's face as she informed them they were driving over. Nevertheless, they were invited in for a quick cup of tea, brewed in the traditional way in an old-fashioned teapot, the tea stewed strong enough to ensure the spoon stood up all by itself, then poured through a strainer into delicate china cups and saucers, ones Lisa remembered her mum using religiously throughout her childhood whenever visitors arrived. The tea would then be taken on a tray to the front room, reserved for special occasions. Her mum was all show, forever conscious of what people thought of her and rarely relaxed around visitors as a consequence.

For whatever reason, her mum, Shirley Meadows, could not accept Clara as one of the family, not only standing on ceremony whenever she visited, but sadly choosing not to acknowledge the relationship the two women had. Lisa had tried on several occasions to have it out with her mum, discussing it both as directly and maturely as she could, but also subtly whenever an opportunity presented it, even simply suggesting they use the everyday mugs that sat in the kitchen cupboard and drank their teas around the kitchen table, but Shirley was not to be swayed, and managed to skilfully change the subject whenever it attempted to veer in that direction. Thankfully, Clara chose not to be offended by her attitude, but Lisa was embarrassed, and whilst she did not want confrontation with her mum, knew that the time would come when she would have to say something at the risk of upsetting her mum.

Her dad Roger, was thankfully a lot more enlightened than his wife, his views not parked in the last century, as he feared his wife's were. He saw how happy his daughter was since she had met Clara, much more settled. He viewed this as a positive, so made every effort to make Clara welcome and included as one of the family, the simple act of which seemed to pique Shirley even more.

Lisa knew she had to accept some of the blame for her mum's position. Growing up she had never felt sufficiently close to her parents to discuss her relationships or sexuality with them, happy to avoid the discussion for fear of it upsetting them, or worse still them rejecting her because of it. She felt it was safer always leaving them to presume what they wanted about what she got up to, and with whom, than for her to elaborate. It was simple, they never asked, so she never confided, and up until Clara, she had never brought anyone home to meet them.

Her parents were of an older generation than Clara's parents. Brad and Jane had welcomed Lisa with open arms from day one, including her without a second thought as their daughter's partner. Whereas Shirley and Roger had automatically assumed one day Lisa would be married and produce grandchildren for them, so over the years became increasingly disappointed when there were no signs of this happening. They had married later in life and had pinned all their hopes onto their only child, and although Lisa understood how they felt, it could sometimes feel very claustrophobic with the weight of their dreams resting solely on her shoulders. She felt she had let her parents, particularly her mum, down, but at the same time felt powerless to do anything about it. 'You can't choose who you fall in love with, can you?' thought Lisa to herself every time she saw that disappointed look on her mum's face.

With hindsight, perhaps Lisa should have been more open growing up, felt more comfortable to have 'that' discussion with her parents, or at least in the case of Clara, give them some indication that she was in a relationship before she invited them down to Bristol to show off her new home.

After they had viewed the one-bedroom apartment, marvelling at the views of Bristol harbour and the ships in the distance from the balcony, Shirley had innocently questioned the sleeping arrangements for Lisa and her flat mate, who she was being introduced to for the first time; so, to be told that they shared the same bedroom had come as more of a shock than a surprise. For Roger, although equally surprised, it seemed to explain a lot, but for him he was able to accept it, and with it accept Clara. He quite liked the spirited American and thought that she was good for his daughter. He tried on several occasions to win Shirley round, but to no avail, so resolved to tread a careful line, maintaining a diplomatic stance between the two whenever the need arose.

'I hope Amanda has the wine chilled, because after the last hour I could do with cheering up. I swear my mum gets worse every time we visit. I don't know why you encourage me to go!' said Lisa as she parked the car alongside Amanda's Audi on the driveway.

‘Because she’s your mum and you love her, and she can’t help the way she feels. We’ll deal with it in time, so don’t worry. I’ll work my charms on her if you like.’

‘Good luck with that. You’ve got a lot more patience than me. I can’t believe she’s so set against you, or more specifically us! You’d think she’d be happy that I was happy – Dad is.’

‘I know, he’s lovely,’ replied Clara pleased at least she was a hit with one of Lisa’s parents. ‘Anyway, changing the subject, what are you going to say to Amanda about seeing Damian last week?’

Being brought back down to earth, Lisa sighed ‘I don’t know exactly, but I’m definitely going to try to broach the subject. Something was not right, but I’m probably reading too much into it.’

Lisa had been in Bath on Tuesday morning the previous week, attending a meeting with a client in one of the less salubrious parts of the city. As a solicitor specialising in family law, it was not unusual for her to conduct interviews at a client’s home. Many of her more vulnerable clients felt much safer and more comfortable in their own surroundings; often feeling intimidated by the plush city offices or overawed by the officious people within them. Within their own space, they generally felt more able to open up and were less guarded with their answers. It also gave Lisa an opportunity to assess a client’s living conditions to understand, if any, the bearings they had on the particular case she was handling. This approach did not work for all of Lisa’s colleagues, most preferring the anonymity of their own offices to conduct business from, but for Lisa over the years it had not only proved an effective tool, but a good use of her time to drive out and see her clients in situ.

On this particular morning, she had finished her meeting and was sitting in her car retrieving emails and messages before driving away from her client’s home, when she spotted out of the corner of her eye a man who she thought she recognised. He looked to be emerging from a terraced house on the opposite side of the street from her client's home. The man looked conspicuously out of place; smartly attired in his business suit and carrying a bag she presumed contained his laptop, leaving a house that not only looked unkempt, but had a garden full of weeds, rubbish and recycling bins, overflowing with all manner of debris, even a broken bicycle on the path and to top it all, a shopping trolley that looked to have made an escape from the local supermarket some months earlier given its general state of repair.

The man was obviously in a hurry to get away, head down as he almost ran to his car, which was parked a couple of vehicles up the road from her own. She instantly recognised the car and its registration plate, leaving her in no doubt that the man was who she had thought, her best friend's husband, Damian. Something in his eyes told Lisa not to attract his attention; apart from his obvious haste, he looked distracted, displaying the body language of a disgruntled man.

After he had closed the car door, Lisa glanced back towards the house, just in time to see a young woman, with a small child in her arms slam the door behind him. The woman from the way she held her body, did not look happy either. Lisa was a professional, someone trained not to jump to conclusions, but something about the scenario in front of her did not feel right. She assumed there would be an innocent enough explanation, but at the same time, knowing Damian and his history, she wondered whether this was something she should look to uncover, or for the sake of Amanda, better let lie.

When she had mentioned it to Clara later than evening over dinner and a glass of particularly good Malbec, she too had become curiously concerned, and after mulling over the various 'what-ifs' between them, they decided they did not feel comfortable to ignore it, but equally they were sensible enough to realise it was not their place to either charge headfirst in on, or make unfounded accusations, particularly as it was probably something innocuous. Both Clara and Lisa would defend Amanda to the hilt, but 'woe betide anyone who upset her' was their combined mentality.

'I suggest you play it by ear and see if Amanda mentions anything before you raise it. You never know, Damian might be planning a surprise for her. It's their tenth wedding anniversary coming up isn't it next month, and we wouldn't want to spoil that if he's got something special planned, would we?' counselled Clara.

'No, you're probably right,' agreed Lisa unable to quell her internal reservations, but equally not wanting to rock the boat. 'Okay, let's go then. You grab the wine and the flowers from the back seat, and I'll grab our overnight bags from the boot. It's time to party!'

Chapter 9

It was Monday evening, as Amanda stood at the sink washing up the final pots and pans after dinner, watching the sun set over the fields behind their house. It was not particularly late, but she was feeling tired after the hectic weekend, and all the entertaining she had done by herself with Damian staying overnight in town. Having everyone round had been a real treat, but it had left her feeling exhausted, so tonight's meal had been a simple chicken pasta bake, a tried and trusted family favourite; something they could all eat, without having to make separate meals, and something that was quick to heat up when Damian eventually returned home.

So, by eight o'clock, with the girls sound asleep, the house reasonably tidy and everything ready for the morning, Amanda felt it was time for a long overdue catch-up with her husband. She put the kettle on to make them both a hot drink, before joining him in the lounge. Putting the mugs down on the table besides him, and seeing his expression, she thought her chances of getting any meaningful conversation out of him were pretty remote. 'I'm fine' was the best she'd had all evening so far, his reply when he had walked into the house earlier and she had checked he was okay. He had arrived home just after seven o'clock, kissed the girls as they were making their way upstairs to bed, quickly eaten his meal at the kitchen table and was now sitting on the settee reading his emails, not only oblivious to the weekend the girls or she'd had, but apparently completely disconnected by his own thoughts.

Saturday afternoon into late evening had been so relaxing, with her, Maria, Lisa and Clara just chatting, slowly getting more drunk as the heat went out of the day and the sun eventually set. The BBQ had been a bit of a disaster, so they had resorted to putting everything in the oven, but no-one seemed to be bothered how it was cooked, as long as they ate something to absorb the copious amounts of alcohol. There was a lot of laughter, an occasional tear as they recounted the various events that had been going on in their lives since they had last got together, but overall, they had all had lots of fun; relaxed in each other's company.

Lisa had mentioned in passing about seeing Damian in Bath a couple of weeks previously, but as Amanda could not add any explanation or think of any reason why he might be in that area, the subject had soon moved on. Looking back now, Amanda recalled an odd exchange of glances between Clara and Lisa as she said she had no idea why he would be in Bath, but as they had all had a few glasses of wine by then, she simply let it pass. To be honest, Damian rarely mentioned his business or his schedule to her, so whether he was in the office, or on the road was a mystery to her most times.

On Sunday morning, although there were a few sore heads, with the help of some very strong coffee, all four ladies managed to put on a reasonable show of sobriety before Maisie and Alice bounded back into the house, the noise levels increasing with each child trying to outdo the other to attract the attention, from not only their mum, but from Lisa and Clara who they both adored, and who in return spoiled them rotten. As Monica and Rob accepted a glass of wine each, they tried desperately to hide their relief at being able to hand the childcare responsibility back to Amanda; having grandchildren was wonderful, but giving them back was even better.

Rachel arrived shortly before lunch, making her own way to the house from the cottage, no more than half a mile away, she would guess. She had walked around the quaint little village the previous day, familiarising herself with its layout; the high street with its convenience store cum post office, the café, the school, the church, even the pub. For a Saturday morning, it seemed busy, with people milling around or standing on corners chatting, occasionally looking at her and smiling, noticing a stranger in their midst.

As Amanda's house was one of the more imposing properties in the centre of the village, it was not difficult to find. Rachel was in awe of its beauty and presence. It was such an attractive building, looking both grand and picturesque at the same time; the formality of the Georgian construct, balanced with the softness of the abundance of spring flowers in the neatly laid out gardens, with colourful creepers crawling around the front door frame, continuing up the walls and around the property. She had no idea what the flowers were, but to see everything in bloom on such a beautiful sunny day was almost magical. At home, their house did not really have a garden, so species of plants and flowers was not something she was familiar with, but nevertheless she could appreciate both the beauty, and no doubt the hard work that had gone into creating the sight in front of her.

The inside of the house was also impressive, with its high ceilings and solid walls, containing a series of rooms that seemed to Rachel to have been tastefully decorated and furnished. She had not been given a full tour of the house, Amanda would do that another day she said, so had only really seen the kitchen, the dining room and the back garden; a haven that was equally as pretty, if not prettier than the front of the house. She spent most of her time chatting to both Maisie and Alice, whilst briefly being introduced to the others, who all seemed interested to get to know her too. Rachel had been briefed a little beforehand by Maria about Amanda's family background, so it was easy enough to pick up on the different relationships and remember most people's names, without getting too confused, but no doubt it would all become clearer over the coming months, she thought to herself.

The afternoon had passed quickly, and before long everyone was on their way, with just Maria staying over, before catching her train into London early the following morning. Rachel had arrived on Monday in time to allow Amanda to run Maria to the railway station, after which they had spent the rest of the day getting to know each other better, and deciding in practical terms how they would manage their days, and more importantly the child care arrangements. Amanda had taken Rachel to both the primary school and to Susie's house so that she could introduce her to both the Headmistress, Mrs Dunmore, for when Maisie needed collecting, and to the childminder for when Alice was being dropped off there. In reality, Alice would not be going to Susie's for much longer, but for the interim whilst they got the girls into a routine and Rachel got herself sorted, Amanda thought it important not to disrupt her daughters too much. Today had gone like a breeze, and as Amanda now relaxed with her cup of tea into the lounge, although feeling a little weary, she was on quite a high after a successful, if not hectic few days.

'Here, I've brought you this,' smiled Amanda, pointing to the mug of tea beside him, before sitting herself down in the chair opposite. Gone was the old furniture her parents had enjoyed, or in her mother's case endured, all the years Amanda could remember, replaced by a more modern leather settee and matching arm chairs, with side tables and lamps that gave a warm glow to the room. She dreaded to think what her dad would have thought as she disposed of his old worn armchair, where he had spent many a year relaxing in front of the fire, watching his television quizzes or doing his crosswords. When Amanda and Damian had moved in, a make-over in the furnishings department had been one of their top priorities. Comfort, modern and stylish furniture replaced the solid and trustworthy pieces; out with the old, and in with the new, were words that would probably have Ken turning in his grave.

'Thank you, I could do with that,' said Damian, looking up briefly from his laptop while reaching for the cup his wife had placed beside him, returning his eyes instantly to the screen as soon as he had taken a quick drink, and the cup to the table, probably to remain there until it went cold. 'What time is it? Are you off to bed?' he asked Amanda, already typing and deep into his own world.

'No, it's not late. I was thinking we could have a chat. I've not seen you for ages and I was going to tell you all about the weekend and how the girls got on with Rachel. You remember she arrived on Friday? Also, Lisa and Clara came over on Saturday and Lisa mentioned she'd seen you in Bath a few days ago, and I didn't remember you saying you were popping over there, or else I would have asked you to do me a favour.'

'Oh right, yes, I do remember about Rachel .... but could it wait until the morning? It's just that I need to finish these emails and get them fired off before I turn in,' replied Damian, managing to avoid the question about Bath in its entirety, not even enquiring what favour his wife had needed doing. Amanda knew that he and Lisa did not necessarily see eye-to-eye, so as Lisa had not embellished on the details of her sighting, it was likely he was a little embarrassed to be caught out avoiding her, so probably felt the least said about that the better.

Recognising that was all she was going to get out of him in terms of conversation for the rest of the evening, she simply said, 'right, I'll leave you to it then. I might as well go and read for a bit, or take a bath. Good night, I'll see you in the morning. If you're going to be a while longer, I'll probably be asleep by the time you come up,' seethed Amanda, adding silently to herself as she climbed the stairs 'but it might be time you showed some interest in me and our daughters before we 'fire off' like one of your precious emails.'

Amanda was starting to get increasingly annoyed with playing second fiddle to his business and often thought she should invest in one of those 'Do Not Disturb' signs and give it to Damian as a present one Christmas as a joke, but the way he was acting at the moment, she presumed he would not see the funny side.

Chapter 10

A couple of weeks later, and a gentle routine had started to form in the Reynolds household around mealtimes, school runs and bed times. Rachel was proving to be an enormous hit with both Maisie and Alice, with both of them treating her like their big sister, doing what she asked of them, when she asked it, with a smile on their faces, never a cross word between them. Amanda hardly recognised her daughters; it was almost as if Rachel had sprinkled fairy dust all over them, or waved her magic wand, transforming two mischievous little imps into two angelic princesses whenever she was around. Amanda had reported back to Maria how good she was with the girls, how natural and relaxed, and how the stress levels in the house were less on the days she worked.

'I think she's related to Mary Poppins!' she said one day when Maria rang, 'she has definitely got them both under her spell.'

'I'm glad she's settling in too. Apparently, she phoned her mum Nora the other evening and spent ages telling her and her younger sisters all about England; what she'd been doing and the different things she was eating. Nora said she had not heard Rachel so excited about anything for so long that it made her finally realise that it was the right thing for Rachel to do. I think Nora has struggled without her – both emotionally and practically as she was a massive help with the other children. They're both very close, and Nora has leaned heavily on Rachel for years, perhaps too heavily, but it's right that she should be spreading her wings and getting more independent.'

'I agree, and I think the cottage is ideal for her,' added Amanda. 'She was off last weekend and went down to the pub, and I believe met up with a few of the locals her age. There aren't too many youngsters in the village, but there are a couple of good kids, so she shouldn't get into too much trouble, fingers crossed.'

'Yes, I wouldn't have thought Castle Heighton was the crime centre of the Cotswolds, although I'm sure it has its characters like all places do if you look deeply enough,' laughed Maria. 'Anyway, have you tracked Damian down recently, or is he still a bit of an enigma?'

Amanda recalled the long conversation she'd had with her husband a couple of nights ago and wondered how much of it, if any, she should recount to Maria.

Damian had come home, reasonably early by his standards, not only in time to have tea with the girls, but happy to help with bath time too. He seemed more solicitous than usual, keen to sit down and chat over a glass of wine after everything had been cleared away in the kitchen. At the time, Amanda thought nothing untoward, simply pleased to have some adult time with her husband all to herself, a luxury that she was not afforded often. Everything was going well, until he deftly steered the conversation onto finances, property prices and specifically their old house, the one they were currently renting out after moving into Monica and Ken's old home.

Damian was suggesting that it might be time to sell; property prices were high and with everything else that was going on, his view was it might be a good time to release some of the equity they held in the property. Whilst Amanda listened, she had never had any thoughts of selling, or of them needing to release equity. As far as she was concerned, they were financially sound, some would even say well off. She had the cottage and her inheritance left to her by her dad, Rob had also made provision for her and his granddaughters in his estate, plus they had no debts or mortgage on their current property, just a small one on their previous house that was more than covered by the rental income. She was also earning a healthy salary and they could afford to live very nicely, thank you very much.

Damian equally had his bachelor flat in Cirencester, plus his business that seemed to be making a good return, so overall Amanda was curious to understand what was driving his agenda, or more importantly its timing?

'Is there a problem, otherwise I don't understand what's the rush to sell? We have good tenants, they pay well and we don't need the money, so why now?' she enquired.

'Well, the last few months haven't been too good at work, and frankly I could do with an injection of cash into the business. I'd thought about a short-term business loan, but why borrow when we have that money just sitting there?'

'How much do you need?' Amanda enquired, immediately mulling over options other than selling the house, particularly if it was a short-term issue. She had savings, and she knew Rob invested in businesses all the time, which might be an option. As Damian's business was pretty sound to her knowledge, he may be prepared to help.

'I'm looking at raising around one hundred and fifty thousand pounds, which is probably the level of equity we have in the house.'

'And you would plough that straight back into the business, would you? What does your accountant advise?'

'I've not had chance to talk to him yet, but I will do once we've agreed what we're doing,' replied Damian, obviously not anticipating that question.

Amanda was not particularly acute when it came to finances, relying on Damian to manage these, but as he continued to outline some of the issues, her gut was telling her there was more to the story than she was being led to believe. She did not know Damian's accountant personally, nor any of his senior team for that matter, as she had never been involved on a day-to-day basis in his business; in fact, the more she thought about it, she realised she had no involvement in the business; no say, power or control whatsoever. Until today, she had never really thought about the implications of that, but the more she listened, the more she realised that effectively he could do whatever he wanted with his company, including any money 'they' ploughed into it.

Almost ten years ago when they had first got married, Damian's business was a relatively new start-up, in the high-risk market of IT and Communications. He had started it initially with a friend, but a couple of years later, was forced to buy his friend out after a minor disagreement on the direction they each wanted the company to take. In the end, the split had been relatively amicable, but to avoid further complications or risks, Damian kept everything thereafter in his own name; thereby keeping Amanda's name, and importantly their joint assets, away from harm's way.

Now, listening to the passion Damian was speaking with, there seemed to be an impetus behind what he was saying that she could not quite decipher, but nevertheless, she felt a need to be cautious in her response.

'Let me have a think about it and we'll have a chat later in the week. I could also speak to the Estate Agents and see what they advise, particularly with respect to the tenants. I presume there's no hurry?' she asked.

'No hurry per se, but I don't want the business to suffer in the meantime. I really need to get my hands on some cash before it's too late,' he replied.

Although Amanda presumed there was no emotional blackmail intended, she had heard something in Damian's voice that indicated otherwise.

Over breakfast the following morning, Damian had suggested she give the Estate Agents a phone call to arrange a valuation. But even having done so, and being advised by Adam, the agent she had spoken to on the phone, that property prices were at a high, so in his view a seller's market, plus confirming there would be no issues with the tenancy agreement, provided the correct notice period was given, she was still not comfortable with what was being proposed.

Deciding to remain on the side of caution for the time being, and whilst not wanting to lie, but perhaps being a little economical with the truth, Amanda eventually replied to Maria, 'Yes, Damian and I are fine. We had a lovely evening the other night, we sat and chatted for ages over a bottle of wine, mainly about his business. I learned a lot, which no doubt I'll tell you about at some stage, but I'll not bore you with it now!'

Chapter 11

By the end of the following week, Damian had become noticeably more edgy in the office, raising his voice or acting completely out of character, with both staff and clients alike. He knew he was on a short fuse, and although no one had called him out on it yet, he sensed from a few glances and murmurs around the coffee machine that people had not only noticed the change in him, but were getting increasingly unhappy with it, and the atmosphere that was being created. He needed to be more careful as he could not afford to lose either staff or business at the moment, and unless he could control his behaviour, he was in serious danger of doing both.

The problem was Amanda had still not given him her decision about selling their old house, with each time he subtly raised the topic, her presenting him with a different question; some of which he was struggling to either respond to, or worse still, defend. Nevertheless, he needed to do something fast and needed to force the issue as he was rapidly coming to the conclusion that if selling the house was not a feasible option, then he would be forced to look at what other options he might have, although if truth be told, these were thin on the ground.

If only he had a time machine like in 'Back to the Future', and turning the clock back was an option, he naively thought to himself, life would be so different. Why had everything gone so wrong for him? Life had been so good, his company was starting to feel established, building itself a solid reputation in the competitive IT industry. He was drawing in a steady flow of business, most of which was making good profits. He had expanded, taken on extra work, and with that more staff, organically growing his portfolio, whilst carefully managing the risks to ensure he did not put his business, or the livelihood it afforded him, in any jeopardy.

Additionally, on a personal level, he had a good family life; a beautiful wife and two daughters he adored. He lived in a perfectly respectable home, with a good standard of living, wanting for nothing materially. Why then had his ego kicked in, his mid-life crisis bitten early, and why for heaven's sake did he risk everything he had for the sake of a bit of excitement? A sordid affair with a girl nearly half his age, that frankly now he looked back on it, was neither particularly exciting, nor did little, if anything, for his ego.

He soon realised it was not in his psyche to 'play around', gaining little, if any, enjoyment from the deceit he created; only his growing anxiety the more it went on and the deeper he got into his affair. After being caught out by his wife 'red-handed' so to speak, and witnessing first-hand the damage he had inflicted on her and their family, as well as finally appreciating the risks he had taken, Damian had done everything in his power to right the wrongs that his selfish behaviour had wrought. Over time, Amanda had graciously rewarded him with a second chance, when she would have been well within her rights to show him the door, but having been given her forgiveness, he was at pains not to squander that again.

Over the last two or so years, he had done everything in his power to rebuild the trust and the relationship with Amanda, working hard not only to rekindle in her the feelings she once had for him, but to get her to believe that although he had acted recklessly, his feelings for her had never been lost. How stupid to reflect back now and think he could get away with wanting his cake and eating it all at the same time.

The last five months though had been a nightmare as far as Damian was concerned; since February, his life had ricocheted around a series of events and circumstances that he was powerless to contain. One-by-one, they not only piled on the pain, but added a further layer of confusion and complexity to what was already an impossible dilemma. It was easy to pin point exactly where his life had begun to unravel and spiral out of control, the point at which he knew all the sterling work of the proceeding two years, not only rebuilding trust with Amanda, but all the investment in his company and the reputation he had built, was to be sorely tested.

The official looking white envelope, marked 'Private and Confidential' had sat innocuously on the top of his inbox throughout the day, being left there unopened, along with the other mail his secretary had already earmarked for his attention. Damian had seen it a couple of times when flitting between meetings, but had thought nothing of it. He had noted it was not a brown envelope, so was unlikely to be a bill, nor did it look like junk marketing material that had been marked-up as private to give it an air of importance, but for some reason his secretary had thought it sufficiently official and inappropriate for her to open. On an impulse, he put the envelope in his briefcase as he was leaving the office, with a view to reading it when he got home, along with the other emails he had not got round to reading during the day.

From the moment he opened the envelope later that evening, relaxing with a glass of wine after dinner, waiting downstairs while Amanda put the girls to bed, and read the letter from Chloe, Damian knew that not only had Pandora's Box been well and truly opened, but that the chances of his life ever returning to normal thereafter were remarkably unlikely.

Now five months on, he had reached the point at which he could not prevaricate any longer. He was out of both options and time, and although he really did not want to push or alarm Amanda, he needed to do something whilst he still had some vestige of control over the situation, because if the latest missive, this time from Chloe's solicitor was correct, that control could suddenly be removed from him.

As Damian entered the house, closing the door quietly behind him, he resigned himself that the moment had finally arrived to come clean. He put his laptop case on the hall floor, draped his jacket over the newel post and headed towards the kitchen, where he could hear Amanda and the girls chattering and the smell of dinner cooking. Realising that he did not have an appetite, he nevertheless put a smile on his face and shouted, 'I'm home!' wondering to himself how much longer he would be able to say those words.

Chapter 12

'Hi, have you got time for a chat? I know it's late, but I really need to speak to someone,' sobbed Amanda into the phone, then looking at the bedside clock and realising it was well after midnight she added 'sorry, if you're already in bed it can wait until tomorrow,' whilst continuing to cry.

Lisa could always be relied upon to not only have her mobile handy, but generally be available day or night in the case of problem or a crisis arising, and listening to her friend as she sobbed at the other end of the line, she presumed today was one of the latter.

'Whatever's the matter? You sound really upset, are the girls alright?' immediately jumping to the conclusion that either Maisie or Alice was unwell.

'No, they're fine, fast asleep in bed thankfully. Damian and I have just had a massive row and I need someone to offload to before I explode,' she replied.

'Anything serious?' enquired Lisa, knowing intuitively that it must be if Amanda was phoning at such a late hour, but also recognising it was very rare for her to actually confide about anything to do with their relationship, so it must be important. When Damian had his affair a couple of years earlier, Amanda had kept the details pretty vague; then once she had decided to forgive and forget, the subject had not been raised again, packed away in a box never to be reopened. But Lisa sensed, and had for some time now if she had read the signs correctly, that all was not as it should be in the Reynolds camp.

'Well, how serious is just finding out your husband has a two-year-old son by another woman?' she blurted out between sobs.

'Wind back, what do you mean, a son?' replied Lisa, suddenly fully awake at the other end of the phone. Even Clara who had been fast asleep beside her when the phone rang was now begging Lisa to put the device on speaker so she could hear what was being said.

'Apparently that woman, well girl really, you know Chloe, the one my darling husband had that affair with, was pregnant when it all finished. He's adamant he didn't know anything about it at the time, but that now she's instructed a solicitor and is claiming compensation or whatever you call it, for constructive dismissal, whatever that is! On top of that, she wants a maintenance settlement for her son, or more correctly their son, or she says she'll go public about who his father is. Can you believe it?'

In her field of work, Lisa was more than capable of believing it, and if she was honest had heard much worse. 'How long has he known?' she enquired, sensing the shock in her friend's voice, but assuming it was not a shock to Damian. Images of Damian emerging from the house in Bath a few weeks earlier, of a girl with a small child in her arms, flooded into her mind. Lisa did not know for certain that the girl was Chloe, but she would bet hers and Clara's mortgage on that being the case.

'Well, according to him he received the first letter from Chloe around five months ago, with an official letter from her solicitor more recently. Five months!' she emphasised. 'He's never said one word to me about this, and I've never suspected a thing. What an absolute fool I've been. The worst is, I thought we were building back trust between us. We've just had a lovely break in Devon, and he couldn't have been more attentive to me or the girls, but this had just blown all that apart, hasn't it?'

'What's she asking for?' queried Lisa, her professional interests now piqued, as she lay in bed thinking through what the scenarios might be.

As a solicitor dealing in family law, sadly cases like these were not unusual. In her early career, whilst dabbling in employment law, she had even had experience in writing similar forms of letters on behalf of her own clients. Although not illegal to have a relationship with someone in the office, most companies did not encourage it. Also, it was not as uncommon as one would think for either one, or both, parties to be dismissed if the situation got difficult. Lisa knew companies often cited how untenable it could become for the individuals concerned to continue working together, how it could impact on wider issues, staff morale, professionalism etc. Some even cited cases of gross misconduct if the relationship was against company policy. It was definitely an area of law where the lines easily became blurred.

In Damian's case, being both the boss and the owner of the business had the potential to make things even trickier. Lisa knew his affair, once suspected, would not only have become divisive among his staff, with the added dimension of becoming awkward in front of clients, but once it had ended, it could easily have turned toxic when the truth came out and feelings were raw. 'The Chloe situation' could have grown into a difficult problem, so at the time, and obviously holding the power, Damian had accepted her resignation, without hesitation. Whether that resignation was offered voluntarily, or whether Chloe was left without an option, was perhaps debatable, and something Lisa feared they would never get to the bottom of.

'Well, that's easy. Apparently, the latest letter says she wants one hundred and fifty thousand pounds as a one-off payment, plus maintenance for the child until he's eighteen or out of full-time education, including back payments for the last couple of years. And would you believe it, Damian has been pestering me to sell our old house, just so that he could use our money to pay her off, presumably without telling me! You couldn't write it!' seethed Amanda, adding 'I knew there was something not right when he wanted to put the house on the market for no good reason. Well, this evidently is his good reason.'

'Does the business not have the ability to raise that money rather than you selling the house? It's his mess, not yours, so why isn't his business picking it up, or alternatively him sell his apartment, that must be worth at least that much?' chirped in Clara.

'Trust me, I've had that argument too, but apparently other than it not being legal, the business is going through a rough patch and there's not that much spare cash floating around. Damian says he's lost a couple of contracts recently to a business that's undercutting him – and reading between the lines, I think he's lost focus whilst this has all been going on. The apartment is already mortgaged, I've just learned, from when he bought out his partner a few years ago, so there's not as much equity there as you'd think. Frankly it's an almighty mess.'

'Where is he now?' asked Lisa, realising that as it was now after one o'clock, and by the tone and volume of the discussion it was clear Damian was not within earshot, he was probably not at home.

'He swanned off back to his apartment for the night, his tail well and truly between his legs. I did remarkably well not to pack his bags and throw him out under the circumstances. Just when I thought we were back on track,' sighed Amanda, feeling drained by the conversation.

'So, what are you planning on doing next?' enquired Clara. 'What are your options?'

'I don't know to be honest, I'm just numb at the moment; it's been such a shock' replied Amanda, adding, 'I was supposed to be travelling over to Boston next week for a few days for business and to catch up with Will and the team. I really don't want to postpose that, especially now that Rachel's settled, and not only are the girls happy with her, but I feel comfortable leaving them. But what that means for Damian and his new family I don't know.'

'Do you want either of us to do anything?' enquired Lisa supportively, 'I could look at your legal options for what it's worth.'

'And I could put a contract out on the son-of-a-bitch and run him out of town' added Clara in her American drawl, which although said in jest, reflected completely her sentiments in relation to what she had just heard.

'No, thanks, I need to work this through in my own mind first, but rest assured if and when I need to call in the cavalry, you two will be top of that list.' Feeling like she had run out of steam, she bade good-night to Lisa and Clara and settled herself in for a sleepless few hours tossing and turning, before it was time to get up and take the girls to school.

Damian had been so delighted when she had been pregnant last time, particularly after what they had gone through, and then finding it was a much longed for son, he had been overjoyed. To then lose Theo so tragically had torn them both apart, but now it seemed Damian had got his much longed for son after all – just without her to share that joy with him. How cruel could the world become, Amanda thought to herself, no longer sure what tomorrow would hold.

Chapter 13

By the end of the following week, whilst the intense heat and uncomfortable atmosphere created by the situation had partially abated between her and Damian, describing their relationship as 'cordial' was possibly as positive as anyone could go. For the sake of the girls, and life in general, they were continuing to follow as normal a routine as possible, each focussing on their work as a way to get through the day. Amanda's emotions felt like they were in a tumble dryer, regularly vacillating between anger and sympathy; anger obviously directed at Damian and Chloe, but sympathy for the little boy caught up in the middle of all this, an innocent two-year old, who probably had no concept of the mayhem his existence had created.

When the red mist descended, Amanda did not know who her anger was most directed at. Her husband for allowing the situation to develop in the first place; having an affair was bad enough, but not taking precautions was pure madness, exacerbated by the fact he had risked her health too, recognising he had still been sleeping, albeit occasionally, with her throughout his affair. But Chloe, suddenly turning up over two years after the event, with a child in tow was almost inexcusable. Her appearance and subsequent demands had in one fell swoop managed to unravel all the hard work Amanda and Damian had put into restoring their relationship; a relationship that had not only been damaged by his affair, but that was tested further following the loss of their stillborn son. Losing Theo at the point when they had begun to make real inroads into rebuilding their family was a devastating and almost unimaginable blow.

Amanda was as certain as she could be that the affair was over, choosing to believe Damian when he assured her the approach from Chloe had come completely out of the blue, but all this did was add to her confusion when trying to work through the mire that the situation had created. Had their affair continued, then by now Damian's bags would well and truly have been packed, thrown through the windows and locks changed, but life was never that simple. No, she had decided to forgive and forget some time ago – but dealing with consequences like these, was not something she remembered signing up for. So, whilst Amanda listened with a degree of sympathy, occasionally voicing her opinions whenever the subject of Chloe veered into the conversation, there was no obvious light at the end of the tunnel. They were both playing for time in their own way.

Damian had finally employed his own solicitor, realising that the approach of burying his head in the sand, whilst praying the issue would simply go away once he 'paid Chloe off', provided he could raise the money, no longer seemed a viable option. He instructed a colleague of Lisa's called Jason Gleeson, whom she had not only recommended, but trusted to handle this in Damian's best interests. Lisa had warned the courts normally favoured women in cases such as these; hence stressed the importance of getting someone who really supported you in your corner. Ordinarily she could have taken the case herself, but where there was a conflict of interest, which recognising her closeness to the family there clearly was here, she needed to rule herself out.

Damian had also come clean that he had already spoken to Chloe, even visiting her at her home in Bath to challenge her after receiving her initial letter. At the time, he did not believe there was a child, purely a scam to exhort money from him. But the debate had become heated, and when their voices woke the sleeping child in the next room, any questions he had, had soon been answered. Chloe had gone to her son, picking him up to calm him, whilst at the same time showing Damian the door, with the parting words of 'you'll be hearing from my solicitor!'

Damian realised now how foolish and naive his pathetic attempt of dealing with it and trying to keep a lid on it had been. Chloe was no longer the young girl with the crush on him, someone who would hang on his every word, but a woman who had been forced to grow up quickly after the shock and demands of motherhood had descended on her. No, he had to accept that somewhere out there he had a son, and like it or not he had responsibilities towards the child, even if he never saw him again. Jason, his solicitor had advised on arranging a meeting with Chloe and her solicitor to understand their options, a kind of mediation session, which given he had nothing to lose, Damian agreed to. The meeting was scheduled for the following week and although Damian was prepared to go ahead with it, he did not hold out much hope for an early, or painless resolution.

Amanda needed to get over to Boston. Her trip had already been rescheduled after she had subtly told Will she had a domestic issue to deal with, and in truth could easily have been rescheduled again, but Amanda needed to get away, for her own sanity if nothing else. She did not relish being at home when Damian returned from the mediation meeting with Chloe, so even though she recognised she was running away, it was her way of coping. Nothing would be decided in the next day or so anyway, so putting a few thousand miles between them seemed a sensible option, particularly as Rachel was now settled and happy to hold the fort in her absence with the girls.

After offloading to Lisa and Clara that first night, Maria had been her next port of call. Maria was now happily in what everyone hoped was a long-term relationship with Will, Amanda's boss but also her Uncle Brad's brother. Throughout her life, Maria had dealt with her own personal and matrimonial struggles, not only being deserted and subsequently divorced with two small children, but left to fend for herself and her children both emotionally and financially as her ex-husband moved onto his new family. Maria had certainly learned the hard way how to survive in difficult situations, coming through all her own personal challenges with not only a smile, but a real appreciation of the bigger picture of life and what it had to offer if you worked at it. Now somewhere in her mid-fifties, very much in love and Principal at a local high school, she was living proof of the adage 'life can only get better'.

Amanda presumed, given Maria's history, that she would have empathy with Chloe, and be damming of Damian's behaviour, but in reality, was relieved to realise that was not the case. She proved to be both non-judgemental, offering a sympathetic ear, even the odd piece of sage advice, but also patient as she offloaded her woes, occasionally passing the tissues as the tears sprung uncontrollably from her eyes.

Maria had collected Amanda from the airport, driving her directly to Rob and Monica's house just outside Salem in Massachusetts. Will was waiting for them there, along with Jane and Brad, all gathered for a family dinner, to be cooked by Monica as it was Mrs Reilly, the housekeeper's day off. Talking in the car with Maria had felt a safe place, where the tears and the conversation could flow freely before she faced the rest of the family. Amanda had given her mum a brief outline of what had happened, and no doubt would be drawn into more detailed discussions over the coming days, but as there were no answers, any discussions would only turn awkward if not handled properly, and that was the last thing Amanda needed right now.

Both Monica and Rob had privately voiced their surprise at the time when Amanda had taken the decision to forgive Damian and move on with their lives. They had assumed after having spoken at length with her that summer, that divorce was the road their daughter would choose following the affair being made public; so, over the last couple of years they had been careful around Damian, never wanting to say or do anything that would unsettle their daughter's fragile marriage; provided that was what she still wanted to protect. They both wanted what was best for her and their granddaughters, and if she felt remaining married constituted the best approach for her family, then who were they to disagree? Nevertheless, they both had their reservations, which so far, they had managed to keep to themselves.

Monica and Rob had only flown back to New England the week before, ready to settle back into their routine of summers by the coast and sailing the high seas. Their apartment in the Cotswolds would remain secured and locked-up for the next three months, before they embarked on the return journey to spend the Christmas holidays back in England. Their routine of flitting across the ocean to spend equal time in both the States and England seemed to be working well enough, but if both were being completely honest, it was not the ideal solution. No matter which side of the Atlantic they were on, there was always a pull from the other side, and neither Rob nor Monica had an easy answer to that conundrum.

Tonight, was their first opportunity to invite friends and family to come over, time for everyone to catch-up and relax over good food and fine wine, taken from Rob's amply stocked cellar. The last thing Amanda or anyone else needed was the dissection of her relationship and the dredging up of the affair that had threatened to destroy her marriage. No, those discussions could wait for a more appropriate time.

'Hello darling, lovely to see you. What a wonderful surprise, we didn't think you'd be here until the holidays in a few weeks' time. This is a real bonus, isn't it Rob?' exclaimed Monica still wearing her apron, as Amanda walked through the door and dropped her bags in the hallway, going straight to her mum and Rob for a hug.

'Wonderful yes, when you rang yesterday to say you were on your way, we were obviously delighted,' added Rob, almost parroting his wife's words, whilst seamlessly handing Amanda a glass of her favourite wine. For a couple that had only got together relatively recently, the way they finished each other's sentences and seemed to be on completely the same wave length was endearing.

Since being reconnected with her biological father, Amanda had spent many weeks at Rob's house and each time she arrived it never failed to impress her. The clean lines, the open spaces, the feeling of calm and serenity created by the colour scheme and the nautical furnishings, and above all the spectacular light that streamed through the house, reflected off the water at the rear of the building were magical. Amanda had always thought the house lacked the female touch though, perhaps a little corporate in its feel, almost like a five-star hotel without the doorman, but now that her mum had become the lady of the manor, it was interesting to notice the subtle changes Monica had made to the décor; those subtle touches that turned a house into a home. Photos of Maisie and Alice now sat proudly on the mantelpiece above the fireplace, alongside graduation photos of Lucas and Ben taken the previous year, but the piece de resistance was the crystal frame displaying the wedding photo of all of them together; one big blended family, smiling at the camera, everyone happy and completely relaxed. Looking around the room now, seeing her Aunt Jane and Maria chatting away like old friends, whilst Rob was proudly showing off some recent snaps on his phone of Lucas's travels around Asia to Will and Brad, Amanda kept her fingers tightly crossed that nothing on the horizon was going to impact their family balance.

'That smells good, what's for dinner? I'm starving,' remarked Amanda as she followed her mum back into the kitchen, leaving the others in the lounge to continue their discussions. 'I didn't manage to eat or drink much on the plane, I just slept, which is so unlike me! I'm normally first at the bar,' she smiled.

Monica noticing the smile did not make it all the way up to her eyes and that her daughter looked emotionally drained, said 'Your body's telling you something then. It's probably the shock that's just starting to hit you. What do you think you're going to do?' enquired Monica, never one to beat around the bush.

'I don't know Mum, but you're right, it has been one almighty shock. Damian and I were getting on so well; this has just scuppered that, and it's not just the trust, but the uncertainty it's introduced into everything,' sighed Amanda, as she took a gulp of the chilled Sauvignon Blanc Rob had put into her hand the moment she arrived. 'It's also worrying that the business has been affected too. I think Damian has been so worried and distracted over the last few months that he's taken his eye right off the ball, and by the sounds of it, some of his management team had too. I'd hate for him to lose his livelihood on top of everything else, when he's worked so hard to establish himself.'

'So, what happens next?' continued Monica, trying to understand the lay of the land whilst she still had her daughter to herself. They had always had an easy and open relationship, with conversation never normally difficult between them, but today Monica had to admit it was a bit of a struggle getting her daughter to open up.

'Well, Damian is meeting with Chloe and her solicitor tomorrow afternoon and we should know more after that. If we have to pay her off, then so be it, and we'll put the house on the market as he suggested to raise the cash, but other than that, I don't know. Frankly, I can't think of anything else or another solution …' Amanda had resigned herself to the fact that although this was not a problem of her making, it was definitely one she needed to take a share in solving if her marriage was to stand any chance of survival; and if it was not destined to survive, then the financial implications were the least of her worries.

'Well, let's see what tomorrow brings, but in the meantime go and get yourself settled ready for dinner. I've laid some towels out in your bedroom if you want a quick shower, but either way, dinner will be in about half an hour.'

'Thanks Mum. It's good to be back; it's really starting to feel like my second home here. Some peaceful few days, a bit of sunshine and your cooking will soon get me back on track, I'm sure,' replied Amanda, knowing full-well how foolish it was to think some home-made cake and a roast dinner would solve all her problems.

Chapter 14

As Damian emerged from Chloe's solicitor's office around mid-afternoon the following day, his mind was reeling from the encounter. He was in two minds whether to head straight to the pub across the road for a quick drink to calm himself down, or lock himself in a cupboard and throw away the key. Jason, his solicitor, who had a calming presence, advised against both courses of action, suggesting instead they head to the coffee shop next door to discuss what had just taken place, and more importantly how this impacted their gameplan.

It was the first time Damian had seen Chloe since his disastrous and ill-thought-out visit to her house in Bath, a house that he had just learned was a one-bedroom flat being rented from the local council, with bad plumbing and drafty windows. In retrospect, running round there, unannounced after receiving the initial letter informing him that he was a father, was a rash decision – taken on the spur of the moment, without any consideration of the consequences or anyone's feelings. He was annoyed at the time that she had barely let him over the doorstep, but listening to her solicitor describe her accommodation, perhaps that was understandable.

That had been almost six months ago; in the meantime, his behaviour had vacillated between hoping the subject would go away if he simply ignored it, to someone living in dread should Amanda find out, always on edge, and never feeling comfortable or relaxed around others. He was fearful of who knew what, or perhaps suspected anything in the office. Keeping up the pretence had been difficult, exacerbated by the fact that his wife was the only person he really wanted to talk to about it, but at the same time, the one that was most likely to be hurt by his actions.

Having finally come clean to Amanda, a weight felt like it had been lifted off his shoulders. Eventually, once she had calmed down, that is, she argued that he should at least seek his own legal advice, give up this macho-man approach of 'I'm dealing with it myself!', and find out what his options were. After all, he was not named on the birth certificate, so claiming he had any responsibilities for this child was going to be difficult, surely, she argued?

After unburdening himself at the time, he had no longer felt so alone or scared. Amanda was there to support, even if she could never condone his actions. But now, having sat through the mediation meeting, Damian realised guiltily that Chloe was not as fortunate; she had no one to turn to, other than the woman who sat opposite him, simply doing her job.

He had listened as her solicitor, a rather officious and rotund woman in her late fifties, who introduced herself as Ms Rawcliffe outlined Chloe's circumstances, and specifically the situation she now found herself in; a single mum, in part-time employment at a local convenience store, unable to get a full-time job due to childcare needs, someone desperately in need of support, both financially and emotionally, with no family to speak of, and on top of all that taking prescription drugs to deal with early signs of depression. Although Ms Rawcliffe was working Chloe's case on a pro bono basis, it was obvious from the outset she had no plans to short-change her client when laying out her predicament.

Throughout the meeting, Chloe sat quietly at the table, rarely even raising her eyes to meet Damian's, visibly twiddling her fingers or picking at her nails under the table. Gone was the attractive, fashionable young woman Damian had risked so much for, replaced by a frightened child, dressed casually in a denim jacket, over what looked like a T-Shirt that had seen better days and a pair of ripped jeans. It was obvious that she was both uncomfortable and completely out of her depth in this situation, but at least she had the sense to let her solicitor do the talking for her.

Chloe had only met Ms Rawcliffe once before, shortly after she had been appointed for her under the Legal Aid process, something she had been introduced to when she visited her local Citizens Advice centre to see if there was anything they could do or advise to help her. From that point, although she had to admit to being quite fearful of the formidable woman, she at least felt a motherly arm had been put around her, with someone not only willing to listen, but willing to help. Since then, her case for claiming compensation, not only for herself but support for her baby, had taken on a life of its own, and now sitting in front of Damian, she was wondering what would happen next. She was the proverbial rabbit in the headlights, just praying the legal process would not hang her out to dry.

At twenty-seven years old, her baby was all she had in the World. Her parents had divorced when she was a teenager, leaving her to live with her dad after her mum left home, swiftly moving abroad to live with her new partner in the sun, without a backwards glance or thought for Chloe. Her dad had not minded his daughter staying around, particularly as she did the majority of the cooking and washing for him, but he had recently died of lung cancer, after years of nagging by her mum to 'give up those cigarettes, or one day they'll be the death of you' finally ringing true. When her baby was born, they shared her back bedroom at her dad's house, begging or borrowing whatever they needed in terms of baby equipment from neighbours or the local charity shops, but after he died the council took the property back, placing Chloe and her baby in alternative, 'more suitable' accommodation, according to the council's housing department's regulations on caring for single mothers.

Life had not been easy, and after eighteen months of living off handouts in a pokey one-bedroom ground-floor flat, with little money coming in for basic food, let alone anything else for her or the baby, and walls closing in on her more each day, there seemed no end in sight. Becoming increasingly tired, after another sleepless night, one morning Chloe finally snapped, shouting at the baby because he was repeatedly asking for 'more'; more coco-pops, more biscuits, more milk. 'More' was something she just did not have. That was the turning point, the realisation she could no longer look after herself or her baby, or keep either of them fed or safe from harm. But equally she could not envisage a life without him, so needed to seek out whatever help or support was necessary to avoid him being taken into care.

When the suggestion of compensation for constructive dismissal was raised, that was an option she had never thought about, particularly as she had tendered her own resignation, rather than awaiting the humiliation of being dismissed. After their affair ended, it was obvious Damian would not want her around the office as a constant reminder of his infidelity. Chloe did not like conflict, and painfully aware he could make things difficult for her, decided to jump before she was metaphorically pushed. At the time, she was oblivious to the fact she was four-weeks pregnant and presumed walking into another job would be relatively easy, after all she had some experience along with a handful of GCSEs to her name.

Within a few days of walking out, morning sickness really took hold, and with that and a visit to the doctor confirming her predicament, the stark realisation that life was going to get more difficult for her. With no job, no parental support to speak of, and frankly nothing going for her, what were her options? At no stage did she consider swallowing her pride and crawling back to Damian. He had made it abundantly clear that it was over, and if she was honest, the sex had never been that good anyway. No, having an affair with a married man was not a hole she was going to fall easily into again.

Ms Rawcliffe had wrapped up her monologue with a reiteration of her client's claims for not only compensation for constructive dismissal and lack of earnings due to maternity, but arrears of child maintenance for the previous two years. There would also need to be a settlement for ongoing child support, which would be set once Mr Reynolds' earnings and financial status had been assessed, but the look Ms Rawcliffe gave Damian, left him in no doubt it would not be an insignificant figure. She went on to outline Mr Reynolds had the right to contest both the claims, or the question of paternity given he was not currently listed on the birth certificate, but either way her client was more than willing to take it to the courts if they were unable to settle.

Now sitting in the café carefully nursing his double espresso, Damian and Jason were weighing up the options, and on the surface, it was not looking good. The session had not gone quite to plan, and rather than it being a mediation session in its truest sense, with both parties seeking an amicable resolution, Damian and Jason felt they had taken a bit of a thrashing, without being given a proper right to reply.

Thankfully, Ms Rawcliffe had not introduced any further categories of claim, over and above what she had outlined in her recent letter, with the one hundred and fifty thousand pounds originally stated for compensation for constructive dismissal remaining on the table, but the worry was that with all the other claims, these were subject to financial assessment. This did concern Damian, because whilst on the surface he appeared quite well off, any money was family money on Amanda's side. Other than his apartment and the share of their house, that he had attempted to convince Amanda to put on the market, he had little if anything to speak of. Most of his spare cash over the years had been ploughed straight back into the business, and currently that was not showing a healthy return.

He had considered denying any responsibility for the child, which both Jason and Amanda had raised as an option, given he was unnamed on the birth certificate, but Damian was not someone to walk away from his responsibilities on the back of a technicality. No, he would undergo a paternity test, so there would be certainty. They had agreed this would be carried out as a matter of urgency within the next day or so, but if the dates all stacked up as Chloe attested, then there was unlikely to be any surprises. In fact, if the little boy quietly playing with the toy cars in the waiting area, being minded by the receptionist while the meeting took place, was Chloe's son, which he suspected to be the case, then paternity would not be a moot point. The little boy, who had glanced up as they left Ms Rawcliffe's office, with his blonde curls and angelic face, was the spitting image of Alice when she had been that age; the mere sight of him, smiling at him as he left the room, left Damian disconcerted. This little boy, his son, was almost the age Theo would have been had he lived – and if he was having difficulty processing this, then how was Amanda going to deal with that, particularly he had just discovered, Chloe had also named her son Theo?

Chapter 15

Mid-afternoon on the last day of her stay in New England, Amanda lay snoozing in the garden on one of Rob's padded sun loungers, a glass of home-made lemonade by her side and a book she had picked up randomly in W H Smith's at the airport before she departed, which she was not particularly bothered about, but was proving easy reading, abandoned by her side. She had just taken a refreshing swim in Rob's pool, and now had nothing more to worry about than allowing the sun to soak into her skin and opening her mind to wander wherever it chose, provided it kept away from thoughts of going home tomorrow. She did not want to think about that yet.

Being at Rob's was almost like going on holiday to a five-star all-inclusive resort; pure luxury, with excellent home cooked food and quality wines on tap. It was delightful, and if she was honest, one of the places she was happiest. For once, she was enjoying the solitude of not having the girls around her, or for that matter Damian. It was giving her thinking time, but all her thoughts did was go around and around in circles, without any structure or control over where they wandered next. This lack of control was something Amanda hated, and no matter which way she considered the dilemma Damian had faced her with, there was no obvious way forward, or one that would allow them to continue as they were. Something within their dynamic would need to change, and at the moment Amanda was at a loss to understand what that could be.

She had borrowed her mum's car and driven to the office earlier that morning, and spent the majority of the time there the previous two days also, desperate to catch up with her colleagues and meet the new managing director Will had recently appointed to oversee the running of the business. Maria had mentioned a couple of weeks earlier that Nicholas Cronshaw had apparently been headhunted from a larger business in Canada, where he had been one of their operations directors; and that by his own admission deciding to work for Will presented a big challenge for him, not only moving to the US for the first time, but taking on the reins of running the business and being the person in day-to-day control.

Will had stepped back a couple of years previously when he had first appointed someone to run his business for him, but that had not worked out as well as he had expected. The two soon parted company as Will continued to meddle, never confident enough to leave his manager fully in control, and the manager, knowing he would never have the opportunity to take the lead he had been promised, could see no reason to stay to take orders from someone who could not let go. Having learned his lessons the hard way, Will now intended stepping back fully and allowing Nick to run the show once he had settled in, but for now, he was showing Nick the ropes and introducing him around to not only the staff, but the businesses' suppliers and customers alike. So far, according to most of the US based team members Amanda had spoken to, Nick had made a good first impression and everyone felt positive about the change at the top.

Being at the office in person, rather than dealing on-line or in emails to her team, and talking to people who knew so little about her life in England, or frankly cared about her personal situation, was the perfect antidote to all the madness that was happening at home. Being able to simply switch off and concentrate on a job she loved, felt more like an indulgence than real work, and for those few days at least she happily lost herself in her work.

'Hi darling, you look nice and chilled,' Amanda turned and saw Rob walking towards her, carrying his towel and obviously heading for the pool himself. 'Do you mind if I join you?'

Since Rob's kidney transplant just over two years ago, his health had gone from strength to strength. Exercise and diet had become important to him, so with the love of a good woman, some great homemade cooking, a regular game of golf and an afternoon swim, he was on top form. Amanda thought back to when she had first met her biological father; the poorly man, widowed and lonely, living a half-life cooped up in his mansion, starved of company for fear of infection and compelled to rest and stay at home to undertake regular dialysis treatment to keep him alive. What a transformation.

Her feelings for him had developed from almost nonchalance when they had first met, to strong affection after a few months, eventually to love. He would never replace her dad, the man who had raised her and for whom she retained so much respect, but Rob had won his own place in her heart, and the hearts of her family. Donating her own kidney to save his life had been a selfless act of love, but at no time did she have any concept of how deep that love would grow over time, or how important a part they would become in each other's lives.

'I'd love some company, any distraction would be welcome if I'm honest,' she replied, smiling up at Rob. 'I'm trying to avoid thinking about what awaits me when I get home, but I'm failing miserably if I'm honest.'

'Have you heard anymore from Damian after his meeting with his solicitor?' he enquired. Both he and Monica were concerned, but as much as they wanted to help felt powerless to do anything other than to provide a listening ear for the time being. The offer of money to help buy Chloe off had been made, but Damian's pride would not accept that; as far as he was concerned, this was his problem, and his to resolve. Rob knew it was rarely that simple, and for him the money was a drop in the ocean, not worth the angst it could cause between Damian and Amanda if they were forced to liquidate their assets to find it themselves.

'Not really, he's done the paternity test and the results should be back either today or tomorrow, but in his mind there's no doubt.' She then added, 'did Mum tell you he thinks he caught a glimpse of Chloe's son in the solicitor's office? There was a little boy there, around the right age, being minded whilst the meeting was taking place, according to Damian. He said he looked surprisingly like Alice as a baby! In terms of anything else though, they're a long way off sorting out the financial details or access arrangements. I'm not even sure what access Damian wants, if any. That's one of the things we'll need to sort out presumably. What this is going to do to Maisie or Alice, or me for that matter, I wouldn't want to even hazard a guess.'

'Well, try not to worry. Your mum and I are here for you, whatever you need, you know that don't you?' reassured Rob as he put his arms around his daughter. He wanted to be there for her, just as much as she had been for him. 'Right then, a quick swim before I get ready for this evening's entertainment. Your mum and Mrs Reilly are deep in preparations in the kitchen, so I'm keeping out of the way,' he laughed, but noticing the confused look on his daughter's face questioned, 'did Will not mention that he and Maria are bringing Nick around for dinner tonight, so that we could meet him? Apparently, he's a bit of a hit with all the ladies already according to Will, so I'd best watch your mum!' he added.

'No, he didn't say anything, but I've been maxed-out pulling all my designs together and catching up before I set off home tomorrow; it's been a bit of a whirlwind trip, so other than a quick hello, we've not had a lot of time together this visit,' replied Amanda, before realising there was probably a good reason she had not been told. 'If you're all having a get together though, don't worry, I'll make myself scarce and give you some privacy. I'll only create an odd number anyway if Nick's bringing his wife, and Mum always says that's unlucky when hosting a dinner party. No, I'm happy to have an early night and give you all some space.'

'Heaven forbid, of course you're included. Monica wouldn't have it any other way, and neither would I. Anyway, Nick's coming on his own, so no need to get all superstitious on that front. I think Brad and Jane have also been invited, so as a group of eight, we should have a great time, and if nothing else give you a good send off before your flight home tomorrow.'

Amanda had noticed a few glances from some of the younger women in the office in Nick's general direction whenever he walked through the office, or stopped to speak to someone to ask a question, but she had been so focussed on her own priorities that she had not given it a second thought, or him a second glance come to think about it. He had been very polite when she had been introduced to him, but other than that, she had not really paid him much attention; perhaps she should have a closer look tonight to see what all the fuss was about.

Chapter 16

The flight home had been uneventful, and taking just hand luggage meant she had been able to waltz through the airport without too much trouble. It was becoming quite a routine journey for Amanda now and something she had begun to take in her stride, even leaving most of her clothes at Rob's, in what had become her designated bedroom. Will, as part of her salary package, approved her to book business class, so not only was she comfortable and well fed on the journey, she was able to get on with some work if she chose, without the disturbance of children whining or playing on their consoles, or worse still the annoyance of people needing her to move while they went to and from the toilet every half hour. Heathrow was, as usual, manic when she landed, but at least Damian had offered to collect her, thereby making the journey home less stressful.

The dinner on her last night had been really relaxing, with Nick proving to not only be good company, but a bit of a raconteur, comfortable to shine the light on himself and his backstory. He was forty-two, originally born and raised in the south of England, but had been living in Canada for the last five years, moving there with his Canadian born wife shortly after they married to live close to her family, in a small town west of Toronto, likened by him to the 'outback'. His wife had recently decided she preferred women, so showed Nick the door when she declared her love for the local Pilates teacher, 'an elfin sized red-head with a pert bum' by his own description. Nick had noticed she had been taking an increased number of exercise classes, but admitted to being remarkably slow on the uptake.

Realising that he was not in the least upset by the failure of his marriage, and having no desire to remain in Canada, he first considered returning to England to be near his own family. He presented his CV to several agencies around London to test the waters; with his degree and subsequent qualifications and experience all being quite generic - in logistics, financial and business management, he did not feel tied to any specific sector, so could afford to stretch the net quite wide. The States was not an option he had considered, but when the head-hunters had contacted him about Will's opportunity, it ticked most of his boxes, and admittedly kicked the inevitable task of looking after his aging parents a few years further out into the long grass. As the son who had not provided them with any grandchildren, and after the recent turn of events was unlikely to do so in the foreseeable future, he 'wasn't in their best books anyway,' he laughed when recounting his story.

As he spoke, Amanda carefully watched not just his mannerisms and behaviour, but those of the others in the room, particularly the 'older' women; her mum, Aunt Jane and Maria, who like her were finding themselves being drawn into his life, smiling and occasionally laughing as they listened to him. He was definitely a charmer, someone comfortable in his own skin, very open and honest; someone you could easily warm to. As the night wore on and the wine flowed, making everyone even more relaxed, she had to admit there was something about Nick that was definitely appealing. He was roughly the same age as Damian, approximately the same height, with the same dark colouring and immaculate dress sense – but that was as far as the comparisons went.

Damian was a good-looking man, there was no doubt about that, but Nick just seemed to have the edge on him, although Amanda had to admit that was not down to just looks alone. His personality just shone through; his natural ability to warm to people, and have that warmth reciprocated was a skill Damian had never mastered, or if it was, was more likely used quite selectively. Damian knew how to turn the charm on with his clients, but how much of that was natural, and how much professional was questionable.

The last couple of years had shown Amanda that although those people closest to her were polite and tolerant towards Damian, that was probably as deep as their feelings went. When his affair was made known, no one had jumped to his defence or encouraged her to work at their relationship, with most people being surprised, albeit supportive when she decided to forgive and forget. She loved him, but was that enough at the time, and more importantly would it be enough going forward if they were to survive this latest set of obstacles to their 'happy ever after'?

Socialising with Nick had been great fun, but as Amanda reflected on the evening during her flight home, she sensed she needed to be careful around her new boss; mixing business and pleasure was something that was not recommended.

'Hi there, hope you've not been waiting long?' Amanda asked as she got into her husband's car, leaning over to give him a quick peck on the cheek before they set off. He had parked exactly where they had agreed to meet when she had texted him thirty minutes earlier to say the plane had taxied to its standstill. 'Thankfully immigration wasn't too busy, so with only hand-luggage I was straight through. I'm dying for some food though - the meal on the flight wasn't anything I fancied, so I slept instead, even passing on the G&T when the stewardess came round taking drinks orders.'

The last few days had taken quite a toll on Amanda leaving her tired; work had been a frenetic three days to get everything done whilst her team was around her, coupled with the fact the previous evening everyone had stayed up until the early hours, chatting in the garden under the stars enjoying 'one more nightcap'. The night air had been so fresh and still that no one had been desperate to make the first move in drawing the evening to a close. All in all, she had been glad of the opportunity to just kick-off her shoes, have a quiet moment to herself and catch up on a bit of sleep on the flight.

'How about we call in somewhere on the drive home and get some food. We could have a quiet chat too. Rachel's already offered to sleep over if we're late back, so we've nothing to rush home for,' asked Damian, as he put the car in gear and headed into the traffic.

Something in the way he suggested a quiet chat rang alarm bells for Amanda. Having spoken to Damian before she left Boston, she knew the paternity results were imminent, but was there something else that was worrying him? Glancing over and staring at his profile as he negotiated his way through the traffic, she suspected there just might be.

Chapter 17

August seemed to come and go without anyone really noticing, or in truth, missing their usual summer holiday routine. Other than the occasional trip to visit Grandad Tom, the time had been spent largely around the village, with the girls playing in the garden with their friends, or taking day-trips to the zoo, even going paddling in the river or having picnics in the park with Rachel. She had proved to be a real godsend, her confidence building day-by-day as she skilfully not only looked after the girls, but managed to fill the increasing number of holes created by Damian and Amanda as the distractions of 'Chloe and the up-and-coming court case' gathered momentum. Normally, Amanda would have taken the girls to New England to spend their holidays with their grandparents and their uncles, enjoying the sunshine and teaching them to sail, a tradition that had begun after Monica and Rob had first married, but this year with everything else that was happening, it just did not seem appropriate for her to be out of the country, and she was not ready yet to let the girls go without her.

Although disappointed, Monica and Rob understood, but it was a long summer for them, made worse by the fact Lucas was still off exploring the Far East, so not at home either, and as Ben always seemed so absorbed by his work at the hospital, they rarely saw him. He struggled to get a weekend off, let alone a proper holiday. The twins were loved equally, but were like polar opposites in many respects; Lucas completely carefree, enjoying the freedoms of youth, travelling around the globe on his healthy allowance, whilst Ben carried the weight of the world on his shoulders, working ridiculous hours on a junior doctor's salary, curing the ills of the world, one patient at a time.

During the first week of August, Damian's paternity test had, as expected, confirmed Theo was his son, so accepting this, he had begun the process to have his name formally added to the birth certificate. His solicitor, Jason, advised this would not help his case when arguing for a financial settlement, in fact it was likely to make Chloe's case even easier, but that was something Damian was prepared to live with. He had a responsibility now, so no use in hiding or shirking from it.

Acknowledging paternity though was a walk in the park compared to Amanda's reaction when he broached the subject of Theo's name, even thoughtlessly adding how alike he was to Alice as a baby. It was almost as if she shrivelled up on the spot, the sandwich she was just about to eat dropping from her hand onto the grass for the birds to peck over. Damian recalled how she had gone completely into her shell, any light leaving her eyes instantly, being replaced by a pained expression that still returned every time the boy's name was mentioned. Invoking memories and pain that would never go away.

In hindsight, he recognised he had not handled it at all sensitively. Having learned it a few days earlier, but wanting to tell Amanda in person rather than whilst she was in the States, he had blurted it out as they had sat outside in the sunshine having something to eat on their return from the airport some weeks earlier, unable to keep it bottled a moment longer. He did not want any more secrets between them, but mentioning it in the beer garden to a wife who was not just hungry but tired after her long flight, was perhaps not his finest hour.

Since then, Amanda had barely functioned; her automatic pilot kicking in whenever anything needed to be done, or decisions made, with any emotions remaining well and truly bottled-up. Everyone has a fight or flight reaction whenever they feel threatened or sense danger, but for Amanda, survival and protecting her daughters was all she could concentrate on as each new day unfolded, bringing with it its own particular drama. The house had gone on the market without a fight; access to Damian's financial status agreed to without a raised eyebrow; and the knowledge that her husband now had his much longed for son, was something that she just had to accept, however painful that was. There was no alternative that she could see, and frankly she had got to the stage that no matter how much she wanted to airbrush the whole experience out of their lives, that was not an option. Chloe and Theo were clearly there to stay and they had to deal with that, whatever the cost.

Having failed to agree a settlement, the preliminary court hearing, to be held in the civil courts had been set for the middle of September, so only a matter of weeks away now. Before then, the new school term was starting, with both Maisie and Alice getting excited at the prospect of seeing their friends again. For Maisie who was going into Year Two, and Alice into Reception class, September could not come around quickly enough. Amanda knew the family's routines would be changing once school restarted, forcing them into a new norm as far as theirs and their daughters' lives were concerned. She and Damian had talked this over, recognising the distractions they would be facing; with Rachel now primed to do the drop-offs and collections, make meals and packed lunches and generally support all the after-school activities in the week, including helping with any homework and reading the girls had.

Whilst Rachel was looking forward to Maisie and Alice going to school, she was beginning to wonder what she would do to while away the hours between drop-offs and collections. She was not one who took well to idleness, never having had the opportunity to experience it at home in Boston, always being called on to help her mum with her brother and sisters whenever she had a spare moment. She had even suggested helping out in the café at lunchtimes, provided Amanda had no concerns with that, imagining that as a way to not only fill her day, but also help her integrate more into village life. Being around children was fun, but she missed adult company, and although there were some people her age around and about, there was no one yet she could call a friend. As much as she loved Castle Heighton, she recognised it was not the social hub of the county, and if she was to stave off those feelings of homesickness that occasionally crept up on her, then having her own distractions was paramount.

'I think working part-time in the café is a brilliant idea,' agreed Amanda when Rachel broached the subject, 'and you'll soon get to feel part of the village if you're serving teas and coffees to all the locals. Most of the gossip comes from there, whether it's true or not, so be warned when you listen to some of the tall-tales you'll no doubt hear,' laughed Amanda, recalling some of the stories she had heard when calling in at the Coffee Pot for lunch, a take-away sandwich or a pie over the years. In all small villages, the church, the pub and the café were the usual hives of activity where everyone gravitated to in one way or another, and Castle Heighton was no exception. 'In fact, if you want, I'll have a word with Gloria, the lady who runs it, and see what she thinks.'

The following day after a visit to Grandad Tom to top up his provisions and check he was not creating more havoc than usual at Willow Tree village, Amanda dropped in at the Coffee Pot and spoke to Gloria, who was delighted at the prospect of Rachel helping her out a few lunchtimes a week. Gloria had met Rachel a couple of times over recent weeks whilst out with the girls or on errands, and had nothing but nice things to say about her. In fact, her regular lady was having a small operation for 'women's troubles', she whispered conspiratorially to Amanda, ensuring everyone in earshot could hear, so the timing was perfect given she was going into hospital the following Monday, provided 'no one mucked up the waiting lists this time,' she said. Gloria went on to add that 'she'll likely be off for a couple of months, what with all the recuperation she'll need when they've sorted her out, so that will give Rachel the chance to get properly stuck-in.'

Amanda smiled to herself as she left the café, with a fresh loaf and a packet of home-made scones under her arm, reassured that the high standard of gossip was being maintained. For some reason, the little interlude and her visit to Grandad Tom had cheered up what was otherwise proving to be a miserable month.

Chapter 18

September arrived and with it the first signs of autumn. The leaves were starting to change their colours, falling from the trees in increasing numbers as the weeks went on, the nip in the air being felt earlier in the evening, and whilst technically it was still summer, the nights were gradually drawing in. Those long hot summer days that ordinarily everyone would have revelled in, brightening up their moods with the fun and sunshine they brought, this year had just faded away, leaving no significant high points to recommend them, just a general feeling of lethargy lingering around the place. As Amanda wandered around the village, the house and even the gardens where she normally felt most at peace, there was nowhere where she felt particularly happy or free of it all.

Unlike those events that had upset the toxic atmosphere in the first place; they remained, well and truly on the horizon and failed to go anywhere, no matter how much Amanda wished and prayed otherwise. The court hearing was scheduled for the fourteenth of September, just under a fortnight away, and no matter how much everyone had sought to avoid it, it nevertheless seeped into everything they did or said, absorbing all the family's energy without any let-off.

As the first day of school arrived, there was no one in the whole universe more excited than Maisie, desperate to get back to her friends and her routine. She had always loved school and was now going into Year Two. With that came not only a different playground, but more responsibility around the school and possibly a chance to join the netball team if she tried really hard. She had been practising in the garden, throwing a ball through the hoop her daddy had put up on the garage wall, and although she needed practice particularly with her catching, she was not too bad. Amanda noticed how much her eldest daughter had grown during the summer, gone was all the puppy fat she had struggled with as a toddler, replaced by long legs and long arms, perhaps a little gangly at the moment thought Amanda, but plenty of growing left to go.

For Alice, there was more of a nervous excitement. She had met her Reception class teacher, Miss Benson, earlier in the year, but other than Maisie constantly telling her what everything was going to be like, she had no real concept of her own what school would involve. She would be five shortly, so as one of the oldest in her class, and with a big sister to copy from, she was already quite mature for her age, able to read some basic words and write her own name. She was perhaps a little quieter and less confident around people than her more precocious sister, but she was a fast learner, with no intention of being left behind.

As Amanda left them both at the gates of St. Anthony's Primary School that first morning with the other mums, waving after giving both her girls a kiss before they ran off to meet their friends, full of stories of their summer holidays no doubt, it was with a mix or relief and excitement, but thankfully not anxiety or apprehension. School was one place she really had no qualms about, and now they were both in full time education it marked an end to one phase of her life, with the start of another, no doubt bringing its own set of trials and tribulations.

'Well, no more childminding needed now Susie,' she remarked to her friend who was waving off her two children, Isla and Josh, both looking equally smart in their red school uniforms. 'Where did the years go? It doesn't seem five minutes since I was dropping Maisie off at your house as a tiny baby for you to look after whilst I went off to college to teach.'

'I know, would you believe Isla is Year Six now. In a couple of weeks, we'll have to decide on a high school for her! It's great that Josh and Maisie get on so well though – just think next year they'll be juniors. I pity their teacher, she's going to have her hands full with those two,' she laughed. 'I remember dropping Josh off for his first day. He was so quiet and shy; you'd just come back from America after your operation if I recall? Look at them both now, so grown up.'

Yes, three years ago, where had that time gone thought Amanda to herself as she drove home. So many changes in her life, some positive and some not so, but all life-changing to one extent or another. Whatever the next few days brings, she needed to remain positive, because the alternative was somewhere she did not want to go.

Putting the car keys on the hall table as she got home, she heard a buzz from her phone, indicating a message had come in. She was expecting to hear from Gloria arranging for Rachel to call into the café to sort out her hours, so was surprised to see the message from Lucas, her half-brother.

> 'Just left Thailand. Decided to change plans and head for Europe. Will be landing in Heathrow in a few hours. Can you put me up for a couple of nights? Text me the train connections. See you soon L x'

Lucas was doing his grand tour, taking a gap year, or two, before finally settling down to become the 'entrepreneur of his dreams'. He had set off for Australia shortly after graduating from Harvard in Business, to initially stay with a friend in Melbourne whom he had met at university, before heading to New Zealand, where he had hired a camper van with two more lads and travelled around both North and South Island, his friends bumming bar jobs along the way if ever their funds got tight, before returning to Australia to spend some time in Sydney. From what Amanda could recall, he had flown to Singapore a couple of months ago to start his tour around Vietnam, Cambodia and the Far East; but by the sounds of it, that itinerary must have been curtailed as she could not recall any stories from Vietnam and that was one of his must-see places. His plans were fluid to say the least.

As much as she loved her half-brother, Amanda initially sighed as she read the brief message. Now was not the best time for Lucas to visit, and with everything she and particularly Damian had on over the next few weeks, with preparing for the court hearing and selling the house, she could not afford the time to show him the sights, or frankly did not have the energy or enthusiasm for it either. He was always a real laugh and a bit of a party animal, but the way she was feeling at the moment, she was sure neither Castle Heighton nor herself would have that much to offer on the entertainment front. Nevertheless, she could not put him off, so messaged over the train connections, suggesting he ring when he knew what time he would arrive at the local railway station and she would collect him.

Maisie and Alice would however be delighted and astonished to see their uncle when they came home from school, particularly given it was a surprise visit. Normally his visits had them excited for days beforehand; both of them waiting desperately at the window for his taxi to arrive, fighting over who would be first in line for the tickles and cuddles he gives so naturally. Although he acts twenty-six going on five whenever he is around them, tapping into their wave length completely, Amanda knew how sensitive underneath all his bravado he actually was, how thoughtful he could be and in truth how intelligent he is. Having graduated with a first from Harvard, there was no doubting his intelligence, just his application perhaps.

'Oh well, his visit will distract Maisie and Alice if nothing else, and by the sounds of it, it'll only be a couple of days before he's on his travels again, so perhaps the timing isn't too bad after all,' and with that thought, Amanda went upstairs to check the spare bedroom had clean linen and towels laid out, after which, and perhaps more importantly, checking there was enough food in the fridge to feed him. Lucas had an appetite like no-one else she had ever met, and that thought finally put a smile on her face at the prospect of seeing her brother again.

Chapter 19

At breakfast the following morning, Amanda sat around the table with Damian and Lucas enjoying a cup of fresh coffee and bacon butties, which for a mid-week morning was a bit of a treat. Normally it was a quick cup of tea and a slice of toast before the school run, but today Amanda was not on duty, so had some time to kill before she went upstairs to her office and started going through the latest designs she was working on. Having started her career designing children's wear, Amanda was now broadening her skill set by concentrating on the teens-wear market, which was growing more than any other sector. She was currently finalising the collection of accessories for next year's spring/summer range that needed to be completed and signed off by the end of October, latest. She was scheduled to fly over to Boston in just under three week's time for a meeting with Will, Nick and the rest of the senior team to get their endorsement, after which she would work through her designs with the manufacturing teams to iron out any questions they may have before they went into production. The fashion industry certainly had its deadlines, and working often two to three seasons ahead of the calendar, was not only a challenge, but could be awfully confusing.

Lucas had just returned from walking the girls to school and looked like he was ready for going back to bed for a few hours' sleep if truth be told, but he sat with them, thoughtfully listening as they brought him up-to-date with what had been happening, including the court hearing, now only a matter of days away. Damian and his solicitor, Jason had been debating how the court was likely to proceed having now reviewed the preliminary information it had been provided with, including the reports on the mediation session they had attended, for what it was worth. There were several routes the court could apparently take when reaching its decision, Damian had been advised. Paternity was not in question, but access rights and maintenance costs were, including a claim for arrears of maintenance. The big question though was how the court would rule on the question of Chloe's claim for constructive dismissal and the subsequent right to damages that could open up.

Damian, through his solicitor, had strongly disputed this, insisting at no stage had he or any of his team ever put her under pressure to resign. But Chloe's case, which stated it was her only option to leave, made it highly debatable and consequentially not a straightforward point of law. Whichever way it went, his solicitor's advice was that any 'ruling' may take several weeks to be reached, so they needed to be patient and remain on their guard. It was all up to the presiding judge and the application, or more likely the interpretation of the law.

Having been travelling for what seemed like over twelve months, but was probably a lot less, Amanda mused, with only sporadic access to emails and messages, she had not been able to share a lot of information, meaning most of what Lucas was now hearing was fresh to him. She could see that he was desperately trying to keep up with what Damian and she were saying, but at the same time realised he was straining to keep his eyes open.

The girls had woken to news Uncle Lucas had arrived the previous evening after they had gone to bed; 'too late to wake you up' Amanda had told them, as they scrambled out of bed and charged into his room, leaping on top of him and putting an end to any lie-in he might have dreamed of after his long journey the previous day. The promise to walk them to school was all they needed to quickly get dressed, brush their teeth and eat their breakfasts, all of which was conducted without their usual arguments or furore.

The Emirates flight from Phuket to Heathrow had been delayed by just over an hour, meaning the connecting train from the airport to London Paddington for the journey up to the Cotswolds had also been delayed. Thankfully the trains were still running, with Lucas managing to catch the last service out of London, and as Damian was at home that evening, he was able to pick him up from the station, leaving Amanda to mind the girls. Other than a quick hello, a cup of tea and a snack before bed, Lucas had not really had any chance to tell them why he was there, or what his plans were. Having listened now, perhaps his news could wait for a while longer.

'So, that's the sorry state of affairs we currently find ourselves in,' sighed Amanda, once they had finished downloading where they were up to, not only with the hearing, but selling the house, keeping Damian's business afloat, their home and getting her designs out in time, adding 'the only saving grace is that Rachel is here to help out with Maisie and Alice, meaning at least we've got the flexibility to come and go should we need to move quickly. It's her day off today, but you might meet her tomorrow if you're staying around for a day or so. She's living in Grandad Tom's old house; you remember it, don't you?' Lucas nodded, without breaking his concentration.

'Yes, and I'm trying to work from home more than I have been doing over the last couple of months, mainly to give Amanda the support she needs,' added Damian smiling at his wife, 'but it's proving more difficult than I thought. Someone needs to keep an eye on the business, but at the moment I've so much else distracting me, I don't know how we're going to cope, and if I can survive,' displaying real emotion in his voice that even Amanda had to admit was difficult to hear. Seeing him now, with the weight of all that was happening firmly resting on his shoulders; knowing it was tearing him apart from so many different angles, was so hard to take in. His business was not just his financial security, but it was like his baby. He had nurtured it from a new start-up, fighting to secure contracts and get a foothold in such a competitive market; so, to see it go from a relative success, to a potential failure in less than six months was heart-breaking. She also knew he felt a responsibility for Theo; a son he had not looked for, but nevertheless had metaphorically been dumped on his doorstep. He could no more deny him than he could Maisie and Alice. Theo was his flesh and blood, and for that he had to hold his hands up. Most of all though, she knew he was feeling a real shit for what he had put her through. They had gone through difficult times before, mainly due to his infidelity, but because of her ability to forgive, they had both come out the other side, ready to weather whatever life threw at them, feeling stronger for it.

These most recent events had thrown them their first serious curve ball since losing their son; nothing felt certain anymore. She had tried to stay angry at him, even angrier still at Chloe for turning up as she had, making threats and outrageous demands; but her 'forgive and forget' mentality meant she was struggling to stay angry. Amanda did not deal well with conflict, and although at times it would have been easier to walk away, than stay and argue, after all this problem was not of her making, for some reason she had opted to stay. She was prepared to continue to forgive, for the time being at least, but with Theo in their life 'forget' might be the harder part of the equation. It was fair to say neither of them was in a particularly happy place.

'Look, I don't want to sound rude, but I need to get some sleep before I collapse. If I don't, I'll be in no fit state for when those adorable little monsters return home from school; but seriously if there's anything I can help with, then just let me know. My plans are flexible, and a couple of calls is all it'd take for me to hang around a bit longer. You never know, it might be time to put my entrepreneurial skills into play – after all, a first-class degree from Harvard must count for something and shouldn't be put to waste!'

As Lucas took his dirty plate and cup to the sink before heading towards his room, Damian and Amanda exchanged glances. Could there be a way forward in what Lucas had said, and if so, were they prepared to find a way to let him in? After all, he was family and who else could they trust?

Chapter 20

The following morning, Rachel arrived early to take the girls to school, wearing her customary jeans and sweat top, but with the addition of a puffer jacket as the weather had turned a little cooler over the last couple of days. She had even had to put the central heating on in the cottage as there was definitely a chill in the air, and Rachel did not deal well with the cold. She was a simple soul, born for comfort, with no airs and graces to talk of, and proud of it. She could not understand girls who spent more time in front of the mirror than was necessary; a quick glance was all it took to check your parting was straight and you did not have spinach in your teeth was her philosophy.

After dropping the girls at the school gates, she was planning on heading to the Coffee Pot to have a chat with Gloria about doing a couple of shifts the following week, or even over the weekend if Gloria was desperate. It was Friday and Rachel had no plans for the weekend; in fact, she had few plans any weekend. She really needed to start doing something about finding a hobby or making some friends she could meet up with, particularly as Maisie and Alice would not be commanding anywhere near as much of her attention going forward as they had done. She loved being with the girls and enjoyed her work, and got on well with Amanda, but there had to be more to life than school runs and packed lunches.

She had agreed to work as the au pair for twelve months initially, but as she did not enjoy being idle, if it got too quiet, then she might have to consider her options, including whether she stayed in England or returned to America. Her visa allowed her to stay, but was that really what she wanted? She was not homesick per se, but she did miss her family; although going back to the way it had been at home was not something she was looking forward to. Having found her independence, including the joys of living alone, deciding what time she went to bed, what she ate for her meals and above all, what she watched on the television, living under her mum's roof again would be difficult – but if she was honest, she could not afford the alternative. Working for Amanda was allowing her to save a little, but without a good job to go home to, with no real savings behind her, to break out on her own yet would just be a pipe dream. She had a good college education, but no university degree to open doors for her. No, she had to think carefully before she threw it all in here.

No sooner had Rachel left to do the school run, Lucas emerged from his bedroom and made his way downstairs. He had spent time helping Maisie and Alice with their homework the previous evening, on the proviso they let him have a lie-in in the morning and let their au pair take them to school. They had reluctantly agreed, but only if he agreed to pick them up from school. They were shrewd negotiators he noted, he had better watch out.

'Good morning, coffee?' asked Amanda as Lucas entered the kitchen. Damian was still seated at the kitchen table, and it was obvious from the papers strewn around him that they had been discussing something before he came in.

'Oh yes please, a big mug. I'm parched. Can I grab some toast and peanut butter too?'

'Help yourself,' replied Amanda, adding 'then have a seat, we've something we want to discuss with you if you've got a few minutes before Rachel gets back.'

Intrigued, Lucas sat down as requested and listened as Damian and Amanda outlined their plan to him; a plan that involved catapulting him into Damian's business to support his existing management team, but at the same time becoming Damian's eyes and ears, reporting back to him areas that were not functioning as well as they should, or issues that were of concern. Over the next hour or so, Damian outlined his operation, his structure and the nature of the business, which given Lucas was IT savvy was not rocket science. In fact, for Lucas it sounded very much like a scenario they had studied at Harvard, where they had gone into a failing business, done a full due diligence exercise, identifying problem areas, valuing assets and basically following the money to see where costs savings and improvements could be made, then making recommendations. He had also done a similar exercise on another company where asset stripping was an option, buying a failing business and breaking it down into its constituent parts to understand the value and the opportunities going forward. With both exercises he had excelled, as well as having a great deal of fun.

'So, what do you think? Does that sound like something you'd be interested in doing for say the next month or so, or at least until we have some clarity here and I can focus back more. I wouldn't just throw you in and abandon you, as I'd always be here, just not there, if you know what I mean?'

'I like the sound of that – in fact, I was thinking how similar the scenario is to some of the case studies we did at Harvard, so it would be great to experience it for real. I'm definitely up for it, and I honestly believe, without being too conceited, that I could really add some value. Listening to a few of the things you've mentioned has already given me some ideas, which I can look into a bit more and see what you think. It sounds a brilliant opportunity – thanks.'

Amanda and Damian exchanged glances, before Damian shook Lucas' hand. 'Looks like we've got ourselves a deal. Let's talk more tomorrow when I've spoken to a couple of the team this afternoon to set things up, then on Monday, if you come into the office with me first thing, I'll show you the ropes. The court hearing starts on Tuesday afternoon, so it will be a real baptism of fire. I hope you're up for it!'

'I'm up for the challenge, I just might need to buy a suit or some smarter clothes – I don't think the shorts and T-shirts I've been backpacking in for the last few months are going to impress anyone, or create the impression you'll need me to make, so point me in the direction of the nearest Bloomingdales, or whatever you have over here,' replied Lucas suddenly fired up by the prospect of the next few weeks working as Damian's mole cum business advisor! His other plans might just need to be put on hold for a little while longer, he thought to himself, realising a couple of calls were in order before he hit the shops.

'Can I borrow your car by the way?' Lucas asked Amanda, 'otherwise I've no means of getting around.'

'You could, but why don't I ask Rachel to run you this afternoon. She knows the way and is also insured to drive Grandad Tom's car, so until we can get you insured on mine, that would probably be easier. I'll give her a ring now, I'm sure she won't mind, and if you're not back before the girls need picking up, I'll go and collect them and explain why you've abandoned them.'

'If I'm here for a few weeks longer than planned, then perhaps I may get away with it just this once' replied Lucas with his fingers crossed.

Chapter 21

As Lucas closed his bedroom door late on Monday evening, after saying goodnight to Amanda and Damian as they sat finishing off their glasses of wine in the kitchen, his mind was spinning after what had probably been the most hectic few days of his young life, and if he was honest possibly the scariest too. Until this point, he knew he had lived a charmed life, never having to work for a living or take life too seriously, with a trust fund to fall back on if ever life got difficult, or he needed to dig himself out of a hole, which thankfully had not happened to date. He was the joker of the family; confident in his looks, his status, his abilities, exuding more natural charm and charisma than was probably good for him.

For the first time in his twenty-six years, the stakes had been seriously ramped up, to a level Lucas was not all together comfortable with. Real life had finally kicked in, with elements of what he had been asked to do capable of impacting people's lives, and importantly their livelihoods, in a very direct way. No longer was it a scenario or a case study that his professor would assess and grade him on, but a real dilemma, with consequences that could be wide reaching if played out to their conclusion. He needed to take stock of what he was being ask to do before he committed himself, because once he was committed Lucas would need to follow it through to its conclusion. Failure for him was never an option.

Earlier that morning, Damian had called all his senior team into his office and introduced Lucas to them as his brother-in-law, recently graduated and looking for some work experience before he returned to the States to start his career. Although that description had not been inaccurate, it had perhaps lacked a little on detail, and had deliberately played down the pedigree or kudos Lucas' qualifications would normally garner. Importantly, there was also no mention of the specifics of the role Lucas had been asked to carry out; only a suggestion he was there to help out and look around, before presenting Damian with any comments or thoughts he might have on the running of the business. Lucas was apparently to have access to all areas, with nothing off limits; but above all else, Damian made it abundantly clear that not only did he have full trust in Lucas, but that he would not be slow to implement any recommendations he felt would drive the business forward. Anyone listening to how Lucas was being positioned was left in no doubt he was to be taken seriously, with any suggestions he made being disregarded, or fobbed off, at their peril.

Lucas had felt a little uncomfortable at times listening to Damian brief his team, but had kept a poker face, careful not to give anything away. Looking around the room, he saw a real mix of individuals and tried to gauge their reactions to what they were hearing. Probably not the Monday morning briefing they had anticipated. Some, many years his senior, were probably wondering what this 'child' had to offer, with others, similar age to Lucas wondering why he was being singled out, seeing perhaps nothing but competition from the young American upstart. A few gave him a wan smile, but mainly they kept their emotions in check, unsure exactly how to react, but sensing things were about to change.

Afterwards, Lucas was shown to an office he could use, introduced to a secretary who would assist him as required and provided with both a mobile and all the IT equipment essential for accessing the management information and customer contracts the business held on its databases. In the space of a couple of hours, he was walking around the building, talking to people and making himself at home; dressed in his new suit, smart shoes and tailored shirt, no one was left under any illusion that he did not mean business.

Discussing over dinner how the day had gone, Damian had given him the option of backing out before he got too involved, if what he was asking was too much, but the deeper Lucas got in, not only did he feel that he could not let his sister down, but importantly the 'job' was something he thought he would really enjoy, and without his normal bravado, he truly felt he could actually provide some real help to Damian.

The business, from what he had seen so far, had potential; but with all the signs of having grown in a way that was neither structured, nor viable longer term. Services were very reactive, rather than planned or thought-out; with opportunities for standardisation and rationalisation crying out to be implemented, changes that could not just drive down costs, but enhance the customer service levels. As a result of the organic way the business had grown, it gave the impression of having lurched from one successful contract to another, but each successive contract appeared to be driving reduced margins, rather than the increased returns you would normally expect to see. Lucas had some thoughts on what the root causes could potentially be, areas he would like to probe more in time, but he was astute enough to know that to gain everyone's support, he needed to be careful how he went. Going in heavy-handed in the first few days would be a disaster, and simply add to Damian's woes.

Reflecting now, less than a week after arriving, effectively unannounced at his sister's front door, he realised he had crammed in as much over these few short days than he had in almost nine months of travelling from continent to continent. Back-packing in the southern hemisphere suddenly felt like a picnic compared with the opportunity he had been given here – and rather than be apprehensive, he felt euphoric at the possibilities it presented.

As he got his laptop ready to dial the other side of the world, the only remaining dilemma was how was he going to explain to Sonia that their scheduled trip to Paris was on hold. He had toyed all weekend with contacting her to let her know his plans were being delayed, but with all the shopping he had done with Rachel, chasing all over Cirencester to acquire his 'business ready' wardrobe, he had run out of time, or more correctly had consigned it in the 'deal-with-later' basket. But as she was due to fly out from Auckland next week, he could not delay any longer. What he could not say with any certainty though, was the nature of the change to his, or more correctly their plans; was he talking a delay or a complete rethink? That was a question he did not feel able to answer.

Dialling her number, and knowing it would be early morning in New Zealand, he imagined Sonia would be bright and breezy, probably sitting on the porch at the front of her parent's property awaiting his call, with a drink in her hand, enjoying the views. Their home was situated in one of the suburbs about an hour's drive north of the centre of Christchurch, and from some of the photos she had shared, it enjoyed amazing views not just of the river, nearby but of South Pacific Ocean on a clear day.

He steadied himself for her answering, but almost instantly her smiling face appeared in front of him.

'G'day Lucas, I thought you'd gone AWOL. I've missed speaking to you all weekend, how are things going? I can't wait until next week……'

Lucas took a deep breath, plastered a smile on his face and braced himself for the task of letting her down gently, glad for once he was thousands of miles away from any fallout.

Chapter 22

Pulling his car into the drive late on Tuesday afternoon, after spending the majority of the day holed up in an airless courtroom, Damian not only felt completely drained and exhausted, but weary of the whole process. Jason had counselled him as they left the court that there was still a long way to go before any judgement was made, advising him the judge could take several weeks before they were called back to hear her summation, particularly where cases were not straightforward. But at least he said the hard work was over, so for now they just needed to get on with their lives as best they could. The platitude had sounded hollow to Damian, after all, it was not Jason's life that was impacted. How could he just get on with everyday life as if nothing had happened, whilst all this was hanging over him?

For most of the day Damian had sat quietly listening as the two barristers, instructed by both Jason and Ms Rawcliffe for their respective clients, outlined the elements of the claim and counter-claim to the judge, providing clarity or detail to the papers she had already reviewed at some length in the weeks preceding the hearing. Judge Donaldson was a distinguished and not unattractive looking woman, perhaps in her early sixties, with silver-grey hair, neatly swept back off her face, wearing what Damian thought were trendy glasses, with bright blue frames, neatly perched on the end of her nose.

She mainly had her head down as she listened to the barristers speaking, but occasionally raised it to note the reactions of both the claimant or the defendant as specific points were being made, even offering a smile he noticed on occasion. Given the claim was constituted of elements that ordinarily would be presented in different courts, for her to agree to bundle everything together and deal with it not just holistically but practically, was progress as far as the court system was concerned.

After speaking to Lisa and getting a feel for what the proceedings would involve, Amanda decided against accompanying Damian to court, even though her support would have potentially been viewed favourably for his case. Lisa had indicated it could get messy, particularly as personal or sensitive information may be discussed, leaving Amanda to conclude she was not only unwilling to sit through the evidence of her husband's affair being broadcast to all and sundry, but also unprepared to watch as Chloe talked about the baby she had given birth to; the baby she had raised especially as Amanda's own baby had been still-born. Listening to stories of Theo and the struggles Chloe had undoubtedly gone through in those early days was something Amanda was not prepared to put herself through. Damian had understood her position, and although he tried to argue against it, wanting her next to him when he went through this, he was not at pains to persuade her otherwise.

With hindsight, he accepted now that it had been the right decision. Watching Chloe in court had been difficult enough for him, let alone for Amanda to witness. Her whole demeanour had been hard to take in. She looked frightened, completely out of her comfort zone, and when asked even the most basic of questions, was struggling to compose her nerves, visibly shaking and biting her nails, failing to make eye contact even with her own team. Damian, not recognising anything of the vibrant young woman he'd had his affair with, wondered at times whether elements of it were an act, coached no doubt by Ms Rawcliffe to win the sympathy of the court; but if it was, it was a good one. It was obvious that she really loved her son and would do anything to not just protect him, but keep him close to her. The fear of Theo being taken into care, now that all her problems were being highlighted so pointedly, must have weighed heavily on her. She had nowhere to hide, and rather than feel anger towards her, Damian's overriding feeling was one of compassion, not just for Chloe, but for his son too. Other than his mother's love, it was clear Theo had not had the best of starts in life, unlike Damian's other children who had wanted for nothing.

Hearing Damian's key in the lock, Amanda made her way into the hall, just in time to see her husband almost collapse onto the floor. He looked beaten, dishevelled; a shadow of the man that had left the house earlier that morning, anxious, but hopeful for the day ahead.

Thankfully Rachel had taken the children swimming after school, so would not be returning for at least another hour; calling in no doubt at the Coffee Pot to get the girls a drink or a treat before heading home. She had started working two or three lunchtimes a week, and today was usually her day for collecting her rota for the following week from Gloria.

Lucas had opted to stay in Damian's apartment in town mid-week, which was not only close to the office, thereby avoiding the need for the daily commute, but allowed him his independence. It seemed to be suiting everyone perfectly; Lucas having access to the social life the town provided, leaving Damian and Amanda to enjoy more space at home, not only for their work, but for the girls and Rachel when she was around. Having visitors was one thing, but if Lucas intended staying a few months, as had been mooted, then having his own space was essential for all of them. Maisie and Alice were the only ones who wanted him to 'stay forever' with them, but the promise of an ice cream, or a trip to the toy shop when they visited him in town, soon won them over. Damian was pleasantly surprised how well and how easily Lucas had settled into the 'nine-to-five' routine, and from some of the comments and feedback he had received, it was clear he was making real progress with the wider team too.

So, with everyone otherwise engaged, and seeing the state her husband had returned in, Amanda was at least relieved they had their privacy, for an hour or so, at least.

'By the look on your face, I presume it didn't go too well?' she enquired, taking Damian's jacket from him and hanging it on the hook before he dropped it to the floor. She noted the colour had drained from his normally tanned face, replaced by an almost ghostly pallor. 'Have you eaten anything all day? Dinner isn't quite ready yet, but I'll make you a sandwich and a hot drink - you look like you could do with it, or even something stronger if you'd prefer. Go and sit down in the lounge and I'll be through in a minute. Then you can tell me all about it.'

With a cup of sweetened tea in his hand, a hand that Amanda noticed was still shaking several minutes later, he desperately tried to summarise the day, but the more he tried, the more he struggled to find the right words, relying eventually on his wife's gently prompting to keep the conversation going. Amanda had so many questions going through her mind, but soon realised that today was not the day to get all the answers she needed. She had to be careful not to push too hard; without sensitive handling, her husband would not survive an inquisition, and as she was heading off to Boston again in a matter of days, she did not want to say or do anything to impact either her trip, or the state of his health whilst she was away.

Sighing, with a mix of frustration and resignation, he concluded, 'to be honest, it's just a waiting game now. We've presented all the facts, answered her questions and provided all the clarifications she needed; now it's just up to the judge. Jason seems to think she's likely to take at least a couple of weeks to reach her recommendations; at which stage we'll no doubt be summoned back to court to hear what she has to say. We then have a right to appeal if it doesn't go our way, or if the value of the damages she awards is deemed unreasonable, but that will add more time into the process, so God knows when it's all going to end.'

'Don't get too disheartened, 'it's not over till the fat lady sings', so the saying goes,' smiled Amanda desperately trying to lift her husband's spirits. She could tell it had taken its toll on him today, more than she or he had expected, and was at a loss what she could do, or say to improve the situation.

'Oh, I don't know; I think the fat lady's sung quite vehemently already,' replied Damian, conscious that Ms Rawcliffe, along with Chloe's barrister had almost wiped the floor with his team, and no matter what his barrister threw back at them, he was always on the back foot. From where Damian sat, it was not comfortable viewing, and nothing Jason had said as they left the court house afterwards had convinced him otherwise.

Chapter 23

'Good morning, and welcome back. Will said you'd flown in last night.' Amanda looked up from her computer to see Nick Cronshaw standing in front of her, a cup of coffee in each hand, a smile on his face and looking so relaxed in his blue chinos and white shirt it was almost criminal. 'If I remember correctly, it's white with no sugar?' he questioned, as he handed her a cup.

'That's perfect, thank you,' she replied. 'You must be a mind reader; I've not had breakfast yet, and was just planning on getting a quick coffee and a bagel from across the street before the meeting started, not only to steady my nerves, but to stop my stomach from grumbling!'

Nick laughed, lighting up his whole face. 'From what I've seen of the designs so far, you've got nothing to worry about. Fashion might not be my background, and I don't have teenage kids to buy for, but I think your designs will really sell. In fact, we're banking on it, so no pressure then!'

It was Amanda's first foray into the teenage leisurewear market, a market Will had only recently decided to focus more of his company's attentions on, so for her to be asked to head-up the design team was a real credit to how far she had come in less than three years. She had learned so much technically about the design processes, had listened to the experts Will had wrapped around her to ensure she benefitted from their collective experience, but had then been allowed, even encouraged to apply her own style when developing her designs. Experience was priceless, but so was a fresh pair of eyes, and coupled with the different perspective that Amanda brought with her British heritage, the results were impressive. To think, only three years ago she had been teaching Art at the local sixth form college, with students the ages she was currently designing clothes for. What would they think of Mrs Reynolds now, would she be 'cool', or whatever kids said nowadays, but importantly would they be seen out in anything she had designed? That was an interesting question, she pondered to herself as she drank the coffee Nick had brought her.

'Well, I'll leave you to get yourself together and see you in the Boardroom in thirty minutes, or so,' said Nick, adding before moving along to talk to one of her colleagues, 'let's catch up properly before you head off though. It will be great to get to know you better. Have you any plans for the weekend?'

'No nothing yet, I'm flying out on Monday, so a couple of days catching up with family was the extent of my plans, but I'm around for a catch-up anytime if you're free.'

Since meeting at Rob's house for dinner on her last visit, Amanda had not spoken to Nick directly in either a business or a social context. He had been involved in some of the video meetings she had joined, and had even copied emails to her with various thoughts and ideas he had as he got closer to the business, but sitting down and chatting had not been on the agenda. She had been impressed so far with his approach, noting that no one seemed to have a bad word to say against him. His ability to gel with the team with such ease; striking the right balance between friend and boss, was flawless, as was his bum in those trousers she thought as he walked away from her. 'Time to stop daydreaming, back to the work!' she chided herself as she returned to her computer and reread her notes ahead of the meeting.

'Well, I don't know about the rest of you,' said Will two hours later, as he was wrapping up the meeting, 'but I'm quite excited about the range Amanda and her team has created. It's really fresh, and with the right marketing, which is over to you guys, I think it could be a winner. Great work guys, have a good weekend everyone.' Smiles and nods came from all directions as everyone agreed. The designs had been wholeheartedly endorsed, with approval to move to the next phase given. Seeing Amanda pulling her papers together, ready to float out of the Boardroom, so pleased was she at the way her presentation had been received, Will called over, 'Can I have a quick word with you please before you leave, oh and you too Nick, I've got something I need to run by you. Meet me in my office in ten minutes.'

That evening back at home with Monica and Rob, Amanda sat around the table on the veranda, finishing off her supper and regaling her parents of the day's events, and specifically the point when Will had asked her to accompany him and Nick to Singapore in a couple of weeks' time to meet with some of the fabric suppliers and agents in the Far East.

'He's asked me to go and talk some of our suppliers through the designs as well as finalise the fabrics and accessories we're planning to use. I can't believe it – Singapore! That's somewhere I've always wanted to go to, but never had the opportunity before.' Monica and Rob watched their daughter's face light up, pleased for once it was a smile rather than a frown she was wearing. She'd had so much to deal with over the last few months, they had become worried about the effect it was having on her, not only physically with her obvious loss of weight, but emotionally as she did not seem her usual positive or bubbly self. 'I know it won't be a holiday, but Will says we can book an extra day into the schedule to have a bit of down time, and we'll be staying quite centrally in a hotel he's used before, so it will be easy to get around. His secretary, Loretta is going to book the flights tomorrow. He says I can fly direct from Heathrow and meet them there, so even better. I'm going to google later and see what the best things to do in Singapore are; a Singapore Sling at Raffles though is a must!'

'What does Damian think of another trip so soon after this one, I presume you've told him?' enquired Monica, unsure what her son-in-law thought about being left at home on an increasingly regular basis.

'Not yet, but I'll ring him later. I'd have thought he'd be okay with it though, as Lucas is proving to be a great help around the office, taking a lot of pressure off Damian, and Rachel will have no problems managing the girls and their routines; she may need to give up her shifts at the café while I'm away though, but that's no biggie. Anyway, with me not around, it's one less thing for him to worry about surely, after all, it's only four days, what can possibly go wrong? ….' replied Amanda, fingers crossed that her husband would agree what a great opportunity it was for her. 'When I've finished off Mrs R's amazing cheesecake, I'll go and call him; but no, looking at the time at home, it's nearly midnight, so perhaps I'll wait until the morning,' suddenly grateful for buying herself a few extra hours to sleep on it and think how best to position the fact she was travelling again to her husband, whom her mum had rightly deduced was not dealing as well with the fact she was a frequent flyer, half as much as she was.

Chapter 24

'What have I done!' Amanda asks herself, waking up to the sun streaming through the floor to ceiling window of her plush hotel room, overlooking the Singapore waterfront, the amazing skyline in front of her. She strains her eyes to look at her alarm, noticing it's not yet six o'clock; far too early to be getting up, but knowing that now she is awake, there is little if any chance of her getting back to sleep. As she moved her head on the pillow, desperately trying to shade her eyes from the brightness, but at the same time trying to open them to locate her water bottle, images of last night came flooding back to her, images she would much rather forget, or preferable erase completely if she had the option.

'Oh God, what a mess,' she repeats to herself, 'I'm not safe to be let out by myself, what have I done!' Feelings of shame and embarrassment quickly rising to the surface, before an urgent need to throw-up had her rushing to the bathroom, cradling her head as she went. Amanda could not remember the last time she was hungover, or in fact ever getting this drunk before. Normally she enjoyed a drink or two, but knew her limits; the main limiting factor being two small children who just did not understand the concept of 'be quiet, mummy has a headache'.

What had she drunk? Thinking back, a cocktail before dinner, a couple of glasses of wine with her meal, a very nice Malbec she recalled, and a brandy afterwards, or was it two? Over the space of a few hours, it was definitely not excessive, but with the heat, her body clock being all over the place, and the fact she had not eaten much during the day, then perhaps that explained it, but it still does not excuse it, or more importantly her behaviour.

The day had started well. It was their final set of meetings with their key Singaporean suppliers, before they caught their respective flights home the following day. She and Nick had met early for breakfast, as had become the norm over the previous three mornings. He liked his food and swore a hearty breakfast set him up for anything the day may throw at him, apart from which, he used the early mornings to catch-up on emails and messages from the office. Being in Singapore, the time difference was working in his favour for once; twelve hours ahead meant any problems fired to him at the end of their day could easily be dealt with and fired back before the start of the next. A perfect use of his time he argued.

When Amanda had been checking into the hotel at the beginning of the week, a message had buzzed in on her phone from Will, advising her that he had been unavoidably delayed and unable to make the flight at the last minute. He had gone on to say that Maria had to attend an appointment at which he needed to support her. He had not elaborated further, just apologised and said no need to worry, they would catch up when she got back. He went on to advise that Nick was aware of the change of arrangements, but had the full authority to negotiate on his behalf; so as far as the business trip went, they should carry on as planned and just offer his apologies. The message had ended by telling her to enjoy her stay, and make the most of the city whilst she had the opportunity.

Whilst Amanda was initially disappointed, she soon felt not only empowered but flattered that Will trusted her, but principally Nick, to continue without him. She had met some of their suppliers previously, but always with a senior buyer in tow. Now she was ostensibly the one with the experience; the one with the background in the fashion industry, and the one Nick would probably look to for a nod from before he finalised any deals. It was shaping up to be a good trip, she smiled to herself as she put her mobile back in her pocket.

The following morning was their notional 'downtime' day, and although Nick needed to carry out some further preparations for his meetings now that Will was not there to take the lead for part of the morning, they did manage a few hours exploring the area around the marina in the afternoon, even venturing up to the top of the Marina Bay Sands hotel to have a drink at their bar and marvel at the spectacular panoramic views from the top of the building. Their roof top infinity pool was a feat of engineering in Amanda's mind, and so inviting; what she would have given to sink into the water with a cocktail in her hand or recline on one of the luxurious loungers. Pure heaven.

She and Nick chatted constantly as they walked along, easily tapping into the other's sense of humour, making jokes and feeling completely relaxed and at ease. She had discovered how easy he was to talk to when they had first met, some weeks previously at her parents' home for dinner; remembering how he could tell a good tale, and how entertaining he could be, his humour quite self-deprecating. She was loving strolling along the harbour, relaxing in a café, or simply sightseeing, but doing it with someone other than her husband, was a whole new experience for her. In fact, she could not recall ever having spent so much one-to-one time with another person before, let alone another man. She felt so happy, so carefree; walking down the street, anyone looking at them would probably assume they were a couple, they just seemed to 'gel' so nicely together.

When the first meeting started the following morning, initially there was a little uncomfortableness before Nick got into his stride, but thereafter the remaining meetings went like a dream. They found they could work well together, and being able to read each other's body language when the negotiations began, meant they not only managed to secure the fabrics they needed, but at prices Will would be pleased with. At one of the supplier's, they even went a little 'off-piste', by securing a selection of products they had not sought out, but Amanda instinctively knew would slot straight into their range, complementing the other designs completely. When they messaged Will to brief him on their 'off-the-wall' purchase, he not only endorsed their decision but agreed with their assessment, making them both sure they had made the right call.

At the end of each day, they met for dinner in the hotel's restaurant and reviewed their progress, before planning the following day's activities, then retiring to their respective rooms. They worked together like a well-oiled machine, and Amanda realised that not only was she having fun, but the troubles and stresses she had been under at home, had been well and truly put behind her, for the time being at least. She felt completely absorbed, not just by the challenges of the day, but if she was honest, the attention she was receiving from Nick. He was forever praising her on her taste, her decision-making skills, her natural abilities and above all her innate flair.

So, why and where had it all gone so disastrously wrong, Amanda asked herself as she lay in bed, after having taken a couple of paracetamols, washed down with half a litre of water to clear her head. Why had she read the signs so badly, and what on earth was she thinking by making a pass at her boss?

They had finished their meals and were in the bar having a final drink before retiring. Nick had ordered them both a brandy, and returning from the bar had sat next to, rather than opposite her as he would normally have done, choosing the comfy chair, rather than the straight backed one he had previously been sitting in. They were both exhausted, but exhilarated after their trip, and that showed on their faces. Talk soon turned to needing to have an earlyish night as they both had flights home the following day; Nick's was departing around eleven o'clock, and Amanda's slightly later at one o'clock in the afternoon. Taxis had been booked to take them both to Changi Airport, Nick's picking him up at seven o'clock that morning, Amanda's two hours later.

For reasons Amanda could still not fathom, she had moved closer, placed her hand over Nick's and looking straight into his eyes, said 'Well, if we're talking about an early night, why don't we go up to my room now, we can take our drinks with us?'

Nick withdrew his hand instantly from under Amanda's, and standing up stuttered out the words, 'I apologise if I have misled you in any way, but that was certainly not my intention. I am so sorry; will you please excuse me. It's probably best we don't meet for breakfast, as my taxi is very early. Goodnight Amanda,' before scurrying off.

The sheer look of embarrassment and panic on his face as he left the bar and made his way to the lift was something she would never forget, and probably never live down. What had she done, and how was she ever going to explain her actions to him, Will or even Damian if this got out?

Later that day, just as Amanda was making her way to the departure gate in preparation for boarding her lunchtime flight back to Heathrow; a flight that would hopefully take her back to some level of normality after the previous few days of living the highlife in Singapore, and importantly maintain a few thousand miles distance between her and Nick whilst she decided how to address the awkward situation she had created, she received a text message from Damian, simply saying 'call me as soon as you get the chance.' She looked at the screen, debating whether to message back, or wait until she landed. The way she felt she was really not in the mood for small talk, or frankly up to talking to Damian about anything that had gone on over the last few days. She needed to get her head straight first, and the flight would give her a few hours to contemplate her actions. Anyway, she would be boarding soon, so would not have much time to talk. She considered just messaging back to put him off, but then realising it must be the early hours of the morning at home, so for him to have messaged, it may be important, decided that was probably not the best option.

'Hi there, I've only just got your message and we're about to board, so can it wait until I get home?' enquired Amanda as soon as her call was answered, but sensing from the fact Damian was not replying she added, 'is everything okay, are the girls alright?'

As she listened to her husband sobbing at the other end of the line as he tried to explain, she realised that the normality she had so longed for, was now a lot further away than she had thought.

Chapter 25

For an early October morning, the weather was unusually warm. The sun was out, the rainclouds for once were absent from the sky, all leaving a crisp autumnal feel to the air. It was the archetypal Indian summer's day, one that ordinarily would lift the spirits, but as Damian parked his car, checking he was in a parking zone where he did not need to pre-buy a ticket, for some reason he was just not feeling it. With Amanda away in Singapore, he had spent most of the daytime alone, unable to focus on work, simply wandering around the house, trying to find anything to distract him until the girls arrived home from school. Then at night, without her next to him, he had tossed and turned, unable to sleep as scenarios continued to form in his head.

He had arranged to meet his solicitor, Jason at the same coffee shop they had met last time, conveniently located opposite the court house, for a quick catch-up before they headed into the building to meet their barrister and stand before the judge to learn his fate. At half past eleven this morning he would know, or at least have a sense of how his life, and the life of his son, would be impacted by what the judge had decided. Over the past few weeks, whilst he had nervously awaited the judge's ruling, his mind had been unable to settle on anything, vacillating from one incoherent thought to the next. One minute he was imagining a situation where he lost everything, was ordered to pay Chloe not only the compensation for constructive dismissal, but the maintenance payments including the arrears, without any access to Theo. To the opposite extreme, where the judge ruled in his favour and awarded him access rights, throwing out any claim for constructive dismissal or any arrears, just ordering him to make an agreement on future child support payments. The shades of grey between the two extremes, and the permutations were mind blowing; but whichever way it went, turning back the clock was not an option, so he had to man-up and move on. There would be a hit to his bank balance either way, but whether the house needed to be sold remained to be seen. It was now up with an agent, and although there had been some interest, so far, no formal offers had been received.

Jason had advised the process allowed for a right to appeal if the ruling was unnecessarily harsh, or had been arrived at without the full evidence coming to light, but in Damian's mind that would be an unlikely scenario. The facts were the facts, and in his mind the only debatable issue was around the reasons for Chloe leaving his employment. He would always maintain that although her leaving had been very convenient for him, given he no longer had to face her, and by association his bad behaviour, around the office, he did not dismiss her. It was her decision to resign. Whether the judge viewed that as a technicality or a subtly that was irrelevant was left to be seen.

The only saving grace throughout the last few weeks was having Lucas around to man-the-ship and stop the rats from deserting it whilst he was otherwise engaged. Any misgivings he might have had about allowing him control over the business were short lived once he got his feet under the table and started to make things happen. He had proved not only a fast learner, but someone who rather than just talked a good job, could actually deliver, and was not shy in either making or implementing decisions once Damian had given them the cursory nod. Already Damian was seeing a vast improvement in staff morale, which in turn drove up productivity, all resulting in enhanced customer service and profitability. There was still a long way to go to turn the business around, but the initial signs were promising, and if today's ruling went the way he anticipated, having a strong business to fall back on was going to be essential, given it would effectively be feeding additional mouths, as well as funding the running of a second household.

'I'll get the coffees if you grab that table over there; it looks pretty quiet today, all the yummy mummies must have already left,' observed Jason as they arrived at the café at almost identical times. It was a regular haunt of his, and usually most of the tables were either full of people on their laptops using the free Wi-Fi, or mums having a chat after dropping their children off at the private nursery or junior school around the corner. 'We've probably got about forty minutes before we need to head over there, so do you want anything to eat whilst I'm ordering? I'm going to get a muffin as I missed breakfast,' he added. Jason, by the size of his straining waist band missed breakfast often, thought Damian if that was his excuse.

'No, you're okay, thanks,' he replied moving to the table in the window. He sat watching the world go by, lost in his own thoughts, waiting for Jason to return.

Five minutes later, carrying a tray with the drinks on as well as a couple of plates, Jason said 'I got you a cookie. You look like you need a sugar fix. I presume you've not been eating too well these last few days whilst Amanda's been away; she's home tomorrow, isn't she?'

'Thanks, but I don't think I could stomach anything at the moment,' he sighed. 'I'll just be glad when today's over to be honest. It's been difficult this last week with her away, but in general, things haven't been great for a while.'

'I know, you've had a rough ride, but once we've heard what the judge has to say, then we can decide the next steps, in terms of your appeal I mean, if necessary.' Jason was generally a happy soul who was normally glass-half-full in his approach to life, taking everything in his stride, but for some reason he did not have good vibes about how today would go.

'Well, let's see,' Damian replied, 'we don't want to get ahead of ourselves, do we?' painting a brave smile on his face; a smile that would have fooled no-one into believing he was happy about the situation.

Feeling the mobile phone buzz in his pocket, Jason looked at the screen, quickly reading the message before turning to Damian.

'Drink up, we've been called over early,' exclaimed Jason. 'Apparently, there's been a new development and they need us to join them in the judge's rooms as soon as possible. It's strange because there's no hint what it's about, and reading the message I've no idea either. Let's go and see what's happened and keep our fingers crossed it's positive, you could do with some good luck mate,' he added, as he wrapped both the muffin and the cookie in a couple of serviettes and carefully placed them in his bag for later. No good leaving good food to go to waste was his mentality.

Chapter 26

Today was going to be a busy day for Chloe, and frankly, one she could well do without, given it meant another day she was unable to work her normal shifts. Attending court was all well and good if you were the type of person with lots of free time and flexible with your arrangements, but Chloe was neither of these. She needed to work to earn a living, and as a lowly store assistant could not pick and choose when she turned up. Her shifts were also planned around the days she could get childcare, with Theo going a few afternoons a week to a local council run nursery where the fees were subsidised. Without this support, she had no one to provide regular cover for him.

To get to court for eleven o'clock meant giving up her afternoon shift at the convenience store, because although she was not due to start until half past one, the court was the other side of town and a bus journey away, and there was no saying how long that would take with the roadworks. She was grateful therefore when the shop's manager allowed her to change her hours to later that day, covering the five o'clock until ten o'clock 'graveyard shift', as his usual assistant had phoned in sick. At least that meant she did not lose any money, but it did mean the additional headache of having to find cover for Theo whilst she was working. The nursery closed at six o'clock, so she had asked a friendly neighbour to pick him up and keep him until she got home. Hopefully she might feed him too and put him to bed at her house as she would not be home until around ten fifteen.

The last few weeks had really taken its toll on Chloe, she felt a little like a rag doll being played with by the system, simply tossed around at other people's whims. Since she had started on this journey over six months ago, nothing had ever really got any easier. She was still struggling to hold down her part-time job, still juggling child care for Theo, and still finding that there was more week than money in her budgeting. She had applied for extra benefits and was now entitled to universal credit, but with everything that needed to be paid for, the last day or so before pay day was always a real struggle. If she never saw another tin of baked beans, or pot noodles she would be happy.

Hopefully after today things might start to get easier, provided the judge ruled in her favour that is. If the judge did not, then she really had no idea what to do next; she was fast running out of options. She could not contemplate living in that one-bedroom hovel they called a flat for a single day longer than was necessary, let alone throughout the winter, that despite today's weather was just around the corner. She was already struggling to find the money for the gas and electricity to not only keep her and Theo warm, but give her the basics for keeping them both fed and clean, saying nothing of the rent she needed to pay. Without further help, keeping warm would not just mean putting on another jumper, or wrapping up in another blanket rather than turning the fire up, but it might mean finding a doorstep to shelter in if her landlord threw her out.

Looking on the bright side, Ms Rawcliffe had been very positive about her case, even saying the odds were stacked very much in her favour; but had not gone as far as saying there was any guarantee. No, she would have to sit in that court room again and pray like she had never prayed before.

'Come on Theo, Mummy's in a hurry now and I really need to get you to nursery so can you please help me and put your coat on,' she pleaded trying to wrestle his arms into the jacket she had picked up from the charity shop the previous week. It was blue with toggles in place of buttons, had a hood with a black trim on and a motif on the back that she could not quite work out, but it did not look offensive. When he had it on, it was obviously a size too big for him, but hopefully that would mean he would not need another one for a few months. He was growing fast, and growing out of everything even faster. New shoes were the worst, as the second-hand shops were little if any help there, meaning every few months she had to shell out more money as his feet continued to grow. If the size of his feet now were any indication, he was going to be a tall man, taking after his father no doubt she thought ruefully. Why had she got mixed up with Damian? A lifetime of regrets would not change anything, but the only good thing to come out of it was Theo, and as she looked at him now waiting at the door with his lunchbox in his hand, she had to be thankful for small mercies.

Ten minutes later, standing outside the nursery ready to hand Theo over to the nursery nurse, with clear instructions that her neighbour would be collecting him before six o'clock that evening, she kissed her son before walking out of the playground. Looking back and waving, she saw him run happily into the room, straight to one of the other little boys she knew he got on well with. He really was no trouble, such a happy little chappie given what life had thrown at them both.

As she left the playground, she saw the number twenty-seven bus approaching. Knowing that if she missed this one, she would be late and possibly miss the start of the proceedings, she ran towards it. The car that was coming in the opposite direction, possibly going faster than was absolutely necessary outside a school, had no chance to react to the woman as she flew off the front of his windscreen into the middle of the road, to be caught a second time by a motorcyclist overtaking the bus that was just pulling up at the bus stop.

Both the car and the motorbike came to a screeching halt, but too late for the woman who by this time lay motionless in the middle of the road, blood surrounding her.

'Can someone call 999 and get an ambulance quickly, this woman needs urgent help, tell them she's been in an RTA, is bleeding and by the looks of it may have fractured her back, so can't be moved,' someone who identified herself as a nurse shouted as she bent down and knelt over the casualty. 'Also, tell them that there are two other drivers injured, so we might need more than one ambulance, and possibly some lifting equipment to get that motorcycle off the driver. The way it's fallen he looks trapped.'

Turning her attention back to her patient, 'Right, dear, my name's Sandra and I'm an off-duty nurse. I'm going to try to help you while we wait for the ambulance. Can you tell me your name? Come on, stay with us, try and keep awake for me please. Help is on the way,' begged the nurse to Chloe as she lay on the tarmac, realising that her pleas were not being headed, as she watched the young lady slowly slipping deeper into unconsciousness.

Chapter 27

Rachel was in the kitchen preparing the evening meal later that day when Damian returned home. It was after seven o'clock as she heard his car pull into the driveway, then the front door open and him dropping his keys on the hall table. Although she had expected him a little earlier, it was none of her business to question his movements.

'Hi, I'm in the kitchen just finishing off dinner, it won't be long,' she called out, 'the girls are in the lounge watching the Disney channel if you want to see them. They've been waiting up for you.' She had told Maisie and Alice that Daddy would be home this evening and would be in charge of bath time, so they had both been on their best behaviour as they waited, staying up much later than normal, anxiously waiting for him to come home.

Hearing no response, Rachel came into the hall just in time to see Damian's back disappearing as he climbed the stairs, looking like all the cares of the world were resting on his shoulders, his jacket slung on the floor, with his laptop bag, both abandoned by the front door. To not even pop his head around the kitchen to see what was for dinner seemed odd, but to not go and see the girls was even more puzzling. Normally he would enter the room and the two girls would launch themselves at him, complete with squeals and shrieks as he tickled them and paid them some attention. He was a good dad, there was no question about that. Perhaps he's just gone upstairs to get changed before dinner, she thought to herself, or maybe he needed the bathroom, so would be down in a few minutes.

Rachel was aware broadly of what was going on with the court hearing, but not the specifics of the case. Amanda had told her enough for her to deduce it was sensitive, so she had decided not to ask too much, and just speak when spoken to on the issue. The less she knew, the soonest all would be mended was her philosophy, and really it was none of her business anyway, she was just the au pair employed to look after the girls. Whilst she got on well with both Damian and Amanda, and felt comfortable speaking to either of them, their conversations had never veered too far from what would be considered polite social chit chat. They always enquired how she was, how she was finding England, any new friends etc. etc., but nothing too deep or personal. Likewise, they never had private conversations in front of her. She was very discreet, and even if she had overheard anything she perhaps should not have done, she would never either ask about it, or mention it to anyone else. Rachel was not a gossip, and certainly not someone who interfered in other people's business without being invited to do so.

After ten minutes Damian had still not returned downstairs and by now dinner was ready, and more importantly it was getting late for Maisie and Alice to still be up. They had school in the morning and being in bed later than half past seven would not bode well for any of them when they woke up. They would be grouchy when the alarm went off and would be difficult to get washed, dressed or fed and out of the door in time for school; and the last thing Rachel needed tomorrow when Amanda was due to return home, was two difficult children on her hands. Amanda would think she could not cope with them, and that would not look good for her job prospects.

'I think it's probably time for bed, you two,' said Rachel as she went into the lounge and picked up the remote control to turn the television off. Maisie and Alice were sat snuggled up on the sofa under a blanket watching Beauty and the Beast. It was one of Rachel's favourite movies and she had introduced them to it, along with most of the other Disney princess films, when she had first arrived in England. They would sit contentedly for hours, lost in the music and story, occasionally dancing around the room if the mood took them. It reminded her of being at home with her own sisters when they were growing up. They were also calmed by the hypnotic effect of these films, and Rachel had frequently had to employ that tactic to deal with them whenever they were having tantrums or playing up, which was a lot more often than Maisie or Alice, who were comparative angels when viewed against her sisters.

'But you said Daddy would be home tonight to see us…' moaned Maisie, obviously disappointed at the way the evening was panning out.

'And you said Daddy was going to bath us. We've not had our bath yet, so how can we go to bed?' questioned Alice, forever the logical one.

'Don't worry, we'll have a shower in the morning before school. I'll come extra early so you can shower and wash your hair before we leave. That way you'll sparkle on the way to school. Come on now, let's get you up the stairs. Last one in bed has to eat kippers for breakfast,' she laughed, knowing that threat was trusted to get them both moving.

'Yuk!' they said in unison, running up the stairs to the bedroom they shared, Maisie reaching it a split second before Alice, who hesitated outside her parent's door for a moment, listening to the gentle mewing noise coming from inside the room.

'Rachel, I can hear Daddy in there, and he sounds like he's crying. Why's Daddy crying?'

Maisie, not wanting to be outdone, came back onto the landing and stood next to her sister, also listening to the strange noise. 'Shall we go in and see if Daddy needs a cuddle?' she asked, reaching towards the handle.

'No, I think it'd be best if you both got quietly into bed and I'll tuck you in. It's late now, so perhaps we can have an extra story tomorrow,' she whispered, trying desperately to placate the two girls and get them into bed without further ado, or without Damian knowing they were outside his room. 'Now I'll leave the little side light on, but I'm going to pull the door to. I'll pop up later to check on you when I've finished in the kitchen. Night, night sweethearts, I'll see you bright and early in the morning,' she said, giving them both a kiss before leaving the room and pulling the door closed behind her, creeping quietly back down the stairs so as not to disturb Damian. Whatever he was going through, Rachel sensed that perhaps it was not something she or the girls needed to witness tonight, but just hoped whatever had upset him would get resolved in the morning.

Rachel was a great believer that things always looked better in the morning after a good night's sleep to get rid of whatever demons were troubling you, so trusted that would be the case here. Damian had been under a lot of pressure recently, and she knew Lucas, Amanda's brother, was helping out, staying around to help him in the business, so perhaps that had something to do with it. But regardless of the reason, she did not feel comfortable leaving the girls in the house under his care. No, she would tidy the kitchen up, pack the meal away in the fridge to be heated through should he come down for it later, and then lock the house up and go to up to her room. Amanda had told her to use the guest room whenever she needed it, and something told her tonight was just that occasion. Her little cottage and the Netflix movie she had lined up to watch later would just have to be put on hold for another evening.

Chapter 28

It was mid-morning and Amanda was sitting at home in the kitchen, nursing her coffee, grateful for whatever peace and quiet she could get. Damian was out walking to clear his head; the girls were both at school and Rachel was doing a lunchtime shift at the café. The radio was on in the background, but she was not listening to it, lost as she was in her own thoughts, trying to process the events of the last few days. She was alone in the house for the first time since she had arrived back from Singapore, almost three days ago now. Seventy-two long hours, but what in reality felt like a lifetime; knowing the life she had left before her trip, granted with all the trials and tribulations they were going through, was not the same one she had returned home to, and probably never would be again. The happy carefree feeling she had experienced in Singapore had long since dissipated.

It was difficult for even her to get her mind around what had happened, let alone try to imagine what Damian was feeling. Shock was the obvious and most natural feeling, but thereafter, it was a mystery as she tried not to second guess where his emotions might be. She just needed to be there, to be as supportive and as empathetic as she could when the floodgates eventually opened and he decided to open up to her.

There was no rule book on what she as 'the cuckolded wife' should feel, or act, in a situation like this.

But knowing her husband, and the way he usually dealt with things that fell into the 'difficult to handle basket', he could continue to bottle his emotions up for some time yet. Her sense though, was he was also attempting to shield her from his real thoughts and feelings, perhaps scared not only where they might take him if he articulated them, but also how she would react. She knew his feelings for Chloe had vacillated considerably over the last couple of years, ranging no doubt from feelings of love, or at least lust, at the height of their affair, to feelings of sheer anger at what she was now putting everyone through with the court case, including accusing him of constructive dismissal. But thrown into the mix were, no doubt, feelings of sympathy for the dire situation she had been reduced to, coupled with the complex feelings he must have for his son, Theo, who until recently did not know even existed, and now had a responsibility for. Given the recent maelstrom following Chloe's accident, where these feelings had now settled was the sixty-four-thousand-dollar question, as far as Amanda was concerned at least.

When she had arrived back from Heathrow Airport after ten o'clock three nights ago, later than she had expected due to both a delay with the flight and a cancelled train connection, the taxi had dropped her outside the house. As she stood in the driveway, looking up at her home now bathed in moonlight, the normal smile she had whenever she saw the attractive Georgian property, was not in evidence. The house was in complete darkness, the curtains left open, which given it was a dark chilly October evening was unusual. There was no welcome at the door for her, no one even looking out of the windows anticipating her arrival. It was eerily quiet and disconcerting.

Digging the key out of her bag and letting herself in, she could hear Rachel in the lounge, the television on in the background, obviously talking to someone on the phone, but in a reasonably serious voice, not the normal tone Amanda had become used to. Usually, if she overheard her chatting with her family or friends, there was laughter and a lightness in the way she spoke, sharing stories about what she had been up to, or making arrangements to meet with one of the friends she had recently made in the village.

'I best go, I think Amanda has just arrived home. I'll speak to you later. Yes, will do, thanks.'

'Hi, I'm not disturbing you, am I?' enquired Amanda, entering the room just as Rachel put her phone down.

'No, I was just talking to Lucas. He was phoning to see how everything was,' she replied with a smile on her face, 'He said to send you his love and let you know to call him if you need anything. Do you want a drink or anything to eat, I've been waiting up for you just in case.'

'Thanks, that's kind of you - a cup of tea would be lovely. How's Damian?'

'I'm not sure, to be honest. He went straight to your bedroom when he came home from court a few hours ago and I've not seen him since. When I put Maisie and Alice to bed though, Alice heard him crying through the bedroom door, so I guess he's upset about something,' obviously unsure from her response what had happened.

'Okay, I'll go and pop my head around the door and see if he needs anything. I'm not clear what's going on either, other than I know Chloe was in some sort of accident earlier this morning. Damian managed to message me just before I boarded, but I've not spoken to him since.'

Climbing the stairs, careful to avoid the ones she knew creaked, Amanda soon realised there was no longer the sound of crying coming from their room, just the more usual noise of gentle snoring her husband made when he was sound asleep; fully clothed on top of the quilt, with even his shoes still on. She quietly moved towards him, not wanting to startle him, carefully placed a blanket over him and undid his laces, gently removing his shoes. There was a chill in the room and she did not want him to wake up from the cold, but looking at him now, he seemed a long way off waking up.

That was three days ago, and now although some of the events of the preceding week had become clearer, there was still a lot that needed to be discussed over the coming days, weeks and no doubt months.

Hearing her phone ring, she picked it up, in two minds whether to ignore it and let it go to answerphone. It was unlikely to bring good news, but seeing it was from Lisa, she decided to answer it.

'Hi there, just ringing to see what's happening and to apologise for not being able to speak much over the last couple of days. It's been one of those manic weeks, but we're home now, so if you're okay to talk, you can fill me in on the latest news,' feeling a little guilty that she had been unable to spare the usual time to sit down and talk to her friend when she had phoned earlier in the week, obviously in distress.

Lisa and Clara had just returned from a two-day fashion event in London, hosted by Clara's magazine and partly her brainchild. It had been arranged to showcase some of the up-and-coming British fashion designers, with not only catwalks, promotions and celebrity endorsements, but a star-studded glitzy awards dinner as its finale. Clara was 'working' the event so had not had too much time to relax and enjoy herself, but Lisa had wangled an invitation and had more than made up for it, even returning home with a couple of samples that would complement her wardrobe perfectly.

'Yeah, I'm okay – but there's not much to report. She's still in a coma, but the doctors, according to Damian this morning when he phoned the hospital, aren't too hopeful. Apparently, she's not showing any signs of responding, and even if she did, they're concerned what the effects might be. I think the car hit her pretty badly, but then when the motorcycle gave her a second knock, how she's survived at all is a mystery. I think it's only a matter of time,' replied Amanda as factually as she could, without displaying too much emotion.

Damian had recounted how he and Jason, his solicitor, had been called into the judge's rooms the day of the accident to hear that there would be an adjournment of the hearing given the recent turn of events. The police who attended the incident had contacted the courts after they had looked through Chloe's bag to establish some form of identity, to find the letter, with the date and time of the hearing clearly visible. Once the police had informed the judge's office of the seriousness of the incident, the judge had no alternative than to call an indefinite halt to the proceedings.

'So, is there any news on Theo, what's happening with him? I bet he's missing his mum, and at two won't have any idea what's going on, poor thing,' sympathised Lisa, obviously well versed in cases of this nature.

'I think he's been put into care for the time being because there's no immediate family close by to take him in. Her mother lives overseas with her new partner, running a bar or something in Spain I think, and isn't apparently in the picture, and her dad died a short while ago from cancer. A neighbour had picked him up from nursery, but couldn't keep him overnight, so Social Services are having to deal with him.'

'That sounds about right,' replied Lisa. 'In situations like these, the courts effectively step in and do what's in the best interests of the child. They have preapproved carers and families that look after children short-term and at short-notice whilst things get sorted out. From what you're saying though, if it's unlikely she'll pull through, then they may need to look at a long-term foster family for him.'

'Yes, you're probably right, but I suppose with Damian now on his birth certificate as his biological father, that might have a bearing don't you think?'

'Well, it would if Damian wanted to take care for him, but that's a big decision and not just his, I presume. Have you spoken about what that could mean, and how would you feel about that, particularly with Maisie and Alice?'

'To be honest, we've not spoken about much. He's gone well and truly into his shell and I can't seem to reach him, and frankly if I could, I'm not sure I'd know what to say. He's out walking, doing laps of the duck-pond for all I know, trying to clear his head. Until we know one way or another, then it's a waiting game,' said Amanda, resigned to the fact that there were no easy answers, and even if there were, she was so out of her comfort zone, she felt powerless to do anything about them.

'Well, just remember we're here for you if you need anything, professional or otherwise, just give me a shout,' said Lisa as she hung up, conscious that her friend was in for a rough ride over the coming days, and worryingly not one she seemed at all prepared for.

Chapter 29

Two days later, it was a bright crisp autumnal morning and Amanda had taken Maisie and Alice to visit Grandad Tom. Sunday morning was one of the best times to visit the village as it was a hive of activity, with a real buzz as the residents prepared to meet up for their roast dinner in the main dining room, generally dressing-up in their Sunday best for what was perhaps the highlight of their week. It was one of those traditions Grandad Tom had readily adopted when he moved into the village, always happy for a roast, but even happier at the prospect of catching up on all the gossip from his other inmates. As he sat opposite his granddaughter today, he was all ready for 'the off'; dressed in a smart white shirt and cravat, his blue jacket with pocket handkerchief on show, grey trousers that perhaps matched another suit, but Amanda did not feel it necessary to point that out, and shoes that looked to have been polished to within an inch of their lives. He had made a real effort, with the twinkle in his eye suggesting he had not gone to all that trouble for no reason; there was obviously someone he was trying to impress.

Amanda knew the routine, so knew how welcome she and the girls would be until quarter past one, but thereafter Grandad Tom would start getting fidgety if she did not start her preparations for leaving. He liked to be downstairs in his favourite seat by one thirty prompt; giving him the opportunity to save a seat before the dining room got busy for whoever he wanted to sit next to that particular week. His companion was normally whichever of the old guys he had spent most time with in the proceeding days, thereby allowing them to continue chatting about whatever hot gossip was doing the rounds, but Amanda had the distinct feeling that would not be the case this Sunday. Although she did not want to pry, she banked it for a later discussion. If someone had caught his eye, presumably one of the new residents she had not already met, she would be interested to learn more.

Today though, with the girls in the room regaling him on what they had been doing at school, and Alice even presenting him with a drawing she had done of a dinosaur that she had named Tom-t-saurus in his honour, conversation had been kept relatively light, without any direct mention of 'the troubles' they were going through at home. Amanda had spoken at length to Grandad Tom last time she visited, honestly voicing her concerns and worries, always assured not only of his discretion, but his sage advice. But today other than saying she had nothing really to report, they kept to safer subjects, ranging from how many and what type of biscuits he needed bringing in, to what the village was planning for its Halloween celebrations, with him even asking if she could get him a costume as he planned dressing up as a werewolf! It was like being in a parallel universe whenever she visited Willow Tree, but it always made her smile.

Whilst she was visiting Tom, Damian was at home, upstairs in his makeshift office desperately trying to concentrate on some papers Lucas had sent over to him the previous evening that he needed his opinion on before work the following morning. Lucas continued to do a sterling job, impressing not only Damian but most of his senior team that he appeared to have won round with a mix of his hard work, his ideas and, above all his charm. It was obvious his Harvard education had not been squandered, and even better that he was getting the benefit of it, Damian thought to himself. Where would he have been without that support? Up shit creek without the proverbial paddle, he presumed.

He was gazing out of the window, focussed on a couple of birds flying effortlessly between the trees in the back garden, day-dreaming how easy life must be for his feathered friends, when his mobile rang. Seeing an unknown number come up on the screen, he was in two minds whether to answer it or not. He was not really in the mood to talk to anyone at the moment, but realising it was a Sunday, so it was unlikely to be one of those annoying cold-calls, he picked up the phone. 'Mr Reynolds, it's Doctor Mullins from the hospital, do you have a moment to talk?'

Damian had last been at the hospital Friday evening, and had spoken to Doctor Mullins at length earlier that day, outlining what he felt pertinent about his and Chloe's relationship, and importantly that with no parents or obvious family around, her next of kin status was unclear. The police had tried to track her mother down, but had so far been unsuccessful. They also discovered that any notes held at her local GP's office had not been updated since her father died some months earlier, so technically there was no one nominated. As such, Damian had assumed the position of next-of-kin for the purposes of speaking with the hospital, but it was not a role he was fully comfortable with.

'Yes Doctor, how can I help you?' replied Damian, unsure what was important enough for him to call him at home on a Sunday.

'Well, it's difficult discussing this on the phone, but I wanted to advise you that I have reassessed Chloe's position this morning. As you are aware, the nurses and doctors on the ICU ward have been monitoring her vital signs regularly to register any changes and determine what the best course of action would be for her, and what her prognosis would be should she pull out of the coma. I'm sorry to have to report that there has been no improvement in the situation, in fact there has been a significant deterioration in the last twenty-four hours, which was why they called me in to offer my assessment. Having reviewed everything personally, I and my colleagues have reached the conclusion that prolonging Chloe's life support is no longer viable.

'Right, what does that mean in reality Doctor?' enquired Damian.

'Well, the recommendation is that the life support machine will be switched off tomorrow morning, unless there is any miracle this evening. I needed to let you know as Chloe's de facto next-of-kin in case you wanted to make any appeal to the courts before that happened, but in my opinion that would not be recommended.'

'Thank you for letting me know,' stuttered Damian, not really surprised by what the doctor had said, or in all honesty unsure why it had taken this long to reach that recommendation. Having visited the ICU on several occasions and seen Chloe's young body wired to all those machines with the constant beeping and flashing of monitors, he had realised that the life had gone out of her some days ago. The machines were technically keeping her alive, but that was not a life by anyone's description. She was no longer the lively young girl he had fallen for, or even the wary opponent he had locked horns with in recent months, and was definitely not the spirited young mum who had protectively held Theo in her arms that time he had called to her house in Bath. No, he would not be appealing; that course of action would be in no one's best interest.

'I know this has come as a shock for you. Do you want any time to consider what we have discussed, or perhaps speak to someone before you let me know what you decide?' enquired Doctor Mullins, noticing the phone had gone quiet for some time. This was one of the elements of his job he did not look forward to in the slightest, but nevertheless it still needed to be handled with as much respect and dignity as any other element of his profession.

'No, thank you, but I don't see any point in delaying it, or involving the courts. They've enough to get on with as it is. I've seen with my own eyes the position she's in, and it's been difficult to see, so whilst it is a shock, it's not unexpected. I knew it was only a matter of time. Do you need anything else from me before tomorrow, Doctor?'

'No, but I suggest you get in touch with the hospital tomorrow afternoon and take it from there. There will be documents to sign, personal effects to collect and the death to register in due course, but someone can talk you through that at the appropriate time,' before adding, 'I know from what you've shared with me about your circumstances that all this is very difficult for you from a personal perspective, so you have my sympathies, but I also wish you well in the future with whatever decisions you make regarding both Chloe and her, apologies, your son.'

And with that, the doctor hit the nail precisely and succinctly on the head. Whatever he thought about the circumstances and how they had come about, Damian now had a son that no longer had a mother; a son that possibly did not even know his father existed, or had given any thought to it. But whichever way you sliced it, responsibility for Theo now rested fairly and squarely on his shoulders. As he ended the call, he heard Amanda's Audi pulling into the driveway, the girls laughing at something as they got out of the car and made their way to the front door.

With all thoughts of returning to his emails long since overtaken by events, he closed down his laptop and made his way downstairs to the kitchen. He could hear chattering and laughter, both of which had been rare commodities over the last few weeks, but as soon as he entered the kitchen, and his wife saw the look on his face, the atmosphere changed. She had just been in the process of taking the food out of the fridge, no doubt to start preparing their lunch, but instead closed the fridge door and said, 'Maisie, Alice, why don't you go and put a film on for a few minutes and I'll bring you a drink in shortly?'

The look on his face signalling that whatever he needed to say, and she had a good idea what that would be, would result in neither of them having much of an appetite for the roast beef dinner she was planning on preparing, no matter how good her gravy or Yorkshire puddings turned out to be!

Chapter 30

Chloe's funeral had been quite a surreal experience. A few people had turned up, but no-one Damian knew, other than a clerk he recognised from his own office, someone he presumed Chloe must have stayed in touch with. To his shame, he had no recollection of her name, or what she knew about his relationship to Chloe, or presumably even why he was there at her friend's funeral. As she made no effort to come over to him, there was no difficult conversation to be had. Since her death, he was aware some in the office had been talking about it, remembering the times she had worked there, even commenting on the fact that she had a young son, and wondering what had happened to him, but so far, to the best of his knowledge and from what little Lucas had fed back, no one had made the connections between him, Chloe and Theo. After today, it would no doubt become common knowledge and Damian had to prepare himself for that.

The only saving grace was that the police had managed to track down Chloe's mother, who at least had the decency to fly over and attend her daughter's funeral, taking some of the pressure off Damian to be lead mourner, a role he had not relished. Her mother, Tracy Jessop, looked like an older version of Chloe, somewhere perhaps in her late forties, but with a complexion aged by too much sun, alcohol, cigarettes, or a combination of all three, thought Damian, a little unkindly perhaps. She was wearing a black mini skirt and knee-high boots, visible under a grey three-quarter-length coat she had probably borrowed for the occasion, as it neither fitted her too comfortably nor looked like it belonged to her usual wardrobe. If ever a woman could be described as rough, then Tracy Jessop fitted that description.

Shortly before the service, Tracy had approached Damian and in no uncertain terms made it crystal clear she had no intentions of taking Theo back to Spain with her. Being a grandma was not on her agenda, and whilst she had been shocked to hear about Chloe, even disappointed to hear she had taken up with a married man, she was in no way responsible for the mess her daughter had subsequently got herself into. As Damian listened to her mouthing off, he wondered what had made her so hostile, what was it about her life that had turned her into this miserable embittered woman, apparently unable to show compassion or grief, let alone any motherly, or grandmotherly concern for members of her family, even at her own daughter's funeral. He felt renewed sympathy for what Chloe must have had to deal with over the years, and was grateful Theo would not have to experience the same.

Social Services had rightly deemed it was inappropriate for Theo to attend the funeral, deciding correctly that for the time being he would stay with the foster family until more long-term arrangements could be made, but once they knew Chloe's mother had been located, had offered Mrs Jessop the opportunity to meet her grandson if she chose whilst she was in the country. Tracy had, none too politely replied, 'thank you, but no thank you,' adding that she had no desire to meet Theo now or ever, and would be heading directly to the airport straight after the funeral. She had no intentions of staying in England a moment longer than was necessary; she had a business to run, a life to lead and a fella to get back to. Her position was duly noted by Social Services and recorded on the file that was being prepared for the courts.

Shortly after Chloe's death, it had been suggested by Lisa that Damian might want to seek a second opinion from a solicitor who specialised in family law, again someone she could recommend if he wanted. There was a senior partner in another practice in Bristol who she knew had recent experience in this type of situation, and he may be able to offer a different or additional perspective to Jason's. As Lisa pointed out, it was in Damian's best interests to talk through the case with someone who not only understood the legal position, but would have a view of what options were available, particularly now that Chloe's mother had effectively washed her hands of her grandson, although Lisa did not use those exact words, or phrase it so bluntly. Amanda agreed this was a good suggestion, and encouraged Damian to make an appointment.

The courts had thankfully dropped all the previous claims originally brought by Chloe, which following her death were no longer relevant, leaving a much cleaner sheet for determining the way ahead. Whilst removing the threat of the constructive dismissal allegation was a great relief to Damian, plus the claim for financial compensation had gone away, the fact remained that the child, Theo still needed support, and without his mum to provide that, then one way or another a solution would need to be found, so perhaps getting some advice would be sensible.

Paternity was no longer a question, with Theo's birth certificate legally amended to include Damian's details, but in terms of anything else, that was still very much up in the air. He and Amanda had discussed long and hard, and late into many an evening, what they felt their options were. In their view, these ranged from leaving Theo in the care system, with the intention of Social Services finding a forever home for him, with an adoptive family in due course, to the other extreme of him moving into their home. The first option would see him out of their lives for good, or at least until Theo reached the age where he wanted to research his family background and seek out about his natural parents, at which stage he would no doubt land on their doorstep, with a list of questions, not dissimilar Amanda thought wryly to her own situation. At that stage, how would they defend the actions they had taken when they abandoned him to the system, no more than a baby?

The other extreme was that they include him in their own family, a brother for Maisie and Alice, bringing him up as one of their own. As his biological father, presumably there would be no issue with that? One of the problems though, was he had no awareness of them; no expectations of being part of their family, and was that a risk they were prepared to take on, bringing up someone else's child, a child who would be damaged in some way by the inexplicable loss of his mummy, a mummy who had kissed him goodbye at the nursery gates one morning, never to return? What harm would that have done, and how would they deal with the fall out? Even as he heard the arguments, and with his logical head on knew they were all valid, he could not help think to himself, 'but he's not somebody else's child, he's mine.'

Damian had no illusions that life would be easy simply inserting his child into their family, like they do with baby lambs when their mothers die and they are palmed off onto another ewe, expecting it to feed the lamb and rear it as their own naturally and without complaint. No, this was real life, not an episode of Countryfile, and he could not expect everyone to just carry on as if it was normal to suddenly have another toddler running around the place. The pressure it would put on both his close and extended family was immense, saying nothing of the pressures it would put on his marriage, a relationship that had sorely been tested over recent months, not only by his affair, but the subsequent and devastating loss of their own baby. That loss had impacted them both immeasurably, but it had brought Amanda so low at the time he wondered whether she would ever return; whether she would ever bring herself out of the depths of the depression she fell into. How could he now expect her to take his new son on; here's Theo mark two, he can replace the one we lost! That would not only be crass, but something he could not inflict on his wife or his wider family.

Always looking for compromise and to steer clear of conflict in any shape or form, as Damian sat in the pew waiting for the rest of the mourners to leave the crematorium, he wondered whether somewhere out there, there was a happy medium, a solution where everyone would be happy and life could simply return to normal. Although he was generally an optimist, today somehow, he did not feel like it was his lucky day.

Chapter 31

The morning of the funeral, Amanda had driven over to see Grandad Tom around ten o'clock, principally to drop off his Halloween costume as requested, but also to have a chat with him. Rachel was at the house today, having returned there after dropping the girls off for school, with the intention of giving their bedroom a good sort out whilst they were out of the way. Both Maisie and Alice hoarded clothes and toys, never wanting to part with anything, but unless it was sorted, Rachel had told them there would be no room for anything new that Santa might bring this year.

Knowing she had a good couple of hours to spare, giving her plenty of time to sit and chat, Amanda wanted to air some of the worry beads that continued to go round in her head, thoughts that were not only keeping her awake at night, but feelings she did not trust herself to express to anyone other than her grandad. She trusted his opinion, and although she did not always like what he said, she knew it not only came from years of experience, but always had her best interests at the heart of whatever guidance he gave.

'Good morning, my darling, come on in,' said Tom as he opened the door to his grand-daughter, full of the joys of spring, and with a gaiety in his voice that suggested he had either been on the bottle early, or had some good news to impart. 'How lovely to see you, and I see you've got my costume – what have you got me?' he asked, like an excited teenager as he took the plastic carrier bag from her.

Having spent hours on the internet searching for Halloween costumes for elderly gentlemen, she had unsurprisingly found little selection, so had opted for a wig, some pointed ears and a set of false teeth, or more correctly fangs, that would just have to do. She had also found a black cape that Tom could drape over the top of whatever jumper or shirt he was planning on wearing, which if nothing else would keep him warm if they were venturing outside into the gardens to do some ghostly ritual or dancing around the bonfire. Although, given this weekend's weather forecast, and the potential thunderstorms, that seemed highly unlikely.

As he rummaged in the bag, trying on the items she had bought, delighted with the booty, Amanda's main thoughts were that if impressing his new lady friend was high on his agenda, then she either needed to have a wicked sense of humour, bad eyesight or equally bad dress sense. Nevertheless, it was good to see that he was entering into the spirit of it and not taking himself too seriously. Moving to the village had definitely brought some fun back into his autumn years, as well as a sparkle into his eyes.

'Grandad, can I ask you a question?' Amanda said hesitantly once they were seated with their cups of tea and custard creams on a plate between them.

'Of course, what's the matter, is everything okay?' immediately sensing all was not well.

'I want to know what you think Dad would have thought to the situation with Damian, and particularly Theo,' she started, 'It's just that the more Damian talks about him and the more he discusses things with his solicitor, I get the sense he's developing really strong feelings for him, and selfishly I don't know how this makes me feel.'

Tom nodded sagely, 'Have you seen the little boy yet?'

'No, and neither has Damian – well not officially anyway. He caught a glimpse of him some months ago at the solicitor's office he thinks, but he's keeping close to what he's doing with his foster family, as well as getting regular updates from Social Services. There's a lady who's meeting with Theo, all part of grief counselling I think, and she's reporting back.'

'And how's that going?'

'Okay, I think. He's apparently settling with the foster family, who have a puppy as well as two other children of their own, so I think they're providing a distraction for Theo. I don't think they are particularly worried about him. Given what he's gone through, he sounds to be quite a resilient little toddler by all accounts,' she smiled, but Tom noticed the smile did not quite reach her eyes.

'Well, if what you said about his mum having to work odd hours is correct, he's obviously been used to being left with friends and neighbours, or people at the nursery, so has presumably become quite adaptive. But I'm sure he'll be missing his mum deep down.'

Noticing she had gone quiet, and deciding it was time to probe a little further, Tom added 'so, what are you worried about, because I can see that something's troubling you?'

Amanda tried to articulate feelings that amounted to not only being scared that Theo was going to supplant Maisie and Alice, and potentially herself in Damian's affections, saying nothing of the memories of their stillborn son, but also that she would be expected to get close to this child too, a child that was the product of her husband's affair. She knew how vulnerable Damian was at the moment, how responsible he felt, but also how guilty he would feel abandoning his child into the system, resulting in her being worried that this might be driving his behaviour and his decisions in a direction she was not fully supportive of.

Passing her the tissues when she had finished outpouring her feelings, recognising this was obviously the first time she had spoken completely honestly to anyone, her grandad reached out and took her hand.

'There's no need to fret. I'm sure however this pans out, there is an infinite amount of love that will mean no one misses out, so I think any worries on that score are unfounded. I would go as far as to say that Damian, since his unfortunate behaviour a couple of years ago, has, to my knowledge at least, done everything in his power to make amends, and I don't think he would risk losing you or the girls again. However, whether you like it or not, Theo is part of his life now, and that little boy is an innocent bystander in all this. He didn't choose to be born, or for that matter have any say over who his parents were. I would suggest though that an accommodation is going to need to be reached somewhere, if you're to remain a happy family, that is.' After allowing that to sink in, he continued.

'You started by asking me what your dad would have thought, well, just remember he took you in under similar circumstances, brought you up as his own, and no one could have loved you or cared for you more than he did. He never blamed your mum; just loved you both until his dying day. I don't think you could ask for a better role model if you were looking for one. If I remember correctly, he told you to follow your heart, so whatever illogical obstacles or other problems are keeping you awake, always keep true to that, and you'll find a way through.'

As Amanda sat in the carpark composing herself before setting off home, she reflected on what he had said. Grandad Tom believed in tough love, and whilst she did not always like his advice, she sensed deep down that it was to be ignored at her peril.

Chapter 32

The following weekend, Castle Heighton was staging its annual bonfire night celebrations. It was one of the highlights of the village's social calendar, along with the Church's Summer Fair, that this year had been a total wash out, and the Harvest Festival that saw not just the children, but some of the more competitive parishioners creating imaginative displays with fruit, vegetables and other such fare for judging by Father Anthony in the church hall, before the food was donated to the more needy or housebound people in the area. But as far as the children were concerned, bonfire night was by far the best, and this year Maisie and Alice were getting themselves very excited at the prospect of going, particularly as Uncle Lucas had offered to take them. 'He'll be a lot more fun than Mum and Dad at the moment,' thought Maisie to herself. She had picked up on an atmosphere at home recently, but had no idea what was wrong, just that both of her parents always looked sad.

Amanda had bought them some sparklers and made bonfire toffee, but other than that was leaving her brother to arrange the treats. He loved to spoil his nieces, and Amanda was happy to leave him to it without wanting to ruin his fun or muscle in with her usual motherly advice and 'be careful, don't burn your fingers' attitude.

Lucas had arrived the previous evening in plenty of time for dinner, cadging a lift back from Cirencester with Damian, who had started spending more time at the office over recent weeks, but returning home each evening, leaving Lucas to continue to use his apartment. Lucas normally alternated his weekends away from the office between either coming back to Amanda's or taking the train into London to catch up with friends. A couple of the guys he had met when back-packing lived and worked in the city, so there was always a bed going spare and a club within staggering distance if he ever needed a little more nightlife than he could find locally.

For Lucas, the last two months had passed in the blink of an eye; now in November, he had no idea where the time had gone. He had originally thought he would be staying around for a few weeks, before resurrecting his plans with Sonia as they had agreed. A few weeks helping Damian out with the business whilst he got his head together dealing with the court case, but with everything else that had gone on since, and to an extent was still going on, he felt in no hurry to leave them in the lurch. Apart from which, he was genuinely enjoying the role he had carved out for himself, pseudo-consultant, pseudo-advisor, with a smattering of 'hands-on' support with anything else that he could direct his skills towards thrown in for good measure. Although he was certainly no geek, IT was something he understood, so marrying that with the business side of running a company, proved the perfect combination for him.

Neither Amanda nor Damian appeared to be in a hurry for him to pack his bags, but even if they had been, where did he have to go to? Home, back to the States, or continue travelling. The arrangements he had made in Thailand had gone by the board now, which probably was fate's way of telling him it had perhaps not been the right plan anyway.

He had met Sonia in Sydney one evening shortly after he had arrived in the city, whilst he was out with a couple of the guys he was back-packing with. They had called into a theme bar not far from the harbour. She was working, running tables and serving drinks, earning whatever money and tips she could before embarking on the next leg of her gap year. The guys were a bit boisterous, having fun and generally making noise, laughing at a group of girls the other end of the bar who by the looks of it were on a hen night. Sonia brought over a tray of drinks and instigated a conversation; never one to be shy, particularly not around a group of good-looking Americans, was her attitude. Throughout the evening they all bantered with the pretty barmaid, but it was not long before the others realised it was Lucas she had her eye on.

The following evening Lucas returned by himself, on the off-chance Sonia might be working again. They had hit it off the previous evening, and Lucas being in the mood for a bit of female company, as opposed to another night of getting drunk with the lads, decided to risk it. There was only so much lager he could take after all, and if she was not around, there would be others he could easily strike up a conversation with. And if all else failed, he could always do some sightseeing. The harbour at night was well worth a visit he had been told.

Entering the bar, he instantly saw her at the other end of the room, balancing a full tray of drinks precariously on her arm, narrowly avoiding dropping them when someone barged past her on the way to the Gents. Smiling to himself, he thought 'that red hair's not something you'd lose in a crowd,' but she must have sensed him watching her as she glanced back and smiled. Her smile seemed to light up her face.

When it was her break, she brought them both over a drink, dropping down into the chair opposite Lucas as if it was the most natural thing in the world, uninvited, but not unwelcome. For the next thirty minutes or so, apart from a lot of mutual flirting, they chatted non-stop, moving from one subject to another without taking breath. They appeared to have a lot in common; similar tastes in music, both enjoyed the social scene, but most importantly had travel and new experiences at the top of their bucket lists. Neither was into sport, but Sonia did confess a passion for the old Hollywood movies, especially the black and white ones, laughing that where she came from, there was not a lot else to do of an evening.

Sonia was a couple of years younger than Lucas, but appeared mature for her age. She had recently graduated in Media Studies, but knew that to get any decent type of career she would need to travel, as opportunities were few and far between where she lived, even if she moved up to Auckland, which according to her parents was a long way from home! She was from New Zealand originally, and told Lucas Sydney was her first port of call, before planning on travelling further west to Perth, then across to the Far East, over to Europe and finally arriving in the States all being well. She was having to earn her keep along the way to continue to fund her travelling, but that was fine, because any work-experience she got must count for something, surely?

The girlfriend she was travelling with however had returned to New Zealand after a family bereavement, leaving Sonia in Sydney until she caught back up with her. That had been five weeks ago, and Sonia was beginning to think her friend had no plans of returning. She told Lucas she had even contemplated returning home herself, which was what her parents were suggesting, not wanting to contemplate the risks of their daughter travelling without a companion.

As they chatted, and it was obvious they were hitting it off, Lucas suggested she could always tag along with them. They were doing roughly the same itinerary, so one more should not be a problem, and she appeared quite easy going, as well as easy on the eye, so what was the harm? They had flight plans for the end of the week, so provided she could manage that, they would be happy for her to join them – well, he presumed they would once he put it to them. They swapped numbers and agreed to speak the following day.

So, Sonia joined them on their travels, and before long her and Lucas became 'an item'; Lucas soon opting to share a room or sleeping bag with her in preference to bunking down with the lads. No one seemed to mind, and whilst their plans continued to align, everything remained harmonious. A serious difference of opinion in Thailand between the rest of the lads put paid to that though, and the group disbanded, leaving Sonia and Lucas not only alone, but at a bit of a crossroads.

Their relationship had become intense over a relatively short period of time; leaving them both under no illusion it was serious, but equally unsure whether living as they were, constantly breathing the same air, was representative of real life. Navigating from one continent to the next was fun and was providing them both with experiences they had never dreamt of, but it sometimes felt a little surreal. Would they survive in the real world, with real pressures and everyday distractions around them; or did they have to wise up to the fact they were in the midst of a holiday romance, emulating a plot from one of Sonia's Hollywood movies?

When they reached their metaphorical crossroads, Lucas had been on the road for several months and although not homesick, was starting to miss some of his home comforts, even some of his family. Travelling was great, but occasionally he wanted to be in the same bed for more than a couple of nights, and be able to have a conversation that had real bearing, other than 'where are we off to next?'. At the same time, Sonia was realising that her finances were not as robust as everyone else's. She sadly did not have access to a trust fund, or any income other than what she earned en route. Her remaining savings would cover flights, but at the rate she was eking into them, day-to-day living was something she was struggling to keep up with, particularly as the guys had not stayed in any one place long enough for her to get a job.

When Lucas suggested they have a break and regroup in a months' time, it seemed like a sensible solution, allowing Sonia time to go home and sort out her finances, whilst giving Lucas the time to reconnect with the real world. He had thought about going back to the States, but that was too far to travel, so hence decided to visit his sister for a couple of days before spending a few weeks relaxing in a nice hotel and exploring London, with soft towels, clean sheets and room service at his disposal!

Okay, perhaps London and everything had not panned out exactly as he planned, and his plans with Sonia were certainly in abeyance, but in terms of reconnecting with the real world, that had certainly happened.

'Right young ladies, aren't you both looking lovely. Are you ready for the bonfire?' he asked excitedly as Maisie and Alice came into the kitchen, already wearing their matching coats, hats and scarves and wearing their jeans tucked into their wellies as the field was likely to be muddy after the recent downpour. Rachel followed behind them, smiling at Lucas as she carried the dirty school uniforms straight through to the utility room, ready to put in the washing machine before Monday morning, and the whole process starting again. Friday night was one of her favourite times of the week; a few hours off, time to catch up in front of the television with whatever Netflix had to offer, a glass of wine and a take away for company. Bliss.

'We are Uncle Lucas, but please can Rachel come too, please? She's never been to the bonfire, and Mum says there's enough toffee for all of us,' pleaded Maisie.

'Rachel, you can have one of my sparklers as long as you wear your gloves and are very careful,' said Alice, now as excited as her sister at the prospect of Rachel coming too.

'Ur mm, well, I could if you want …. but this is Uncle Lucas' treat, and he doesn't need me tagging along,' replied Rachel, desperately trying to find a way to get out of going, without either upsetting the girls or offending Lucas. After all, the wine was chilling in the fridge, she had already decided what meal she would be ordering from the Chinese take-away and a night in front of Netflix with her feet up and the fire on was preferable to standing in a muddy field getting cold, surely?

'No, it would be lovely for you to come too,' smiled Lucas politely, adding with a laugh, 'shall we give you five minutes to find your coat, gloves and matching wellies!'

Rachel saw no alternative but to tag along.

Chapter 33

Two weeks later, and it was a cold, damp autumnal morning. By eight thirty, the sun had still not risen, and looking at the clouds overhead, there was nothing to suggest it intended making an appearance at all that day. The pavements were still wet from the heavy downpour through the night, and although the girls would have loved nothing better than donning their wellies and splashing in the puddles on their way to school, Amanda had other ideas.

'Come on you two, let's get a wiggle on. I'll run you into school today, don't forget your P.E. bags, come on, you don't want to be late,' shouted Amanda from the bottom of the stairs, their packed lunches in hand, urging her daughters to hurry up. Although it was a midweek day, Rachel was away, so she was doing the drop off, leaving Damian to clear away the breakfast plates and cereals, before making his way upstairs to his make-shift office. He was working from home today so that he could manage the school pick-up at home time. She had even left instructions for dinner that evening, something simple that he could prepare without any hassle; although why she felt it necessary, she was not sure, as Damian knew his way around the kitchen as much as she did, but it eased her conscience a little to think she had thought about it.

Nothing was going to put the dampeners on Amanda's spirits today, so after having eventually deposited her daughters at the school gates, she pointed her Audi east and headed down the winding country roads, until she joined the M3 towards Bristol. As Amanda listened to Zoe Ball on the Radio 2 breakfast show chatting away to one of her guests, she mused happily that provided the traffic was not too bad, within the hour, she would be sitting in a café enjoying a fresh coffee and a fancy pastry with her best friend Lisa and her cousin Clara. A whole day of relaxation, some retail therapy, plenty of girly gossip and a swanky lunch in one of the trendy new wine bars Lisa had found, thrown in. Plus, a day free from worrying about Damian or the girls; what more could she ask for? Pure indulgence!

'Amanda, over here,' she heard Lisa calling as she entered the café. She looked over to see Lisa and Clara waving over to attract her attention, already sitting around a small table, reclining in comfortable armchairs, each with a coffee and Danish pastry in front of them. They both looked so relaxed and cosy that Amanda feared their shopping trip might be put on hold in favour of remaining indoors and keeping warm. Lisa and Clara's winter coats had been draped over the back of the fourth chair, leaving them both casually dressed in simple jeans, boots and tops, but there was nothing 'simple' about the way either of them carried off the casual look. Fashion was obviously Clara's business, but also Lisa's passion, so between them they managed to create a look that was not only completely on-trend, but complemented each other perfectly, which given their body shapes and sizes were so different, was a feat in itself.

Clara was a statuesque blue eyed blonde, over five-foot, eight inches tall, with legs that seemed to go on forever and natural curls that tumbled down her back, whereas Lisa was only five-foot, three inches on a good day, so much more diminutive, with brown eyes and brunette hair, currently worn short in a fashionable, edgy style that accentuated her features perfectly. Amanda would have been happy to master elegant, understated or stylish; but no matter how hard she tried, she never successfully pulled off any one of these, let alone all three with the ease or naturalness that Lisa or Clara managed.

Seeing there were already three coffees on the table, she by-passed the counter and walked straight over to join them, giving each a kiss before following their lead and dumping her coat. As she fell into the chair and took a mouthful of the awaiting cappuccino, she visibly relaxed for what seemed like the first time in a long time.

'Boy, do I need this!' she said, replacing the cup in the saucer. 'I have been so looking forward to today. You won't believe the sheer joy I felt leaving the house, knowing I'd got a full day all to myself, no kids or husband to worry about. The way I feel at the moment, I might not go back!' she laughed, only half joking Lisa and Clara sensed.

'Yes, we really should do this more often, but with one thing or another I don't know where the weeks, no months, have gone recently,' replied Clara.

'Would you believe it's five months since we last properly met up - do you remember when Maria flew over and brought Rachel, and you both called in after visiting your parents, Lisa?' Amanda prompted them both.

'Don't remind me, that situation is not getting any easier. Mum's still being peculiar with us, but Dad's been well and truly won over by Clara. In fact, he's even started to subscribe to her magazine, which given his idea of fashion is wearing matching socks, is hilarious.'

'And we've not seen you since your visit to Singapore,' added Clara, 'you never really told us what happened there.'

'Oh, please don't remind me! That was a nightmare and I'm not sure I'll ever live it down. I made a drunken pass at Nick; would you believe it?' said Amanda sheepishly. 'Working with him these last few weeks has been embarrassing to say the least. I did at one stage consider offering my resignation, but didn't know how I'd tell Will!'

'Wow,' they both seemed to laugh in unison, 'well, he's a good-looking guy I'll credit you with that, but what were you thinking?' enquired Clara, struggling to keep her face straight, that being the last thing she had expected Amanda to either say or do. Her cousin was normally the sensible one.

'I think I read all the signs wrong; he was being so kind, so supportive, he's so easy to talk to and just such great company. When he suggested an early night, I got the wrong end of the stick and thought he was suggesting we go back to his room, and at the time I was certainly up for it! Looking back now, I don't think I was thinking at all. With everything that's been going on, I just felt so vulnerable and was probably just grateful someone was paying me some attention for once. But he was a complete gentleman and didn't take advantage …. although I sometimes wonder what would have happened if he had,' she added wistfully as a bit of an afterthought.

'Well, having met him at Will and Maria's in Boston last time I flew home, I can certainly see the attraction, but perhaps he's a complexity you should perhaps avoid for the time being. An affair might even-up the field, so to speak, between you and Damian, but I'm not sure you're up for that level of excitement at the moment, and the fall out could be horrendous,' warned her cousin. Although she wanted Amanda to be happy, Clara sensed that a casual and meaningless fling with her boss might not be the best way to achieve that.

'No, you're probably right,' accepted Amanda, but not prepared to concede yet added, 'but perhaps I'll keep him in reserve in case Damian steps out of line again.'

'Is there something wrong?' probed Lisa, obviously aware that now Chloe was permanently out of the picture, she was no longer a risk, but that did not mean something else was not going on.

Trying to keep the conversation as light as possible, she updated her friends on the recent meetings between Damian and his solicitor regarding Theo, as well as how Theo was coping with his foster parents, including feedback from the bereavement counselling and grief therapy sessions that had been arranged for him; things that until now Amanda had not even been aware existed. The more she spoke, she realised how much of their lives were now revolving around Theo, and how matter-of-fact it was becoming to talk about him. Chloe's death had created a strange response from Amanda. She had not grieved her loss per se, but nevertheless had been touched, directly or indirectly, by all stages of the grieving process. There was certainly shock at the unexpected nature of her demise; followed by a mixture of guilt and anger that Theo was now an irrevocable part of their lives, replacing in some way the son she had lost; followed by no end of 'bargaining' with both Damian and Grandad Tom about what the right thing was to move forward. Grandad Tom had even offered his views of her dad Ken's perspective; views that had given her some serious food for thought. She was not sure depression had hit, but there were certainly a growing number of days when she wondered how they would cope as a family; and if they would ever get through this.

'So, have you still not met Theo yet?' enquired Clara, aware from earlier conversations that Damian had on a couple of occasions visited him at his foster parents' home.

'No, but I think I'll have to soon,' replied Amanda thoughtfully. 'I'll need to see through all that's gone on, and just accept that Theo is the innocent party in all of this.

He's Damian's son after all, and no matter how hard I fight it, my heart won't let me ignore that fact.'

'Everything will work out in the end, I'm sure,' said Lisa empathetically, knowing from the numerous cases she had handled over the years, that it was never going to be easy, but equally time was a great healer, and generally a solution was found.

'Well, shall we order more coffees or hit the shops? I'd prefer the former, but know that unless I start Christmas shopping today, it might never get done, and I don't fancy having two disgruntled daughters, let alone a sour-faced husband when Santa doesn't bring what's on his list,' Amanda smiled, keen to move the subject along.

'I'm with you on that, I really don't feel like moving, but equally if I'm to make any inroads into my list, we're going to need to get a move on. I've a few ideas for Maisie and Alice, but could do with your help on sizes. I also need to find some things to take to Boston for Jane and Brad; but given the amount of clothes and shoes I've already earmarked to pack, they will need to be smallish,' added Lisa, before looking at her watch and reminding everyone, 'the table's booked for two o'clock, so we'd better get a move on. That champagne I've ordered to celebrate isn't going to drink itself!' she added with a wink in Clara's direction.

'What are we celebrating?' asked Amanda, with a puzzled look on her face, whilst at the same time noticing the look that was being exchanged between her friends. 'More importantly, what have I missed, what aren't you two telling me?' immediately assuming it was an engagement announcement. Her friends had been together now for over two years, and making their relationship more formal would not be too much of a shock; but there had been no hints at it, well, none that Amanda had picked up on anyway. Although, having been so distracted lately with her own problems, perhaps that was not too surprising.

'No, it's nothing like that,' laughed Lisa, suddenly realising where Amanda's mind had been going, 'it's just that I've been offered a senior partnership at the law firm; they only asked me last week, so I was as surprised as you. I've been ironing out all the details over the last few days, you know, important things like how big the lettering is, or where 'Meadows' features in the firm's name; alphabetically, it should be before Yates or Walker, but I don't think I'm going to win that argument,' she laughed, 'but it's great to think that after all these years of slogging and working my fingers to the bones to make money for the firm, I can finally start making it for myself!'

'But I thought you were already a partner?' questioned Amanda, slightly confused.

'Well, I was a junior one, or what you'd call an associate, but that didn't really confer many benefits, but now as a senior partner I get to have my name in lights! We've been quite small until now and relatively specialised, but as 'Walker, Yates & Meadows' we're growing, planning to take on some more associates and rebranding the business to get a wider footprint, which overall will be great for business,' she said, struggling to keep the pride out of her voice.

'Well, congratulations and that's brilliant news Lisa, you certainly deserve it. You've worked so hard, I'm so proud of you,' she said, getting up from her chair to give her friend a huge hug, 'but next time you've got some earth-shattering news, please give me a heads-up first; I nearly had a heart attack thinking I'd missed something,' at which both Clara and Lisa laughed, knowing how much their friend liked to feel in control.

'Right then, now we've got that sorted, lead the way,' smiled Clara, easing herself gently out of the chair and putting her coat on to ward off the cold that would undoubtedly hit them as soon as they left the warmth of the café, 'and on the way, you can bring us up to speed on what Lucas and Rachel are up to in Boston. I spoke to Mum last night and she dropped it into the conversation like a bombshell. I certainly didn't see that coming, and by the look on your face neither did you!'

Chapter 34

Late Monday morning, the first working day after bonfire night the previous Friday, Rachel was making herself a coffee in the kitchen, ready for a well-deserved sit down and a chance to catch up with her social media feeds. She subscribed to Facebook, Instagram, Twitter, Snapchat, well basically all of them; anxious to keep in touch with what was happening not only to her friends, but all the entertainment channels she watched, or programmes and celebrities she followed. She rarely posted anything of interest herself, because frankly she did not consider herself doing anything that warranted posting, but nevertheless was an avid follower of other's exploits.

She had arrived as usual at seven-thirty in the morning, allowing plenty of time to get the girls up and dressed, ready to be dropped off at school, before returning to the house to do whatever else needed doing, depending on the day of the week, or the diary. Over the last few months, she had developed a routine that not only worked for her, but seemed to suit the rest of the family too. Monday was her day for restoring order to the girls' bedroom; picking toys up, hanging clothes back in the wardrobe and generally clearing away the mayhem of the weekend. Dressed in her trademark jeans and hoodie, with her hair tied back in a ponytail, her face completely free of make-up, she had no qualms about crawling on the floor or under the beds in her attempts to return everything to its rightful place.

She had finally finished tidying the kitchen, when Amanda came downstairs and joined her, heading straight for the fridge to get the milk out when she heard the kettle was already boiling. They had not spoken all morning; her office door had been shut, a clear indication that she was busy and would prefer not to be disturbed, unless it was an emergency. Rachel was not one for idle chit-chat, so was more than happy to get on with whatever needed doing, leaving both Damian or Amanda alone, unless they asked her for anything specific.

'Hi, Rachel, did you have a good weekend, I've not seen you since Friday night?' enquired Amanda. 'How was the bonfire? I gather from the girls everyone had a great time. They were certainly tired when you dropped them back home, but they never stopped chatting when I was getting them ready for bed, although as soon as their heads hit the pillow they were out like a light.'

'Yes, it was good, thanks, and the girls I think had fun,' replied Rachel, unsure how much she wanted to say about either the evening itself or the weekend that followed. It had not panned out at all as she had expected, she thought to herself as she continued to wander around the kitchen in a bit of a daze.

'Well, Lucas seemed to have a good time too from what he said when he dropped them off, but I've not seen much more of him this weekend, so haven't got a clue what he's been up to, or where he went afterwards. I presume he returned to the flat on Saturday or down to London to see his mates, but no doubt we'll see him later.'

'Yes, no doubt,' Rachel replied with a smile on her face, knowing full well where Lucas had spent the majority of his weekend.

Rachel recalled the bonfire had been fun, with both girls waving their sparklers, squealing whenever a firework had been lit or a 'loud bang' had been heard. They had clung to her and Lucas, laughing and dancing around, competing for the attention of each of them; both happy to be the centre of attention, revelling in being spoiled by both adults. Lucas had bought them all mugs of hot chocolate from the refreshments van, along with a big bag of marshmallows to share, which Rachel promptly showed them how to dip into the chocolate to render them gooey, making the girls laugh even more as the marshmallows either dropped into their mugs, onto the floor or down the front of their jackets on the way to their mouths. By the end of the evening, although the girls' faces were covered in sugar and chocolate, their hands sticky from too much treacle toffee, and their jeans and wellies dirty from all the mud in the field, they were the picture of contented, if not extremely tired children.

After dropping them off at home, Rachel had said goodnight to Lucas and Amanda on the doorstep before heading in the direction of her cottage. It was just after nine o'clock, so if she did not dawdle, she would still have time to order the Chinese she had planned, and the bottle of wine was still in the fridge, so not a wasted evening after all.

'Rachel, do you fancy a drink before you head home? I think that's the least we deserve, don't you?' she heard Lucas say as he caught up behind her, a little out of breath after obviously running.

Looking at her watch, but not wanting to appear rude, she replied, 'Yes, thank you, that would be nice,' thinking a quick drink, then straight home would not delay her plans too much.

They had walked to the pub, falling easily in stride with one another, chatting away, happily reliving the fun of the last couple of hours. Lucas had gone straight to the bar and ordered their drinks, along with two of the Friday night specials, Fish and Chips, leaving Rachel to find a quiet booth at the rear of the pub, away from the juke box and the dart board.

'I hope you don't mind, but I've ordered us both some food,' Lucas said, placing a large glass of white wine in front of Rachel. 'I think we've earned it, and as nice as those marshmallows were, I needed something more substantial to eat, they've worn me out. I don't know how you cope every day with those two!' he added, laughing.

'Oh, thanks, but that wasn't necessary,' she replied, thinking about the Chinese take-away that would now have to wait for another day.

The next couple of hours seemed to fly by; they talked about everything and nothing all at the same time, neither with any agenda, other than to relax and chill after a long week. Without realising it, they were soon hitting it off like old friends, completely at ease. It was almost as if they had known each other for ever, whereas in reality it was the first time they had spent time alone; just the two of them, without the children or Damian and Amanda, or work itself to distract them.

At the end of the evening when the landlord called time, neither had realised how late it had become, or in fact how gloomy it was outside. The night sky was obscured by thick clouds, preventing the moon for shining any brightness to light the way home. Lucas offered to walk Rachel safely back to her cottage, taking her arm naturally as they manoeuvred their way along the dark and damp country lanes, giggling like schoolchildren as they avoided the puddles that had arrived whilst they were in the pub, or got caught as a car splashed them as it drove passed.

Arriving home around twenty minutes later, her offer of 'coffee' was eagerly accepted, but once inside, the offer turned into 'something a little stronger if you prefer', but as there was no beer in the cottage, the two of them shared the bottle of chilled wine that had patiently been awaiting her return all day. 'At least it's not going to waste,' thought Rachel to herself as she poured.

The fire was lit, Netflix was switched on and tuned to a series they were both following, but before long, with the warmth of the fire, the effects of the wine and the result of a long week, Rachel started to nod off. Noticing her breathing had changed, Lucas considered getting up and going home, but as she was comfortably reclined against his shoulder, and being careful not to disturb her, he instead moved his arm, wrapped it carefully around her shoulders, and moved into a position that would ensure she was comfy. Lying there in his arms she looked so angelic; without thinking, he kissed her forehead, nestled down and before long he too was asleep.

It must have been around five o'clock in the morning when they awoke, both startled by a loud noise outside, but instead of being embarrassed by falling asleep with a strange man she was not even dating, Rachel did something she had never done before in her life. She simply took Lucas' hand and led him straight upstairs to her bedroom, saying as she drew the curtains, 'If you're going to stay the night, we should at least get ourselves comfortable,' before giving him the type of kiss that suggested going straight back to sleep was not at all where her mind was.

'I like the sound of that .....' replied Lucas with a smile on his face, wrapping his arms around Rachel and returning her kiss with a passion that was not only unexpected, but felt entirely natural.

On Saturday it rained all day, but as neither of them was showing any intention of getting out of bed for too long, it did not worry them at all. When they woke up around ten o'clock, they had taken a long steamy shower together, before making breakfast, wearing nothing but a towel and a smile. They returned to bed with a tray of tea and buttery toast, which was soon abandoned on the bedside table as they once again fell into each other's arms, laughing at something one of them had said, tumbling back onto the sheets, still crumpled after their nocturnal activities. It just felt natural; they were so relaxed together, that neither of them had stopped to question their behaviour, or what it might mean.

Rachel had only had a couple of boyfriends before, so although she was not a virgin, she was not particularly experienced in that department; sex was something she had previously thought was overrated, but now as she lay naked with Lucas besides her, wrapped in his arms, with her head nestled against his chest listening to his heart beat, her perspective had completely and unexpectantly changed.

What surprised her most, was she had not seen it coming. Until last night, Lucas was just Lucas; the girls' uncle, Amanda's brother, the man who was helping Damian out at the office. Whilst she had obviously been aware of him, for in truth who could miss those tall dark handsome looks, she had never given him a second thought romantically. He was well out of her league, and from what she had overheard, sensed there was a 'significant other' waiting for him somewhere. Nor, to the best of her knowledge, had he given her a second glance either. She was the type of inconspicuous girl who faded into the background, happier to watch the world go by than play a central part in it. Throughout her life, she had never dressed or done anything to attract attention to herself, content to just be one of life's bystanders.

But Lucas had noticed her, noticed the way she was with people, her natural ability to ease a situation, her kindness, her patience. There were so many small qualities that he admired, none of which amounted to love, or even lust in the first instance, but there was something so reassuring and wholesome about her that over time he could not help but be attracted. There was something in the way she was with Maisie and Alice the night of the bonfire, that made him realise he did not want the evening to end once they had taken the girls home, but even in his wildest dreams he had not anticipated what had subsequently taken place.

Sunday followed a similar pattern, with neither leaving the bedroom, let alone the house, for longer than was necessary. By the time the evening arrived, Lucas realised that he needed to head for the railway station in order to catch the last train if he was to keep up the pretence for work the following morning. The last thing Rachel needed was for him to turn up on Amanda's doorstep saying he'd spent the weekend sleeping with the au pair! That would not do his or Rachel's reputation any good, and if the way he was starting to feel about this girl was anything to go by, then managing that situation was very important for both of them.

His other concern was Sonia and the crazy situation he had unwittingly created there. He had recently begun to feel guilty that he had perhaps strung her along without realising it; keeping her on the back burner month after month, leaving his options open until he was ready to make his next move. She was waiting back at her parent's home in New Zealand for the call to resume their travelling, no doubt harbouring romantic ideas of their reunion. She had talked of meeting up at one of the iconic landmarks reminiscent of a Hollywood movie; the top of the Empire State Building perhaps like in Sleepless in Seattle, or even an Affair to Remember; or Heathrow Airport in Love Actually, ready to be swept into Lucas' waiting arms as she entered the Arrivals Hall, even sitting at the bar in Harry's in Casablanca, with a gin in her hand, with Lucas saying 'here's looking at you kid!' as they toasted their future. However, if the way he was feeling about Rachel was anything to go by, and without wanting to labour the Hollywood metaphors more than strictly necessary, to avoid a bloodbath reminiscent of a scene from Halloween, and exit stage right with all his bits still attached, then he had better come up with a plan pretty quickly.

Chapter 35

It was early evening at home in the Cotswolds, when Amanda decided a call to her mum was long overdue, as unusually, they had not spoken for nearly a week. She had the house to herself; dinner was all cleared away, the girls tucked up in bed, hopefully now fast asleep, and there was nothing particular that she wanted to watch on the television. Damian had phoned earlier to say he would be home about eight o'clock, a meeting had overrun; so, all being well, she had around an hour of undisturbed time for a catch-up.

'Mum, hi, I just wanted to wish you both Happy Thanksgiving, or whatever they say over there,' said Amanda as Monica picked up the phone; her daughter imagining her sitting on the terrace, with the sun shining and the yachts bobbing along on the water. In reality though it was nearly the end of November, and the weather in New England was definitely heading fast towards winter. The trees had changed their hues, the autumnal colours now in their full glory, with the promise of snow not too far off.

Monica was sitting in the lounge, with a cream cashmere throw draped over her legs, the fire blazing and a good book on her lap. She had been stealing a quiet moment reading whilst she had the house to herself, a pastime she had resurrected since her recent marriage. As a student, English Literature had been her passion, the subject she had got her degree in, but over the years, reading was something she had always struggled to find enough time to do, other things competing for her time.

'Hi darling, lovely to hear from you, and thank you, I'll pass that onto Rob when he gets back. I'm not sure I'm fully up to speed yet with all these traditions, but I know Mrs Reilly has gone to town this last week preparing more food than I would know what to do with.'

'That sounds good, where's Rob anyway? I thought he'd be home at this time, entertaining his guests perhaps.' Amanda had struggled to call Rob 'Dad', as for some reason even though she occasionally tried it for size, it simply did not roll off her tongue, so they had settled on 'Rob'. That way, she did not feel disloyal to her dad, Ken, but neither did it diminish her feelings for Rob, who as her biological father she had now developed a strong love for.

'Rob, oh yes, he popped into town about an hour ago, he shouldn't be too long. I think between you and me he's getting me a surprise, but I'm not to let on I suspect anything,' Monica giggled. Amanda smiled at her mum's reaction, happy to see the positive change that being married to Rob had brought to her; life was fun again, she was no longer a pensioner tending her garden and visiting the Women's Institute in an afternoon, but a vibrant woman with a renewed passion for life. 'Yes, we've got a houseful that's for sure, I think with Brad and Jane, Will and Maria and Greg, we've got either nine or ten for lunch. I'm just sorry you and the girls couldn't get over too. This year seems to have been so disjointed in terms of holidays. I've really missed seeing you all, but with everything that's been going on, it's understandable you've stayed at home. We'll see you at Christmas though won't we, it's only a month away? I've already started packing, and most of it seems to be presents for Maisie and Alice,' she laughed, hardly taking a breath as she spoke.

'So, what did you think when Lucas turned up, were you surprised?'

'Oh, yes. I'd forgotten about that. Yes, we were a little. He just phoned from the airport and said he'd be arriving in an hour or so, and was there a bed free. Rob and I hadn't expected to see him until Christmas; we knew Ben was planning on coming for Thanksgiving, but not Lucas, and certainly not with Rachel in tow. How did that all come about? I'd no idea they were an item.'

'Well, to be honest we're not sure either. One day they just nodded politely whenever they passed each other in the corridor, the next Rachel was asking if she could have some time off, as she was planning on visiting her family for Thanksgiving, and was intending flying over with Lucas. At the time, we just presumed it was convenient in terms of travelling arrangements, but reading their body language soon put us straight on that,' Amanda laughed, adding 'I don't think they intended letting on, particularly around the girls, but it was so obvious, it was laughable. Maisie and Alice keep breaking out into the K-I-S-S-I-N-G song whenever they are around.'

'So, is it serious, do you think? I thought he had someone waiting for him in Australia or some other place he'd been travelling to. I lost track after the first few months if I'm honest.'

'Well, there was definitely a girl in New Zealand that he was keen on a while ago, but I presume that must have fizzled out. I think her name was Sonia, but he's not really mentioned much about her to us, and every time we enquired about his plans, she never really featured. How serious it is with Rachel though, I wouldn't want to guess – we all know Lucas isn't one for settling down, so only time will tell. I just hope he doesn't hurt Rachel because I think she's quite a sensitive soul deep down.'

'From what I've seen of her, I agree she's lovely; Maria can't speak more highly of her or her family, and you and the girls have no problems with her I presume? I think Maria might be dusting off her wedding hat in anticipation of a big announcement over the turkey,' laughed Monica, obviously enjoying the latest episode in her step-son's love life, without taking it too seriously. She had seen several ladies come and go over the last couple of years.

'No, we've no problems with Rachel, but I don't want to lose my au pair due to him messing her around,' replied Amanda, partly in jest, but partly serious. Rachel was invaluable to both Damian and her at the moment, and with everything they were going through, she did not want Lucas scuppering that. 'Anyway, has Ben arrived yet? When he messaged me the other day, it seemed a bit touch-and-go whether he'd be able to make it. He's never off duty; he seems to think the hospital will collapse if he's not there to shore it up,' enquired Amanda.

'I know, but yes, he arrived late last night. He's only stopping until Friday afternoon as he's back on call over the weekend, but at least we've got him for a few days. I think Mrs Reilly intends fattening him up as she thinks he's losing weight. He mentioned something this morning about potentially looking for a move to another hospital, somewhere nearer here Rob and I are hoping. He still wants to do paediatrics, but Chicago's so far away and I think he feels like he's missing out by not being home so often. I know Rob would be happy with that.'

'I think Rob'd be happy if we all moved into the annex, and he had us all under one roof, where he can keep his eyes on us, especially his granddaughters. They can't wait until they see you both again. But they have loved having Lucas here these last few months, and he truly has been a godsend, what with everything that has been going on; so much so, we might have to consider paying him eventually,' laughed Amanda.

'How are things going on that front? Any developments yet with the solicitors?' enquired Monica cautiously. She received regular updates from Amanda, but generally waited to be told rather than run the risk of being accused of prying. She knew it was a sensitive subject, with her daughter's feelings complex, particularly where they related to Damian's son, Theo, but nevertheless she wanted to provide as much support as she could, even if it was from thousands of miles away.

'As it happens yes, I've agreed with Damian today that I'm going to visit Theo with him next time he goes, provided Social Services approves it of course. They're looking into what clearances I need, which I guess is normal procedure, given I'm not a direct blood relative. Damian says they're having to play everything by the book, what with safeguarding and everything.'

'And how do you feel about that?' Monica asked, conscious that to have reached this stage her daughter will have given it a lot of thought. Although she was well aware Amanda had jumped in with both feet when searching for her biological father, neither planning nor pre-thought being top of her agenda on that occasion, her approach then had been completely out of character. She always prided herself on being methodical, careful and guarded; doing little without considering the risks or the consequences first, a trait she had probably inherited from her dad, Ken who after a lifetime of working in insurance never jumped into anything without assessing the risks. Having reached the decision though, Monica mused to herself, what did her daughter think she would gain from meeting him?

'To be honest Mum, I don't mind admitting I'm pretty scared. I'm scared what I will say, what I'll do, but more importantly what I'm going to feel when I come face-to-face with him. He's only a two-year-old little boy, not yet three and probably still in nappies, and I'm scared of meeting him! What does that say about me, a grown woman?'

'I think it says a lot that you want to meet him, for both his and Damian's sake, as well as your own. From what you've said already, if Damian wants Theo in his life, then to my mind he's got to be in your life too. You can't make Damian choose; because if he chooses you and the girls, he would still never forget his son, and over time would grow to resent his actions; and if he chooses him over you, then where would that leave you, Maisie and Alice? I think you're right in trying to find a compromise. I'm sure it will work out in the end; you just need to be patient and not expect too much. Time is a great healer; we know better than most what that means, don't we darling?' she said almost echoing what Lisa had said a few weeks earlier.

'You're right Mum, as always, thanks.'

'Anyway, I'd better make a move or I'm going to get rooted to this settee, I can feel my legs going numb and I could do with a warm drink,' Monica said, suddenly feeling a bit sore after sitting for so long. 'I probably need to go and check on Mrs Reilly too, to make sure she hasn't ordered any more food. At this rate when we fly back home next month for Christmas, they'll not just be checking our luggage in as cargo, but us as well, given we'll weigh so much after all we've eaten,' laughed Monica.

'Well, give Rob and everyone my love when they arrive and tell everyone we can't wait until we see them again,' adding as a bit of an afterthought, 'and if in the meantime you find out any more about Lucas and Rachel and their big romance, don't hesitate to call me. I can't wait to find out what's really going on with those two!'

Chapter 36

December arrived in Castle Heighton in a blaze of glory, with colourful fairy lights, decorations and Christmas trees appearing almost overnight. The main tree, a Norwegian Spruce, standing over fifteen feet high, stood proudly in the village square, directly across the road from the parish church, in full view of anyone passing by; anchored down by a set of weights and guy ropes to prevent it going skywards, should a sudden gust of wind take hold. There was also a series of perhaps a dozen smaller Christmas trees lining the pavement outside the main parade of shops, each planted in matching wooden beer barrels, donated presumably by the local pub or the brewery from the neighbouring town; the barrels garishly painted in seasonal reds, greens, golds and silvers. All the shops were decked-out in their finery too; with spray snow or stars glittering their windows, holly and mistletoe adorning the door posts, and an abundance of plastic Santas or snowmen on view no matter which way you turned. It was like one giant cheesy grotto; not just good for business, but morale too, and by the looks on most people's faces it was making everyone smile.

Well, perhaps not everyone. As Damian drove through the town that crisp winter's morning on the way to Stroud, a distance of around twenty miles away, Amanda sat quietly in the passenger seat next to him, nervously twiddling her fingers and staring out of the window; lost somewhere in her own thoughts. She appeared oblivious to all the bustle going on in the village, seeing straight past the villagers who were ambling around, happily getting ready for the Christmas season. Today she did not pip her horn as she saw Gloria opening up the Coffee pot, or at old Mr Thompson coming out of the post office, carrying his morning newspaper in one hand and a loaf of bread in the other, no doubt hurrying home for his breakfast. He had been Grandad Tom's next-door neighbour, as well as one of his regular domino partners down at the pub, and by all accounts still travelled up to see him at Willow Tree village on the bus at least once a month, no doubt to swap gossip and keep his hand in with the dominoes. The two were like a couple of old women when they got started!

Amanda had got up early that morning, well over an hour before the rest of the household stirred; unable to sleep the previous night, tossing and turning as each hour ticked by. Reaching for her slippers and her dressing gown, she had eventually gone downstairs to make herself a hot drink, careful not to disturb Damian, who slept peacefully beside her, his face looking like he did not have a care in the world. As she pulled her dressing gown tighter to her, she shivered as she went into the kitchen, switching the under-counter lights on to minimise the glare. The heating would be kicking in shortly, but for now it was chilly.

Nursing a mug of coffee, she sat staring into space, and for some bizarre reason began worrying about what to wear. Unlike Clara or Lisa, clothes were never top of her agenda, so why was it bothering her so much today; why did it matter what she turned up in, she was not on trial or being assessed was she, so why did she feel the need to make a good impression?

'Try to relax, darling, it's going to be okay; there's really nothing to worry about,' said Damian, smiling over at his wife, gently placing his left hand on her leg to reassure her, noticing as he did, the slight tremor in her knees. 'We should be there in around thirty minutes, so just sit back. Shall I put the radio on?' he asked rhetorically as he switched the station to one of the smooth music channels; the more relaxing music she normally preferred to listen to when driving. Instead of one of the usual ballads though, the ten o'clock news headlines came on. The reporter was talking about something to do with Brexit, citing the Prime Minister and his latest exploits; Members of Parliament being interviewed about their views on this or that. Damian was not in the mood for it today, and he knew Amanda certainly would not be, so flicked between the channels until he found something more relaxing. Politics was one of those subjects they both steered well clear of; not that their views differed particularly, but it was just not something either found exciting or engaged with.

'Ah, that's better,' he said eventually finding a channel that was playing half decent music, but glancing over at his wife, he realised that she was completely uninterested, a blank expression on her face. 'Are you sure you want to come today, I can always turn round and take you home if it's too much for you?' he asked, concerned that he was perhaps putting too much pressure on her.

'No, I'll be fine. I'm just wondering what I'm going to say when I get there, and what they'll think of me,' her voice quivering as she answered.

'No one is going to think or say anything, so please don't worry. We'll only stay for a short time, and as soon as you want to go, then we'll say good-bye and head off,' Damian said as reassuringly as he could manage, adding 'you look lovely by the way, is that a new top?'

'Yes, I treated myself to it in Bristol when I went shopping with Clara and Lisa last month, along with these trousers. They twisted my arm into buying it, it's not my usual style, but they said it suited me, and apparently it brought out the colour in my eyes. Given my eyes are bloodshot at the moment from not sleeping last night, plus all the worrying, I'm not sure it was the right choice today,' she replied, smiling over to her husband and trying to add a little humour into an otherwise difficult situation.

The midnight blue wrap-around top, with flecks of red and cream running through it, had been teamed with a pair of off-white denim trousers, a pair of black kitten heel booties and a three-quarter length grey jacket, creating a look that was smarter than Amanda would normally wear for a drive out in the country, but perfectly on trend. The trousers were also a size smaller, clearly indicating how much weight she had lost over the last few months. Every cloud, she thought to herself.

Before long, with the country roads now behind them, Amanda noticed they had entered a housing estate and were starting to slow down, eventually stopping in front of a small semi-detached house, with a neat garden at the front, a red Polo car in the drive and bright lights in the bay-fronted downstairs window. The white UPVC door remained closed, but not for long, as soon a kind looking middle-aged woman, somewhere perhaps in her early-fifties, opened it and walked out to greet them.

'Mr Reynolds, how nice to see you again,' the lady said, smiling at Damian.

'Good morning, and it's Damian, please,' he said before adding, 'and this is Amanda, my wife. Amanda, this is Mrs Wilson, Theo's foster mother.' Damian continued politely, 'I hope we're not too early. Traffic was relatively light today and we got here in no time.'

'Hello, no, you're perfectly on time,' Mrs Wilson replied with a reassuring smile, at the same time offering a welcoming hand to Amanda, 'Pleased to meet you, it's Susan. My husband, Denis, is inside with Theo watching cartoons.'

Susan Wilson and her husband had been fostering children for nearly twenty years, and were highly regarded by their local Social Services team, but no matter how many children she cared for, one of the things she prided herself most on, was her ability to read people and situations. Looking at Mrs Reynolds now, she clearly saw a woman who was completely out of her depth; and someone who clearly given the choice would have probably chosen the firing squad rather than having to stand outside her front door on this particular morning. But it was neither her position to judge, nor jump to conclusions, so she just welcomed them into her house, indicating they take the door on the left as soon as they entered the small hallway.

Denis Wilson was perched on the end of the three-seater settee, obviously straining to listen to the conversation that was taking place outside, whilst at the same time keeping his eyes on Theo, who was sitting on the rug in front of the television playing with a couple of small matchbox cars, running them up and down the carpet with the obligatory 'Vroom-Vroom' noises. Denis should normally be at work by this time of the morning, ferrying people to and from the railway station, or into town to do their shopping, but with Susan having visitors he felt he should stay and lend his support. Being a taxi-driver meant he was his own boss, therefore allowing him greater flexibility in the hours he worked, which was essential given the frequent calls they got usually at short-notice, requesting them to take children who needed urgent care. He struggled to recall the number of times the phone had gone off in the middle of the night asking if they could take a child in; some children staying as little as a few hours or overnight, whereas others perhaps months, or on the odd occasion years before they found their forever home, or went back to their family. One thing was for sure, all cases were different and usually difficult; many harrowing depending on the individual circumstances, but he like his wife, did not judge. They were just there to look after the child, an innocent little person who had been caught up in something that was not of their making.

Denis stood and smiled as his wife led Amanda and Damian into the small lounge, allowing her to make the introductions. He and Susan exchanged a brief glance, 'I'll go and put the kettle on whilst you both sit down and say hello to Theo if you like; is a cup of tea okay, white no-sugar I recall Damian, what about you?' he asked looking directly at Amanda.

'Thank you, we'll have the same,' replied Damian for both of them, his wife still rooted in the doorway, her eyes clearly focussed on the little boy sitting on the rug, wearing his Paw Patrol tracksuit and Paddington Bear slippers, with his wispy blonde curls just tickling the back of his pale neck. He had stopped playing with the cars and was now looking up at the two of them, with clearly some recognition of Damian, but perhaps wondering who the new lady was. She was not his mum that was for sure, he thought as he returned his attention to the cars. 'Perhaps she'll come another day.' Theo wondered to himself.

Denis and Susan had been briefed on the situation with Theo, so had real empathy for Amanda. They knew, not just from their own experiences, but from what Damian had mentioned the last time he visited, that today would be difficult for her. No one had any preconceptions on how the visit would go, but secretly as they sat there watching the scene play out in front of them, a lot of prayers were hanging on its outcome.

Chapter 37

As Amanda sat in her regular pew at St Anthony's Church on Christmas Eve waiting for the vigil mass to begin, she looked around and counted her blessings; namely her family. Damian was sitting to her right wearing his black overcoat, wrapped up against the cold, with Grandad Tom to her left wearing his smartest herringbone suit, displaying a matching cravat and pocket handkerchief, proudly guarding the aisle seat. His head was on a constant swivel to ensure he did not miss any of his friends or old neighbours hobbling up or down the church on the way to take their seats, no doubt wondering where his next bit of gossip was coming from. His overcoat had been draped over the pew in front, where Monica and Rob sat, quietly talking to Maisie and Alice, who were tightly wedged between them, excitedly wearing their new matching red winter coats, complete with fake-fur trims and hand muffs on a silky cord around their necks. Amanda thought they were a little over the top, and not something she would personally have bought for them, but Monica had insisted when she and Rob had turned up with them the previous weekend, that they were perfect for the season, and the girls had agreed.

Rob was not particularly religious, but as his eyes wandered around the old building taking in the atmosphere and the artefacts that surrounded him, there was a lump in his throat. He knew how important it was to his wife

Monica, particularly this church where she had spent so many happy years with her first husband, Ken; both of them playing a pivotal role in the life of the parish community. He also knew how much he had to be thankful for, as such, had no qualms accompanying her to church whenever they were in England, even if asked, joining her as she lay flowers on Ken's grave. In fact, he had even started joining in with some of the prayers and hymns, although listening to him sing loudly in his distinct American accent, it was safe to conclude he would never have been chosen to be a choirboy in his day.

Next to Damian were Lucas and Rachel, still in the first flush of their romance, holding hands and whispering to each other. Amanda noticed how lovely Rachel was looking. She had ditched her usual padded jacket, opting for a smart green fitted coat, with a wide belt that accentuated her slim waist, worn over an aubergine-coloured woollen dress and black knee-high boots. Since starting to date Lucas, there had definitely been an upturn in her wardrobe and clothes selection whenever she ventured out, Amanda thought to herself with a pleasant smile on her face. Gone were the student jeans and hoodies that had appeared to be de rigueur, regardless of the occasion, replaced by a stylish elegance, that coupled with the merest hint of make-up, seemed to make her blossom. Whatever was happening between them, it had certainly brought out her natural beauty, leaving her positively glowing.

Lucas, recently more used to wearing formal attire and smart suits for work, now enjoyed dressing down whenever he had the opportunity, but his idea of dressing-down still involved him covering himself in designer labels from head to toe, tonight wearing his pale blue cashmere jumper over distressed jeans that probably cost more than most people earned in a week, if not a month, teamed with a leather flying jacket that would not have looked out of place on a second world war pilot, or the set of Top Gun. When he had travelled, he had consciously left his designer labels at home, relying instead on whatever 'stuff' he could cram into his back-pack, easily replaceable items that could be washed and worn without worrying about how good they looked, or whether they would be ruined or stolen. Returning home for Thanksgiving though had given him the perfect opportunity to replenish his wardrobe, his check-in luggage on the return leg overflowing with clothes; some new after hitting the malls, but mainly old favourites.

Lucas, like his dad, was not particularly religious, unlike Rachel who had been brought up in the church, regularly attending Sunday school with her siblings. Although she would probably now consider herself more of a lapsed than a practising Catholic, she did occasionally join the family at Mass, especially on high days and holidays. The two of them had arrived late, sneaking into the back of the packed church just as the organist started belting out the first carol 'Oh Come All Ye Faithful'; both having had a couple of drinks before the service started, so it was fair to say, they probably had a little more Christmas spirit in them than most.

Looking around, Amanda marvelled at how spectacular the altar looked; the Christmas tree to its right, decked out with festive lights, with wrapped presents beneath it that had been donated by some of the village's shops and businesses and would subsequently be delivered to the local children's home; the Advent wreath to the left, now with all its candles ablaze, and in pride of place in the centre, the crib awaiting the arrival of the baby Jesus. It was a tradition dating back as long as Amanda could remember, and probably many more years before that, that the children of Year Six brought the model representing the baby Jesus up at the start of the Mass, carefully placing him in the manger. The children would process down the aisle, each carrying a small lit candle, before the crib was blessed by the priest and they were asked to return to join their parents in their seats. It was one of those magical moments that always brought a tear to the eyes; parents and congregation alike, with most parents visibly only relaxing after their child's candle had been extinguished.

Throughout the service, Amanda tried desperately to concentrate on the words of Father Michael Tate, the long-serving parish priest and family friend who had been at St Anthony's for more years than people cared to remember; the priest who had not only married her and Damian, baptised both of their children, celebrated her dad's Requiem Mass, but also married her mum and Rob just a couple of years ago. He had been there through the highs and lows of not just their lives, but the lives of most of the people in the church too. Listening to his melodic voice wash over her, the Christmas messages he was trying to convey were nothing new, but try as she might, she struggled to focus. Her mind kept wandering to places she would prefer it not to go, to thoughts she would prefer to 'park' rather than acknowledge or bring into existence.

The last few weeks since meeting Theo for that first time had been difficult for her emotionally; trying to understand and process the feelings he had evoked in her was an ongoing battle, and one she was unsure who was winning. Feelings that if she was honest, she would have preferred not to feel. She had tried her utmost to block her emotions, to ignore them; desperately trying to lose herself in the practicalities of preparing for the season, buying presents for her family, sorting out the food and drinks, decorating the house. All those everyday distractions that she could have easily delegated to others to help with, she threw herself into, in the hope that they would absorb her completely, and stop her from thinking about anything else. But try as she might, this year Theo was an ever-present thought in the back of her mind, and a thought that would not go away.

Driving home from the foster parents' house after meeting him, Damian had naturally asked her how she felt, concerned whether it had been too much for her; but no matter how much she tried, she struggled to properly articulate her feelings. Words like 'fine', 'lovely', 'he's cute' somehow did not seem to cut it. The little boy she had seen looked angelic, there was no doubt about that, with a twinkle in his eye that suggested he had a real personality about him, and the way he laughed a sense of fun. He appeared bright for his age; apparently, he had turned three the previous week, something Damian had not realised, and throughout the hour or so they were there, he engaged with Damian, both talking easily as they played with his toys or read stories. He was a proper chatterbox, but also listened quite intently when he was spoken to. When they had left, he had given Damian a hug and waved good-bye from the door, holding tight to Susan's hand.

Watching how he interacted with both his foster parents and Damian gave no indications that there was a grieving child in the room, or a child damaged by the loss of his mother, or even one having suffered recent tragedy of any nature. He had occasionally looked over at Amanda sitting nervously in one of the armchairs, her hands clasped tightly on her lap for fear of giving herself away, sheepishly raising his eyes in her direction, but never once said anything directly to her, or attempted to draw her into any of his games. She was silently relieved at that, having been on edge all the while wondering what she would have done if he had attempted to talk to her, what would she have said?

Throughout the hour, Chloe's name was never mentioned by Damian, the foster parents or Theo, and at no stage did Theo ask where his mum was, or when she would be picking him up. He just seemed sub-consciously to accept she was no longer around and that Susan and Denis were now looking after him, something that did not appear to present him with a problem. He was a happy little boy.

Deep down, Amanda was curious whether that was a temporary situation, or whether in time something could happen to trigger or evoke those memories, bringing them sharply to the surface to either haunt him, or at least create a painful episode in his later life that would affect his behaviour. She had read enough on-line recently to know that no one really had the answers to those questions; how deep hurt, or in fact memories, went in those early years of a child's life was difficult to quantify. The only thing for certain, was that everyone responded differently, so for Theo and those around him, it would be a waiting game. But from the reports Damian had shared with her, none of the grief therapy or counselling sessions had raised any red-flags so far, which had to be a promising sign, surely?

For the time being at least, Amanda had to acknowledge that although she had never met Chloe or been one of her fans, and knew little about her, other than what had sadly been brought to light following her death, she had done a remarkable job in raising what appeared to be such a well-balanced little boy; made no easier she surmised by the unenviable financial and home environment she had found herself in, without family, support or money to see her through. She might not have liked the thought of the girl, but she could not criticise what she had done by way of mothering skills.

As Amanda's thoughts were brought back to the Mass, she sensed Father Michael was beginning to wrap up his sermon, conscious no doubt that a number of the children in the congregation were starting to get fidgety, as well as several of those adults who were not obvious or regular church goers. He had also noticed some of the dads looking subtly at their watches, wondering presumably how much time they would have to sort the presents out after the children had been tucked into bed, or more likely whether they would still have enough time for a quick pint before the pub closed. Father Michael charitably overlooked whatever their reasons were, just grateful to see so many in attendance. He was well aware being in church was not everybody's cup of tea, and for some who had probably been dragged along tonight under sufferance, knew they would only feel comfortable once they were back out in the fresh air. The church tonight felt warmer than usual; a result of more bodies tightly packed in, or perhaps the extra lights and candles throwing off additional heat, even the consequence of being dressed in more layers than was strictly necessary given it was a relatively mild night outside for the time of year, but whatever the reason, even he was starting to feel a little warm under all his vestments if he was perfectly honest, and he hoped he was not sickening for something.

Nevertheless, as Father Michael finally brought his sermon to a close, a few of his words kept resonating around Amanda's head; 'the holy family', the innocent baby, the role Joseph played bringing up the baby Jesus, in the full knowledge it was not his son. None of these messages of Christmas were new, they were the same messages repeated year in, year out, regardless of wherever in the world you happened to hear them, but as Amanda sat in the quiet church, in the beautiful village she called home, with her family all around her, this year, there seemed to be greater significance than ever to the words that were being said.

Chapter 38

The antique grandfather clock in the hall, that had stood proudly in the same place since Ken's grandfather had bought it over a hundred years ago, was just about to chime the midnight hour, heralding in the new year; a year like all others, full of promises and hopes for all, with resolutions being made that would undoubtedly be broken. Some resolutions would perhaps not even see the end of the week, never mind lasting the month, before they were resigned to the recycle bin along with all the bottles and cans that kept mounting up. The house was full of friends and family, neighbours and old acquaintances, all gathered and happily celebrating the season, glasses primed ready:

'Ten, nine, eight ....', Damian counted down, soon to be joined by everyone until it reached its natural crescendo.

'Happy New Year!' went up the cry as the clock eventually struck the hour, cheers being heard from throughout the house, people grabbing whoever was closest, and engaging in the age-old tradition of kissing, as if their life depended on it.

Amanda sought out her husband among the crowds, approaching him with a chilled glass of champagne in each hand. She had been in the kitchen, refilling her drink and chatting to one of her neighbours about the new by-pass that was being proposed, when she realised the time and made her way to find her husband,

'Happy New Year, darling, here's to 2022!' she said as she handed him a flute and reached up to kiss him, adding, 'I love you,' feeling happier and lighter than she had in some time.

'Happy New Year to you too, my darling, and I love you, more than you could ever imagine,' he replied adding, 'have I told you how gorgeous you look tonight in that dress with your hair up, very sexy?' returning her kiss with an added passion, possibly fuelled by the numerous beers he had been drinking throughout the evening, but clearly indicating that regardless of everything they had weathered over recent months, his love for her had not diminished. He was proud of the way she had stood by him through it all; knowing it had not been pretty or easy for either of them, but realising how especially hard his wife had taken most of it, and none of it her fault, or of her creation.

Looking back now how had she coped? The thought of having to sell their house to pay off Chloe's demands; the risks of losing his business because he had completely lost focus; the court case and all the legal distractions that created; the aftermath of Chloe's sudden and traumatic death, and all the uncertainty that injected into an already confusing landscape, the list went on. But most of all, dealing with the prospect of a child in their lives; a young boy who could never replace the one they had lost, but at the same time a son who could not be ignored. He truly loved his wife, not only the way she handled herself, staying strong and unstintingly continuing to put the needs of their family above her own; most importantly, how she ensured both Maisie and Alice were protected from all the fallout. Life for them, with the help of Rachel of course, who Damian had to accept had been a star throughout, had continued almost unaffected by the maelstrom playing out around them. At no stage were

Maisie or Alice left in any doubt they were loved by both their parents, and would always remain their priority.

As Damian now held his wife, trying desperately to stem the small tears that were starting to form in his eyes, he knew for certain how grateful he felt. Other than the one monumental glitch in their relationship, a stupid affair he would prefer to forget and ideally erase completely from his life if he had his way, from this point forward he vowed to do whatever it took to make her life happy, for as long as ever he could, and hopefully make her as proud of him, as he was of her. 'If only someone would invent a rewind button to deal with life's disasters,' he said to himself wistfully, 'now that would be a real money spinner!'

Feeling playful, he asked 'have you any New Year's resolutions you might want to tell me about Mrs Reynolds, before I whisk you off to bed and remove that exceptionally beautiful gown you are wearing tonight, and show you my resolutions?' nibbling the back of her neck quite suggestively, whilst twiddling the tendrils of hair that had escaped from the diamanté clip she had used to secure it up.

Amanda stood there, content to be in her husband's arms, also feeling grateful they had weathered the storm so far, but in her mind, there was still some way to go before life would return to normal, or whatever their new normal would consist of, she thought ruefully. The week between Christmas and New Year had given her some quality time to focus and reflect, a quiet interlude when the children could be left to play with their new toys, or watch the endless Disney films the programmers had scheduled to repeat over the holidays.

Damian had decided to have a Christmas shut-down, allowing not only the staff but himself and Lucas a few days off to recharge their batteries, leaving him at home to help out around the house, including indulging his passion of making imaginative meals from left-over turkey. With Lucas' help the business was not only showing real signs of recovery, but his fresh acumen and business drive was opening up some new and promising opportunities that Damian was giving serious thought to introducing.

Amanda had also worked extra hours in the run-up to the holidays concentrating on those designs that needed finalising before the year end, leaving her not only ahead of schedule, but able to switch-off for a few days before the demands of January and planning for their next collection resumed with vengeance. She had spoken to Will a couple of days before Christmas as part of a regular discussion, so nothing untoward; but was surprised at the end of the call when he asked her to make arrangements to come over in the new year as he needed to have a private talk to her, something that needed to be discussed face-to-face. A little intrigued to what he might want to say, and hoping it was not fall-out from her disastrous trip to Singapore with Nick, she had agreed to fly over early-January, once the girls had gone back to school. It was no use worrying about it now, and if nothing else it would give her a chance to reconnect with Maria and her team, and if she timed it right, possibly fly home with her mum and Rob, once she had checked what their plans were. Either way, Rachel would be perfectly able to manage, and given the way she was feeling about Lucas at the moment, she obviously had no plans for returning back stateside any time soon. Her visa was still valid for another eighteen months or so, so whatever worries Amanda did have, that was not one of them.

But the more she reflected, the more the messages of Father Michael's sermon remained with her; leaving her more disconcerted than she realised possible. Everything was on the up, they had weathered the storm, so what was there left to worry about?

Christmas morning had been frenetic; the usual toys and gifts littering the lounge, surrounded by the brightly coloured bows, wrapping paper and boxes that had contained them just minutes earlier, discarded in the race to open everything in record time. Maisie and Alice scrambling from present to present, with no real appreciation of the gift or who had lovingly chosen it for them. How many hours had gone into the planning and preparation of those presents, Amanda had thought to herself, for it to turn into a bombsite within minutes, but seeing the smiles on her daughters' faces, as they marvelled at each new gift, she could happily forgive them.

Just before lunch, Monica and Rob turned up; Rob parking the 5 series BMW he had hired for their visit in the driveway alongside Amanda's Audi, Damian having garaged his own car to leave them room knowing they were picking Grandad Tom up from Willow Tree village en route. Monica linked arms with Tom as they gingerly navigated the path to the front door, whilst Rob brought up the rear, cradling even more gifts in his arms. They had already dropped off their main presents the evening before, so Amanda wondered as she stood to greet them, what else could they possibly be bringing. As they entered the house, glad of the warmth, they promptly removed their coats and shook off the snow that had arrived from nowhere overnight. After Mass the previous evening, everyone had commented on how mild the weather was, and how unlikely a white Christmas would be, but waking up to it the following morning had been magical, for the children at least.

Lucas and Rachel arrived shortly after, both ladened with carrier bags full of presents as they entered the house, similarly shaking the snow from their shoulders and stamping it off their boots. From the glow in their cheeks, they had obviously walked the short distance from

Rachel's cottage, where Lucas seemed to now be basing himself whenever he was not making use of Damian's apartment in the town. Since returning home from New England after Thanksgiving, Amanda had noticed most of his 'bits and pieces' had gradually been moved out of the bedroom and bathroom he occupied at their house, with Damian commenting that Lucas rarely stayed at the apartment in town any more, preferring he said to commute in as Damian had done for years, either on the train or cadging a lift whenever one was available. Whichever way you looked at it, the two of them had become inseparable, spending whatever time they had together, either holed up in the cottage, no doubt cuddled on the couch or watching Netflix, or when weekends allowed, visiting Lucas' friends in London, catching a show or perhaps visiting the cinema before having a meal out. Rachel had really come out of her shell, discovering a new level of confidence among Lucas' friends, as well as interests she had not previously known she had, or afforded to enjoy. She had never been a great socialiser, happy to be the one who faded into the background, but now chatted away easily, even singing along to the radio as she worked, leaving Amanda to wonder where the reserved and shy girl she had picked up from the airport less than six months ago had gone.

The feelings of joviality and love were palpable around the house, everyone simply relaxed in each other's company, enjoying the good food, the copious amounts of wine, even the corny jokes that came out of the Christmas crackers were making everyone giggle.

Grandad Tom was on top form, regaling stories over lunch of the Christmas party the management had laid on for the inmates at the village the previous week, even admitting with a twinkle in his eye to pinching a sprig of mistletoe from the floral display on the bar and catching Mrs Seymour unawares with a kiss on the cheek; receiving a playful slap in return for his efforts. Rather than letting that deter him, it in fact encouraged him to invite her to join him for afternoon tea the following day, to which she had readily agreed.

'Well, now I know who that box of chocolates was for, the one you asked me to pick out specially,' laughed Amanda, 'and I thought they were a thank-you gift for one of your carers!'

'Ha, ha. I thought that would have you guessing, young lady,' he laughed, wagging his finger at his granddaughter mischievously, 'there's life in this old dog yet, I'll have you know. I might even get her to play dominoes with me one day, if I'm lucky,' he added with a cheeky grin, the innuendo not lost on the adults.

'Well, I'll definitely look out for the merry widow when I next drop your provisions off, check you've not got her locked up in your wardrobe, or worse still tied to the bedpost,' she joked as everyone joined in laughing at Tom's exploits whilst tucking into their turkey.

Now, nearing the end of their New Year's Eve party, with the girls safely snuggled in their beds upstairs, hopefully fast asleep by now regardless of the noise below, her parents waltzing away on the makeshift dancefloor in the dining room, to the 1960's classic Moon River from Breakfast at Tiffany's, without a care in the world, while Rachel and Lucas smooched alongside them, failing to make any real effort to co-ordinate their feet in tune with the music, Amanda scanned the room with a contented smile on her face, happy to just absorb it all. She revelled in the atmosphere, taking more than a little pride in the scene before her eyes, something she had orchestrated, a happy family tableau. But no matter how much she tried, she could not rid herself of the feeling that something, or more correctly someone was missing. There was a hole, and no matter how much she tried to ignore it, it would not go away.

Turning to Damian, speaking so quietly she could hardly hear herself utter the words, let alone believe she was saying them, she whispered, 'I wonder what Theo is doing tonight?'

'I hope he's in bed like Maisie and Alice are,' he replied, not paying any heed to her question, or looking deeper into its meaning.

Damian had called round to the foster parent's home the week leading up to Christmas, taking some token presents with him, but at no stage had it been suggested that he call in over the holidays. He presumed they would have enough with their own family, without having visitors calling as well, and at no stage had Amanda given any indication that she felt he should call over to see him either.

Amanda, then added, with more courage than she felt possible, 'do you think it's about time we brought him home?'

Damian smiled back and looked at his wife, unsure whether he had heard her correctly over all the noise, but on seeing the look she gave him, a smile suddenly lit up his face.

'Are you sure?' he asked.

A simple nod was all she could manage, but the message was clear. If that wasn't a New Year's resolution for him to ponder, then what more could she do?

Chapter 39

Damian had driven his wife to Heathrow airport early Wednesday morning of the following week, leaving plenty of time for her to catch her eleven o'clock flight to Boston, before continuing across country to Bristol to meet his solicitor, Jason Gleeson at eleven thirty later that morning. He had arranged a meeting with him to understand what wheels needed to be put in motion now they had decided what they wanted to do about Theo; assuming after all, as his father everything should be relatively straightforward. If the traffic was in his favour, and there were no hold-ups due to the weather, within a couple of hours he should be sitting in Jason's office ticking whatever boxes were needed to bring his son home. At this time of year, at least the roads were unlikely to be clogged with caravans, motorhomes, or tractors, but some of the country roads did get effected by black ice, so he needed to be careful and avoid letting his mind wander too much as he drove.

The problem was, since Amanda had whispered in his ear on New Year's Eve, 'isn't it about time to bring him home', he had not managed to remove the inane grin from his face, never daring to accept until that point how much he wanted Theo to come and live with them, but had never been brave enough to say it out loud, or in his wildest dreams imagine Amanda would feel the same way. He had resigned himself to being an arm's length dad, someone who would visit as regularly as he could, take a level of financial responsibility for his son's upbringing, but never be able to play as close or as active a role in his life as a father should. He knew it would be difficult, but had vowed that if that was the price he needed to pay, both to maintain his wife's love and the love and respect of his daughters, then so be it.

Over the first few days of the New Year, they had talked it over, both carefully checking each other's feelings to ensure it was not just the champagne that had been talking, or the rashness of their seasonal resolutions, but a real intent to permanently change their family dynamic. They both knew it would not be easy, and that there would need to be a lot of adjustments made to their lives; let alone how they were going to explain Theo's existence to Maisie and Alice, or the concept that he was their half-brother. But the more they spoke, the more they knew they would manage it, because as Amanda so generously reminded him, it was the right thing to do.

A couple of days later, having driven over to their apartment, Monica and Rob had listened as Damian explained their plans to them, with Amanda sitting opposite on the settee as he spoke. Rachel and Lucas had diplomatically offered to take the girls for a day out to Bristol Zoo to see the hippos and elephants, among other such creatures when Damian had suggested they needed some alone time to talk a few things over without 'little ears' listening in. Her parents had sat quietly, all the time scrutinising their daughter's face for signs that this was something she truly wanted, rather than something she felt obliged to do, or worse still found herself being pressured into, but saw no evidence of that. Whilst neither was particularly surprised that Damian would want to do this, Theo being his son after all, they both had reservations that this was not what Amanda needed, particularly having lost her own baby so recently. Her career was taking off, the girls now both at school and her life was settled. Did she need this extra dimension in her life for now, was their primary concern, but mainly was she strong enough to cope with bringing up someone else's child? They both sat quietly, intuitively knowing that this was not the time for them to voice their concerns.

Having left Rachel ostensibly in charge in her absence, with the girls now back to school and Lucas and Damian beavering away at the office, both refreshed after the Christmas break, Amanda relaxed into the flight, knowing that in a few short hours she would be heading towards her new spiritual home. She loved returning to New England, but this was her first visit 'home' when Rob or Monica would not be around to entertain her, so it felt a little strange. They had decided to stay in the Cotswolds for the foreseeable time, with no definite plans of when they would return. Mrs Reilly had graciously agreed to look after her in their absence, so a few days of relaxing and being pampered after a hectic Christmas would not go amiss, plus there was always her cheesecake to look forward to. Also, if her timings worked out as she hoped they would, and what Will needed to tell her was not bad news, she might even get a day or so to visit Lisa and Clara, who last she heard had agreed to extend their Christmas holiday at home with Aunt Jane and Brad.

As she sat back, took a mouthful of the chilled champagne the stewardess had kindly handed her as she had taken her food order, she tuned into the entertainment system, homing straight into the boxset of 'Luther', one of her all-time favourites crime drama series. Oh, for a steamy night with Idris Elba, she allowed her mind to wander, as DCI John Luther's hunky form filled the screen, and the plane soared higher.

Chapter 40

Sitting outside Will's office on Thursday evening, after the rest of the team had left for the day, Amanda could not stop her hands from shaking, or the tears from falling from her puffy eyes into the cup of cold coffee she was still holding, having hardly taken a mouthful since Will's secretary, Loretta, had handed it to her nearly an hour previously. Loretta was a quiet girl, with a beautiful smile; someone who made you want to smile in return. She had only joined the company the previous year, and other than speaking to her occasionally on the phone, Amanda had not had many dealings with her. But from what she gleaned from the rest of the team, Loretta was already proving to be a real asset in dealing with the majority of the admin that no one else really wanted to take on, and from the way Will spoke to her as she closed the door behind her, you could tell he had a lot of respect for her, and that the feeling was mutual.

What Amanda, Nick and Will had discussed after Loretta had left them was so far from what she had been expecting, that the shock was too much for her, and sitting opposite Will she had visibly deflated as he spoke, sinking further into her chair. Nick sat next to her, trying to be as supportive as possible, but equally concerned by the recent turn of events. He had guessed there was something Will had wanted to discuss, having picked up on the vibes in the office since coming back from the Christmas break, but he had never had an inkling Maria was the cause of Will's concern.

Amanda had arrived the previous evening, a little tired after the flight, but upbeat at the prospect of catching up with family, having a few days away from the pressures of home life and especially being able to throw herself back into the job she loved. Meeting up with the team again face-to-face was something she was really looking forward to; taking the opportunity to all be in the same room again rather than at the other end of a video call. Exchanging ideas and bouncing off each other creatively was so rewarding, and preferable to working remotely if she was honest, but given her current situation there was really no alternative.

Mrs Reilly had been at the house awaiting her arrival as she pulled into the driveway a little after seven o'clock, parking the hire car she had collected from the airport in front of the impressive front door of Rob's waterfront mansion. A hot dinner was already prepared, a glass of wine chilled, her bed made up with fresh linen and an arrangement of winter blooms sitting on the dressing table, their sweet perfume filling the room. It truly was like staying in a five-star hotel, but without the over-priced bill at the end of the stay.

'I'm going to leave you now if you don't mind,' Mrs Reilly said a little flustered. 'It's usually my night off tonight, and unfortunately, I've got something arranged for tomorrow that I can't move, but I'll be back the day after tomorrow, sometime around lunchtime. There's enough food and provisions in the fridge and larder to see you through until I return, so you should be fine, but ring me if there's anything urgent, here's my number,' she said panicking a little as she passed Amanda a slip of paper, her mobile number scrawled on the reverse of it. 'The keys are over by the table in their usual place, and everywhere is locked up at the back, so just put the alarm on when you go out and everything should be good.'

'Thank you for staying around to wait for me, that was very kind of you, but please don't worry, I'll be fine,' Amanda smiled in response, sensing the housekeeper's concerns at leaving the house in her care, whilst walking her to the door so she could lock it up straight after she left, 'and thanks for whatever smells so delicious in the kitchen, I didn't eat much on the flight, so I'm ravenous. Have a good day off, and I'll see you soon.'

Being in the house all alone felt a little unusual, but Amanda had stayed so many times now it really was beginning to feel like her second home, a happy place where she felt relaxed. She wandered around the downstairs rooms, gently touching pieces of furniture or fabrics as she went by; the elegant hall with its clean white floor tiles and mirrors, all designed to reflect the natural light that normally flowed through the house; the comfortable and spacious lounge where the spectacular views of the water that ran along the back of the property, although not visible tonight due to the darkness of the sky, would return in the morning, although perhaps with fewer boats bobbing along, given the sailing season had come to an end; the formal dining room, with its modern table, large enough to seat an army, she smiled, remembering the many happy meals they had shared there as a family, including that first meal when she had met Lucas and Ben for their birthdays nearly three years ago. As she made her way through to the kitchen, she noticed a more feminine feel to the house, little touches Monica had made, happily recognising some of the nick-nacks her mum had obviously brought from England, including a framed photo of her and her dad on one of the side tables, a casual snap taken when Amanda had graduated some years ago from university, proudly wearing her cap and gown over the calf length navy dress she remembered scouring the shops for, her mum insisting she needed to look smart for the occasion. It had been such a happy day, both of them smiling as Monica took the photo, her dad looking like the proverbial cat who had got the cream. Such happy memories to cherish, but thankfully Amanda reflected, there were many more happy memories still to make.

The following morning as Amanda was munching her way through some cereal she had found in the cupboard before heading into the office, she was surprised to receive a telephone call from her brother, Ben.

'Hello stranger,' she replied, desperately trying to swallow the food in her mouth as she reached to pick the mobile up as soon as she saw who was calling, 'how lovely to hear from you. Is everything okay?' she added quickly, knowing Ben rarely called just for a chat.

'Yes, everything's fine, stop worrying,' he said, adding 'It's just I spoke to Dad yesterday and he mentioned you were at the house all by yourself, so as I've got a few days leave I thought I'd fly down later today to join you. After the last couple of weeks, I could do with a break as well as a bit of a distraction, plus it'd be good to catch up, and I'll even take you out for dinner if there's nothing in - unless you've something else planned this weekend that is?' he questioned, thinking that perhaps he had been wrong to just presume his visit would be welcomed.

'No, that would be lovely. I'm going into the office to see Will later today as he wants to talk to me about something, but other than that I'm all yours. I do want to catch up with Clara and Lisa in the next couple of days as they're still over at Aunt Jane's since Christmas, plus hopefully see Maria while I'm here, but so far, no firm plans made.'

Ben laughed, 'by the sounds of it, you've a busy couple of days ahead of you; are you sure you can fit me in, or do I need to make an appointment?'

'No, I'll always make time for my little brother,' loving the way that sounded, and the easy banter they enjoyed. 'And we'll be able to swap stories about what Lucas is up to too, as I'm sure you're more in the know than the rest of us!'

'Yes, that sounds like a plan; I'll message from the airport when I arrive, but I should be at the house between seven and seven thirty. I'll have my keys with me, so don't worry if you're not home. Right, got to go and sort out a flight, see you soon,' he said ending the call abruptly, which was not unusual for Ben. He was always in a hurry.

Ben had been a junior doctor at one of Chicago's main hospitals, specialising in paediatrics since graduating, moving slowly up the ranks and assuming greater responsibility as his residency period matured. Now, with nearly three years behind him, and an unhealthy number of hours under his belt attending to some really sick children, often under harrowing and impossible situations, he was beginning to think that a change might be in order. A fresh start, some new challenges, plus an opportunity to experience a different hospital, with a lifestyle change thrown in if he was lucky. Still only in his mid-twenties, he was too young to settle or stagnate, and seeing what his twin Lucas had done with his life recently, including finding a partner, who Ben had to admit sounded too good to be true, left him wondering whether it was time to spread his own wings. He did not want to be left behind, that was for sure, and hearing about Lucas with Rachel had really spurred his competitive side.

As Amanda pulled into the drive later that evening, after finally pulling herself together sufficiently to navigate the short journey back from the office to the house, she was initially surprised to see lights on, both in the hallway and some of the upstairs windows, feeling scared she had forgotten to lock up behind her, and assuming they had been broken into, with perhaps the burglars still in the house. She considered remaining in the car and locking the doors whilst she phoned the police, before relaxing when she saw the front door open, revealing Ben standing in the door way, a reassuring smile on his face and his arms open ready to give her a massive hug. How could she have forgotten he was arriving today, she thought to herself, but immediately answering herself, that given the day she'd had, forgetting something like that was the least of her worries.

'Hi Sis, what's the matter,' asked Ben, automatically adopting the concerned voice he so often used at the hospital when talking to patients or their parents, as soon as he saw the way Amanda got out of the car and walked towards him, slowly, but looking as if the weight of the world was on her shoulders. Her body language spoke volumes, and the look in her eyes instantly alerted him to something not being right. He had dealt with enough people to know what shock looked like or when people had received bad news.

'Come on in, I'll get you a drink. You look like you need one,' he said, supporting his sister's arm as he led her into the house, eager to learn why she was so upset.

Chapter 41

On Friday morning, Amanda sat in the kitchen across the marble countertop from Ben, both bleary eyed and tired after not having slept much the previous evening, drinking the sweet milky coffees he had prepared, and playing with the wholemeal toast that sat on the plate between them, unbuttered and hardly touched. Neither had eaten the previous evening; Amanda had no appetite when she returned back from the office, with Ben not being bothered to cook for himself, or even simply warming up one of the numerous meals Mrs Reilly had left in the fridge. He had last eaten on the flight, a 'plastic sandwich' he had grabbed from one of the food stalls in the airport whilst dashing across the concourse as the final call was being made for his flight. But it had sat heavily on his stomach all journey, leaving him a little nauseous, so until that settled, he had not felt like eating much anyway.

Once they had exhausted themselves talking, and drank the generous brandies Ben had poured for them, knowing brandy was good for shock, they had each gone to bed. Amanda, obviously spent by the day she had experienced, and Ben physically drained from providing a much-needed emotional crutch. He knew it was unavoidable, accepting he needed to be there for his sister, but felt a little irked that his break was turning into a bit of a busman's holiday. He had wanted a few days away from talk of death and illness, and by the looks of it, that was not going to be the case.

Amanda had as succinctly as she could, but without wanting to over-dramatise it, or break down into even more tears, told Ben what Will had discussed with her and Nick, namely that Maria had a relatively uncommon form of gynaecological cancer, and as a result he was stepping down whilst she underwent treatment. He did not go into the specifics, but said it was something that had come on recently, adding the consultants were optimistic of the prognosis, but felt he needed to stand back whilst Maria went through the treatment, to ensure he could give her the support she needed. He wanted to be there when the going got tough for her, as undoubtedly it would do over the coming weeks, months, or years, because as yet no one could put a timeline against her full recovery.

He continued by asking Amanda to work alongside Nick to keep the business afloat, assuming a senior position as Nick's deputy for all intents and purposes, making those key decisions on the range they would stock, the designs they would manufacture, the fabrics they would use. He felt she had the fashion expertise, giving her the edge over Nick in that department, but his business acumen would balance her creative side. He felt reassured he could trust her judgement, secretly admitted to himself that he had been grooming her for this type of role for a while, so had every confidence in her ability. After all, she was family and who better to trust than family? The circumstances and the timing under which her 'promotion' were taking place though were perhaps not what he would have chosen given the option, he added wryly, but there was nothing he could do to change either regrettably.

As Amanda listened, her thoughts were all over the place. Maria was one of her best friends, so why had she not seen it coming, how had she been so absorbed in her own problems that this was the first she was hearing about it? She felt guilty that after Will cancelled his Singapore trip because Maria needed to attend an appointment, that she had never thought to follow up, or taken the time to ask what that was all about, assuming perhaps naively that if it was anything she needed to know, her friend would tell her. Well, now Will was letting her know, but was it too late for her to do anything about it? Some friend she turned out to be, she thought to herself, chiding herself.

Memories of receiving similar news when her dad was first diagnosed with stomach cancer came flooding back; her and Damian sitting in their kitchen at home over three years ago now, while they made their dinner unaware that their lives were about to be blown apart; these memories obscuring what Will was saying, his lips were moving but she was not catching most of what was being said. A rare form of cancer, he said, but that was what her dad had contracted, but sadly in his case it was inoperable; Maria's was apparently treatable, but they had said that about her dad too; with the right treatment, his prognosis was that he could live a relatively normal life for perhaps another five years. But they had not been right, had they? Within a couple of months, he was dead, leaving her and her mum not only broken hearted but devastated with the shock, so much left unsaid between them. Ken had been taken far too soon. What happened if they got it wrong with Maria, what if the treatment they had lined up for her did not work either? She was a relatively fit woman, still in the prime of her life, with so much to live for. Her relationship with Will was going from strength to strength, they were so happy having found love a second time around; her career as one of the most respected school principals in the area, a career she had worked so hard to achieve against all the odds. Maria's whole life, well, it just enriched everyone she touched, she was one of life's truly genuine people. Life could sometimes be so cruel.

Amanda knew cancer was no longer the automatic death sentence it had been viewed as when she had been growing up, when people were even afraid to voice the word, calling it instead the 'big C', in hushed tones on the off chance it might be contagious. Today there were lots of treatments out there, with more drug therapies being discovered every day thanks to all the money that was being pumped into research, leading to millions of people making full recoveries, going on to lead healthy and fulfilling lives. But, sadly her experiences to date were not good, and for the time being at least she was allowing those to cloud her feelings, rather than homing in on the positives Will had been keen to point out. Maria would receive the best treatment possible; they had caught it relatively early, and given her general state of health and wellbeing the doctors expected her to eventually make a full recovery. All in all, a lot to hold onto surely?

What Amanda needed to do was support both Will and Maria in the only way possible, by throwing herself into keeping the business side going with Nick; leaving the doctors and specialists to deal with the difficult bits. But for someone who was one of life's natural worriers, eager to take control whatever the situation, or at least have a say in what was going on, taking one step back was not going to be without its challenges.

Chapter 42

Over the weekend, rather than partying with Clara and Lisa, or dining out with Ben at some swanky restaurant as she had hoped, Amanda found herself locked in the office from dawn until dusk with Nick, going over everything they needed to do during the coming few weeks or months whilst they were effectively steering the ship. Will had left the building shortly after speaking to them on the Thursday evening, handing Amanda the keys to his office and leaving them in no doubt that he needed them to step up with immediate effect; what he had said was serious, and unless it was urgent, and without using 'gallows humour', a matter of life and death, they just needed to deal with it. Loretta had been briefed and would support them with whatever they needed administratively; saying he would be in touch in due course, kissing Amanda as he left, adding that he would ask Maria to phone her when she had a moment.

On Friday morning, work had continued as normal, without any of the staff either noticing or commenting on anything different. Will was not in his office, but that was nothing surprising. He was frequently on the road, so his office being in darkness raised no suspicions, and anyway, Nick was the operations director, the one in day-to-day control, so provided he was around, everything ran smoothly. Nick held his usual end of week briefing with the senior team, congratulating them on the week's progress, before outlining the priorities for the following week, ensuring no one came in on Monday morning unsure what was expected of them. Today's briefing though was cut short, but again no one paid any particular attention to that; given it was the first week of the new year, it was bound to take a while to settle back into a routine.

Amanda arrived early and sat with her team, logging onto her laptop and catching up with some of the emails she had missed over the previous couple of days. She did not want to arouse any suspicions by moving into Will's office until she and Nick had decided how they were going to play it. They had met briefly that morning and agreed that once everyone left at two o'clock that afternoon, an early Friday finish being something they all normally looked forward to, they would convene in his office and start to plan. There were short-term priorities that would need to be focused on, including briefing the senior management team, and no doubt addressing their questions and concerns, but thereafter there were suppliers and customers who had meetings in Will's diary. Nick had met with most people now, so felt confident to pick these meetings up, with Amanda's support as necessary, but whatever they did or said would need to be addressed sensitively, because if the company was to retain the reputation it had worked so hard to achieve, they could not blow it. Will may not be hands-on, but it was still his company, still his name over the door, and importantly his reputation that was on the line.

By Sunday evening, they were shattered, but pleased with the results of their combined efforts. They had worked late into Saturday night, ordering a Chinese take-away to be delivered to the office, and not leaving until after ten o'clock that evening, by which time it was pitch black outside, frost had settled on the windscreens of their cars and the roads were icy.

'Are you okay to drive home, or do you want me to order an Uber?' he asked, realising how tired Amanda was, but also seeing how bad the conditions were. The roads although good and well-marked in the city could get a little more treacherous as you drove nearer the coast.

'No, I'll be fine, I'll take it easy, but thanks anyway,' she replied smiling back, conscious of how considerate Nick was being to her. There had been no mention of the 'Singapore episode' by either of them, both presumably grown-up enough to realise that in the scheme of things, it no longer ranked particularly high on the scale of what was important. Nick had briefly discussed Amanda with Will on his return from Singapore, complimenting her on the way she had handled the business and their clients, and if he was honest doing some subtle 'fishing' to find out more about what made her tick. They had got on really well from the first time they had met at Rob's house, and having worked with her since and travelled together, he was intrigued to know more. When she had made the pass on him, he was shocked, but also aware she had perhaps drunk too much, and under no circumstances was he prepared to take advantage of her when she was in that state.

Will had confided a little of some of the personal challenges and pressures she was up against at the time, full of admiration of how she was continuing to stay focussed with all the issues Damian and his newly discovered son were creating in their lives, leaving Nick to conclude her behaviour was probably driven by the stress she was under; an isolated incident, and something best forgotten. Whilst under normal circumstances Amanda was exactly his type and someone he'd really gelled with, mixing business with pleasure was never recommended, and particularly not where the boss' niece was concerned; so, backing-off before it got complicated was probably his best approach, for now at least, he concluded sadly. But that would not stop him caring for her, or being alert should the situation change, he thought, ever the optimist.

Early Sunday morning, Amanda was just unlocking the building when Nick's car arrived and parked alongside hers. She watched as he got out of the vehicle carrying two paper bags, having called off en route at one of the few local delis he knew opened on Sundays, to collect coffees, bagels and a selection of pastries to see them through until lunchtime. Loretta had proposed she join them in the afternoon to go over some of the plans they had developed, offering to bring with her a couple of pizzas as lunch, plus doughnuts to keep their sugar levels up. She wanted to ensure she would be up to speed the following morning when the rest of the workforce turned in, no doubt wondering why Amanda was occupying Will's office. As a secretary, she knew her role was many faceted, but a big part of it was to act as gate-guard to her boss, and for the foreseeable future, that was a combination of Amanda and Nick.

Carrying the pizza boxes, she arrived just after one o'clock in her denim jeans, tucked into her black UGGs, the sleeves of her oversized knitted winter woolly rolled up. Her positive mental attitude was working overtime as she proceeded to deal with whatever they threw at her, with the ease of someone who had been with the company years, not just a matter of months. She was a calm and confident twenty-nine-year-old woman, highly organised, and no matter what they suggested, she smiled on, not shy to either offer a suggestion or a comment if she felt it added to the discussion, but equally knowing her place.

By the end of the day, rather than being apprehensive by the new management structure, Loretta was actually looking forward to it.

Chapter 43

January soon turned into February, the cold winter finally giving way to milder and longer days, less rainfall and the occasional glimmer of sunshine, if you happened to be looking skywards at the right time. The forecasters were suggesting the worst of the weather was over, time to pack away the snowshoes; spring was finally on its way. Locals were commenting favourably on the weather wherever they met, pleased that it had not been anywhere near as bad as previous years, with recorded temperatures slightly higher than expected, rainfall lower and a noticeable absence of snow and ice, adding further argument to the impact global warming was having on climate change.

Being British and knowing it was an accepted pastime to obsess about the weather, Amanda would have normally joined in, but she could honestly say she really had not noticed the weather or been adversely impacted by it, spending the majority of her time cooped up inside the office, or behind her computer screen trying to keep ahead of the work that continued to mount up. Her routine was house, car, office, car, house repeat, with minimal variation from day-to-day, unless of course it was her turn to stop off to buy the pastries or the doughnuts on the way in.

For Nick, there was no doubt he had taken on extra responsibility with Will being effectively out of the picture, but it felt like volume rather than variety or complexity that drove his schedule these days. His normal responsibilities for all the internal operations and business performance were now augmented by those elements Will had previously retained, namely being the face to the outside world, dealing with any key customers, along with any legal or financial issues Nick brought to his attention that required his involvement. Even after his appointment, Will had always retained the final say on anything strategic; because after all the company was his baby, his reputation, but not any longer. Even the strategic decisions were being trusted to Nick, and of course Amanda to deal with.

For Amanda though, she was now getting involved in activities way outside her normal comfort zone, taking on the ultimate decision-making role in terms of anything product related, in addition to staying close to what her team was doing on a day-to-day basis. It was not that she could not delegate, but more there was no one particularly to delegate to. Taking on additional designers to cover the unspecified period of Will's absence would neither be cost effective nor an efficient use of people's time; frankly there were no spare bodies around to train someone new up.

Once Nick had briefed both the senior team and the wider workforce on the situation, making it clear that he did not want people to speculate, or engage in idle gossip about Will or Maria, their response had been amazing. Everyone rolled their sleeves up and committed to supporting both Nick and Amanda, agreeing that they would work with the resources they had, until it got to breaking point, at which time someone would shout. Thankfully they had not reached that point so far, but on some days, Amanda thought that was by sheer luck rather than judgement. By the time she left the office most evenings, exhausted and hungry, with her head spinning to the extent she did not know which way was up, the thought of going home to one of Mrs Reilly's warm dinners and a chilled glass of wine was the only thing keeping her going.

By the end of the third week of February though, Amanda's mind was beginning to turn to thoughts of returning home; back to England, to Damian, her daughters and real life. It was now nearly eight weeks since Will had first implored her to stay, knowing how much of a hardship it would be for her to be away from her family so long, but at the same time arguing that he could not step back without her support. Nick had proved invaluable in the six months he had been running the business side of the operation, but he did not have the innate flair and passion that Amanda had. Over the last couple of years Will had proudly watched from the side-lines, taking close interest in her development, careful all the time not to show favouritism among the others. Everything he saw, or was told, left him pleasantly surprised, not only by the aptitude she brought to everything she turned her hand to, but the 'natural manner' she had with people, the way they reacted to her and trusted her direction made her an effective leader.

He had discussed it with Maria, admitting that one day he would like Amanda to succeed him, whenever the time came for him to retire that was. After all he had no children of his own to leave his business to, so what better than leaving it to Amanda, and letting her enjoy the fruits of his labours. Over the recent years whilst getting to know her better, his admiration for her, her generosity of spirit and the general way she had handled herself throughout, knew no bounds.

Rather than it being the hardship Will had predicted, Amanda had revelled in her time in New England. The weeks had flown by in a whirlwind of activity, creating a frenzied routine, but one that brought fresh challenges every day; her feelings of confidence growing as each new boundary was pushed, her comfort zone being replaced by the full glare of the spotlights and the centre stage position she had moved into.

By the end of February, Maria was well into her treatment cycle, and although the chemotherapy was gruelling, demanding more of her than she thought possible, she was at least ticking off the days, with a glimmer of light at the end of the tunnel. The consultants were pleased that the early signs from the regular tests and reviews they conducted were showing the treatment was having an effect, and with the combination of drugs and some minor surgery they had undertaken, the prognosis was as they had anticipated; their patient would make a full recovery. Amanda had initially respected Maria's privacy, but over time had started calling in during the weekends to visit her friend, giving Will a bit of a break as she sat with Maria, either gently holding her hand as she rested, or simply amusing her by talking about incidental things that neither taxed her nor gave her anything to fret about. Being there for Maria was important to her, and that would not stop regardless of which country she happened to be living in.

'Will, I've been thinking that I probably should head home for a few weeks,' she mentioned one Sunday afternoon as they sat in his lounge enjoying a quiet cup of coffee and a catch-up whilst Maria rested in the other room, the effort of having eaten a bowl of soup and nibbling at a small sandwich tiring her out. Amanda had turned up earlier with a take-away lunch for the two of them, correctly presuming that the chances of Will cooking for himself were zero. He had hired a lady to come in to do the cleaning and cooking during the weekdays, preparing nutritious meals for Maria to help build her strength, but at weekends preferred to manage by himself. 'I've discussed it with Nick and we believe that with the processes we've established, and the support from the team, which as you know has been amazing, that it will be manageable. I can be on hand from the UK to pick up anything that's needed, and also fly back if anything becomes urgent. What do you think?'

'I think you've been absolutely amazing,' he replied with tears in his eyes, whilst avoiding the direct question. 'What you and Nick have done I can never forget and I owe you both so much,' he said rising from his armchair to give Amanda a hug, careful not to spill coffee down her back, adding, 'I don't think I could be prouder of you if you were my own daughter.'

'Thanks, but I'm not walking away from what you've asked me to do, it's just I think it's time I showed my face at home. Damian, Rachel and Mum have managed to prevent the ship from sinking admirably in my absence, and Lucas has been great helping out with Damian's business, but I think there will be a collective sigh of relief when I walk back in the front door and they can hand back responsibility for the girls to me. Also, it looks like the courts are due to make a decision regarding Damian's son, Theo, and I should be home for that at least,' she added, trying to impress not only her continued support, but the importance of returning home for a short time if nothing else. 'So, what do you think?'

'I trust your decision making implicitly, why shouldn't I after all you've achieved in the last few months? If you're both on board and say it'll work, then who am I to question it?' Looking directly at her, and with a smile she had not seen for so long, he added 'You certainly don't need my permission young lady, you're running the company, not me!'

Chapter 44

It was around six thirty in the evening when Damian eventually pulled his Volkswagen estate into the driveway. The roads had not been too bad, but as he stretched getting out of the car, his back aching from sitting, he realised how long a day it had been; leaving home that morning around six o'clock, allowing a few hours in the office to cover a meeting he could not avoid, before driving to the airport to meet his wife's mid-afternoon flight's arrival.

'Hello. Mummy's home,' shouted Amanda as she dropped her handbag and coat in the hallway as Damian closed the door quietly behind her, carrying the bright yellow suitcase she had acquired whilst she was over in America, now full of the emergency clothes she had bought to support her unexpected and extended stay, as well as presents for the girls, plus a few bits from the house Monica had asked her to bring back. Leaving home at the beginning of January, Amanda had only planned on staying three or four days maximum, so had travelled light, taking little other than a change of work shirts and a couple of more dressy outfits for going out with Lisa and Clara in her little wheel-on case. Now two months later, by necessity her work wardrobe had expanded, but sadly her party clothes remained unworn, languishing in the bottom of the case.

'Mummy, Mummy,' screamed Maisie and Alice in unison as they came running from the kitchen, still dressed in their school uniforms, but with their polo shirts untucked, their socks around their ankles and the ribbons dangling from their ponytails, looking like a right pair of ragamuffins. Rachel had unsuccessfully been trying to get them to eat their meal before Amanda got home, hopeful that she would have the kitchen tidied away and the girls at least presentable before their mum walked in. Instead, there were two half eaten bowls of spaghetti Bolognese going cold on the table, dirty pots and pans littering the kitchen and homework still to be done. Today had not gone to plan!

'Hello my darlings, come and give me a big hug,' said Amanda as she crouched down, just avoiding being knocked to the floor as they ran towards her. 'Have you got us a present?' enquired Alice, turning her attention to the suitcase that now stood at the bottom of the stairs.

'Well, that depends on whether you've been good girls for Rachel and Daddy, or not. Shall I check with them first?' she replied playfully as the girls giggled. Having been in almost daily contact with home, she knew there had been nothing to worry about, being regularly reassured that everything was running like clockwork in her absence.

'Welcome home,' said Rachel, smiling as she popped her head out of the kitchen, wearing Damian's apron, now splattered with tomato sauce, over her clothes and looking a little frazzled, 'there's some dinner prepared when you're ready and I've just popped the kettle on for you, or would you prefer something stronger?' Damian had phoned Rachel from the car to let her know they were on their way, asking for something to be left out for dinner if possible. He had left the office to drive down to Heathrow just after lunchtime, so was starving, and Amanda rarely ate much on the aircraft, so would need feeding too.

'No, a cup of tea would be perfect. Give me ten minutes and then we'll come through to eat,' she replied returning Rachel's smile, but noticing how tired she looked, 'actually Rachel, why don't you get yourself off, you look exhausted. I can take it from here. Thanks for everything, I'll see you in the morning and we can catch-up properly then.'

'If you don't mind, that'd be great,' she replied, relief sweeping over her face as she untied the apron. 'It's just Lucas rang earlier, and apparently, he's invited a friend to stay over this evening, someone who's driving up from London to the Lake District for a wedding I think, so I should be there when he arrives. We're then going to the pub for dinner as we've no food in, so I'll need a shower and some clean clothes if I'm going to look anywhere near presentable' she added, sweeping her hair from her eyes and looking down at the state of her clothes. 'I hope he's tidied up, because we both left the house in a hurry this morning!' Damian and Amanda both laughed as she picked up her bag and coat from the rack and made her way out of the house, waving to the girls as she almost ran down the driveway towards the cottage.

In the privacy of the car driving home from the airport, Amanda and Damian had talked non-stop, in a way they had not be able to do with other people around, or little ears listening in, vying for her attention. He had brought her up to speed on where the solicitors were in terms of Theo, pleased and relieved that all the steps had now been completed, and subject to the final hearing in the family court in a few days, his son should be coming home with them. Monica and Rob, along with Lucas and Rachel were all well aware of what was happening and had been very supportive, but they needed to find a way of speaking to the girls about it. They were still very much in the dark about what was going to be happening, but Damian and Amanda knew how important it was to tell them together, and put on a united front when answering the questions they would undoubtedly have. They also needed to prepare a bedroom for Theo. Damian had looked at some furnishings, but wanted his wife to make the final decision. He was very sensitive to the fact that taking Theo into their home was their decision, and not just his. She had to be fully on board and involved in every step along the way, apart from which, she had the eye for décor, and left to him it would probably be a disaster.

He also brought his wife up to date on how his business was doing, commenting on the fact that in his view they had turned a corner. Orders were up, costs were down and morale seemed to be back to where it should be. They had stemmed the loss of key team members to rival companies and had even managed to inject real mojo back into the workforce. Lucas had been a revelation, neither of them realising that he had the capability or the work ethic to do what he had achieved. He had worked tirelessly, taking responsibility well above what anyone would have expected and really thrown himself into it.

'Do you know, he's never accepted a penny for all the work he's done! Other than providing him free board and lodgings and access to the apartment, he's paid for everything else himself,' observed Damian, 'I don't know how we'll ever be able to repay him.'

'We'll have to think of something, although we have introduced him to the love of his life, so that surely must count for something,' laughed Amanda, but not diminishing the fact that they owed her brother a huge dept of gratitude.

Lucas and Rachel were however inseparable, leaving Amanda to wonder what would be next for them as a couple, but also pondering what it would mean for her in terms of losing her au pair. She knew Rachel's position had always been a stop-gap, but now that there was more at stake with Amanda working longer hours, taking on greater responsibility including more frequent travel, apart from another child shortly being introduced into the household, one who was still not school age, then the need for support had never been greater. Thinking aloud she mused, 'we really should start considering what support we're going to need with the house and the children. Rachel won't be around for too much longer is my guess, and with Theo still pre-school it's going to be difficult. We probably will need to think about engaging a proper nanny or a housekeeper like Mrs Reilly, because I don't think Susie is going to want to take on more children now hers are at school, and we probably will need a lot more than a bit of extra childminding. What'd you think?'

'I don't think my waistline would support Mrs Reilly coming to live with us, that's for sure,' he joked, 'from what you tell me about her cheesecake, I'd be the size of a house before too long, but yes, you're right. Let's add it to our growing to-do-list.'

Amanda had also brought Damian up to date on Will and Maria's position, but importantly stressing what it meant to her, and the work she was continuing to do to support the business.

'I know it's not helping and just adding more pressure into the mix, but I really can't walk away from Will at the moment, or leave Nick in the lurch on the design side. He's still picking up a lot, and as good as he is on the business side, fashion is not his forte. Looking at Will this last weekend, he's really taking it badly; it's aged him quite a bit, loads more grey hairs, and his focus has gone completely. My guess is we've another couple of months hard slog ahead of us before next year's collection, after which things may calm down a bit, but I wouldn't want to bank on it. The range last year just took off; demand has never been higher.'

'We'll find a way to cope, don't worry,' reassured Damian, smiling over at his wife and patting her hand as he changed gear. He too worried that they had a lot of plates spinning at the moment, but for once all the issues they had to address seemed to result in positive changes to their lives; no longer in problems that had the ability to pull them into the mire, or worse still tear them apart. They had a strong marriage, one that had certainly been tested, but it had survived against all the odds. They now had two successful careers that they loved, earning salaries that afforded them a nice lifestyle, which was surely better than the alternative; being in a job you detested, or struggling for money to pay the bills. They also had a family network and friends who had supported them through thick and thin, rallying around and putting themselves out to help in whatever way they could. There was no price that could be put on knowing that support and love was there come what may; never having to fear being abandoned or alone when times get difficult. And having an extra mouth to feed on top of two lively, healthy and beautiful daughters, well, that was probably the best problem of them all.

Yes, their lives were busy, but busy in a nice way, thought Damian to himself, as he'd pulled the car into the driveway, a contented smile on his face.

Chapter 45

Monica was quietly reading her newspaper in the conservatory of the apartment complex they lived in, overlooking the grounds, admiring the daffodils that were just starting to pop their heads above ground, promising to give a colourful display once they came into full bloom. Spring was just around the corner, and for Monica it was the most beautiful of all seasons, but also the most poignant one, remembering that was the time she had lost Ken four years ago. He had loved to spend every spare moment in the garden, pottering around endlessly to make it pretty for her to look at from their big picture window, as she watched the birds at the feeder he had built, or the insects as they buzzed from plant to plant collecting nectar. Although she loved their new modern living, she missed having her own garden when she was in the UK, so regularly came down to the conservatory, just to sit and watch the changing seasons.

Rob was sitting next to her, working away on his laptop, an untouched cup of coffee in front of him, forgotten no doubt as he became engrossed in what looked like a spreadsheet, but she could not be certain, and if she was honest not really interested either. She knew her husband had an investment portfolio and a series of properties he owned that were managed in various ways, but other than that she paid little interest in his business affairs. She had not married him for his money, so other than a passing curiosity on the odd occasions when he mentioned something about particular stocks or shares, or needed to catch up on some paperwork, she left him to it.

His mobile was on the table beside him, on silent mode, for fear of disturbing some of the other residents who had come down for a quiet nap after lunch, or perhaps to escape their partner for a while. There was quite an eclectic mix of people that lived in the complex, some of whom kept themselves to themselves, preferring to read in the library, whilst others liked to socialise, perhaps playing games in the lounge, or enjoying a drink on the veranda. Monica and Rob were a bit of both, happy to chat if anyone came along, or join in a hand of cards, but equally as happy in their own company.

Monica was only half reading the paper today, distracted as she was by thoughts of her daughter. Today was the day they were due to meet with the courts to hear whether their application to take custody of Theo was approved. Whilst there was little chance of it being rejected, given Damian was Theo's biological father, and someone who wanted to formally take responsibility for him and bring him up, there was always the chance of a hiccup at the last minute, an unforeseen complication or a technicality that needed to be addressed. She hoped that would not be the case for Theo and Damian's sake at least, but at the same time could not fail to worry about what this would do to her daughter. Was she strong enough to bring someone else's child up, and was her motivation for doing so the right one?

Amanda had told her of the conversation she'd had with Grandad Tom, where he had indicated what he thought Ken would have done, and in fact did, but was that colouring her views here? It was different times then, different circumstances, and just because last time it worked out, did not mean there was any guarantee that it would be the case here. Her and Rob had talked it through on many an occasion, sharing similar views, but each time concluding that it was not their role to interfere, simply support, and that if this was what Amanda wanted, then so be it. Theo would never be their grandchild in the same way Maisie and Alice were, but that would not stop them developing a certain warmth towards the child over time, they presumed.

Rob's phone started to vibrate, and picking it up he saw it was Will.

'Hi there, what do you think then? Is it a goer?' Rob enquired, a sense of excitement in his voice as he balanced the phone at his ear, whilst trying to do something with his laptop at the same time.

Monica could not hear what Will's reply was, but from the tone of the conversation it seemed that Rob was quite happy, so she zoned out and returned to the cryptic crossword she had started that morning. Ken would have finished it within the hour, but for her it mostly took all day, and even then, she did not always get it finished.

'Okay, that sounds like a plan. I'll be in touch in a couple of days,' Rob said after about five minutes. 'Give our love to Maria by the way, glad to hear that everything is moving in the right direction. Monica will no doubt be in touch with her in the next day or so for a gossip,' he said, smiling in his wife's direction before ending the call.

'Is everything alright dear?' enquired Monica, pleased to see her husband's smile, but still unsure what all that was about.

'Oh yes, just something I wanted to run past Will. Nothing for you to worry about my dear,' he replied, obviously pleased with himself about something, but at the same time wanting to keep it close to his chest. 'I'll go and get us both a fresh coffee shall I, mine looks to have gone cold,' he mumbled to himself as he wandered over to the cafe.

No sooner had he left, his phone started vibrating again. Presuming it would be Will, no doubt having forgotten to tell Rob something, Monica picked it up and was about to answer it when she saw it was an unrecognised number, so thought better. They were invariably scam calls or cold-calls trying to sell you something, but if it was someone important, they would leave a message or call back.

Shortly after returning with two cappuccinos and a blueberry scone he could not resist; the phone rang again. It was the same unrecognised number, but Rob picked it up, curious to who was phoning.

'Hello, Rob Mason's phone' he answered quite formally.

'Hi Dad, it's Ben.'

'Oh, I didn't recognise the number,'

'Sorry, but I've misplaced my phone, so I'm using my colleague's mobile,' he explained. 'Just wondering if you're around at the moment, as I'm only a couple of hours away and thinking of popping over. I'm planning on catching the train if you could pick me up from the station when I get in. I've got some bags, so could do with a lift.'

'That's wonderful news, yes certainly I'll come over when you let me know what time your train is arriving. Where are you staying tonight by the way, are you staying long?' asked Rob, curious to learn not only why his son was in England, but also why this was the first he or Monica had heard about it. Was someone keeping secrets from him? They had only spoken on the phone the previous week, and he was certain nothing had been mentioned about a trip to the UK then.

'I'm not sure at the moment, but I'll tell you more when I get there. Got to rush, speak later,' he said hanging up, leaving Rob with a perplexed look on his face, but a wife who was not only wondering what was going on, but importantly whether the second cup of coffee was going to be left to go as cold as the first.

'That was Ben on the phone,' Rob explained to Monica, who noticing the quizzical look on her face asked, 'Is everything okay?'

'Apparently, he'll be here in a couple of hours and wants me to collect him and his bags from the railway station. I'm not sure what's happening, but he didn't sound his usual self.'

Ben was normally the one who was so organised, never taking risks, everything meticulously planned out or well-thought through ahead of schedule, unlike his other son, Lucas who seemed to live by the seat of his pants, never ceasing to amaze anyone with his exploits. There was something going on and Rob had every intention of finding out before he arrived back home. Monica and Amanda had enough to cope with today without another set of problems arriving at their door.

Chapter 46

Later that evening, Amanda phoned Monica and Rob to let them know how the court hearing had gone earlier that afternoon. The girls had finally gone to bed and Damian had popped out for a quick drink to the pub with Lucas to unwind after what had been a stressful day.

'Hello darling,' replied Monica when the phone rang around seven thirty, at the same time pressing pause and turning the volume down on the television handset. She had been catching up on a couple of episodes of Coronation Street whilst her husband was out. 'I was thinking that might be Rob. I've not heard from him for a while, and was expecting him back by now.'

Amanda noted concern in her voice. 'Is everything okay Mum, I thought he'd be there with you. Where's he gone at this time of night, although to be fair it's not that late?'

'Oh, there's nothing to worry about, well I don't think there is, but we got a call from Ben earlier this afternoon asking for his dad to pick him up from the railway station. He's apparently over here and Rob didn't know anything about it.'

'Me neither,' said Amanda, adding thoughtfully, 'I only spoke to him the other night and I'm sure he didn't mention anything to me, and Lucas certainly hasn't mentioned anything, but saying that he's only got eyes for Rachel at the moment, so the rest of us just fade into the background whenever she's around. If fact, I doubt he's spoken to his brother for a while.'

'Anyway, how did you get on today? Was it quite stressful or did everything go as you expected?' enquired Monica, keen to understand what had transpired at the courts.

'Well, it was a long day as we waited around for quite a while, but eventually when we got into the judge's rooms, it was relatively straight forward. Damian said it was the same judge who had dealt with the early stages of the previous claim, so she was familiar with the case and had already met Damian before. She asked a couple of questions, some actually directed at me, which I wasn't really expecting, but after a while she said in her opinion it was in Theo's best interests to come and live with us.'

'And how do you feel about that now that it's all over?'

'A little bit apprehensive if I'm honest, as I've only met Theo once before, but otherwise I'm pleased for Damian. He's spent quite a lot of time with Theo recently getting to know him at his foster home, and I think that went in his favour. By all accounts he's a lovely little boy. The social services team reported back on how well the two interacted and how comfortable they would be to support the court's decision, so it was all very positive in the end. Damian would've been devastated if he'd lost though; he'd worked himself up into quite a state over the last couple of days.'

'So, what happens next?' probed Monica, interested to learn more.

'Well, we collect him in four days' time, so on Monday. That gives us a bit of time to sort out some of the practicalities at home, but it also gives the foster parents and the social services team the opportunity to talk to Theo and let him know what's happening. At three it's unlikely he'll appreciate much of what they say, but nevertheless he'll get upset when he's moved from his foster parents into another home. He's been there almost five months now and is remarkably settled, so although he gets on with Damian, any new circumstances are bound to unsettle him. We just need to be extra careful in those first few weeks and look out for any worrying signs that he's not settling.'

'When are you planning on telling Maisie and Alice? I presume they still have no idea he's coming to live with you?' Monica had always been conscious that a third child in the house could present a real threat to her granddaughters and the relationship they enjoyed with their parents. They already showed signs of competing for their parents' attention, and were both very much daddy's girls, but with another child in the house, how would that play out? Would the fact that Theo was not Amanda's biological son, but Damian's, split them when it came to taking sides, which inevitably it could with children on occasion?

'We're going to sit them down tomorrow after school and tell them together, which gives them the weekend to think about it and ask us questions before we pick him up. Social Services said they have a counsellor who can talk to the girls and help them if we need it, so we may take them up on that, depending on how it goes. I'm hoping neither will be a problem, but you never know. Generally, if one kicks off the other does, so we'll have to watch out as they're as thick as thieves when they get together, as you know,' she laughed, having no need to explain either of her daughters' behaviour to her mum. 'Anyway, they've both been asking for a rabbit or a puppy for so long now, that presenting them with a brother might at least stop them moaning about pets for a while.'

'Well, let me know if you need anything from us, and we'll be straight over. Right, I'm going to ring off now as I can see Rob's car pulling into the car park outside. I'll speak to you tomorrow. Good night, darling,' she said hurriedly, as she went to the window to get a closer look, just in time to see Ben heaving two suitcases from the boot of the car, in addition to the back pack he'd already been carrying. It obviously wasn't just an overnight stay, Monica thought to herself, wondering not for the first time what was going on.

As Amanda started to run herself a bath about a couple of hours later, she heard the front door close and footsteps slowly climbing the stairs. She came out of the bathroom to see her husband tiptoeing up the stairs, carefully avoiding those steps that were known to creak, mindful of waking the girls, but also by the look on his face, and the way he put his fingers to his lips to say 'shush' when he saw her, a little tipsy.

'What on earth are you doing?' she asked laughing at the sight of him, his jacket flung over his shoulder, one hand holding onto the banister rail, while carrying his shoes in the other hand. 'I presume by the look of you, you've had a couple of drinks to celebrate.' Damian was not a big drinker, so it did not take much to tip him over the edge, but thankfully he was a happy drunk.

'I have, and you'll never guess what or who we saw in the pub,' he said in a conspiratorial tone that suggested that no matter how many tries she had, she would never guess his secret.

'Now, let me think,' wondering whether to play along or cut straight to the chase as her bath was getting cold, and deciding in favour of the long soak said, 'could it perhaps have been Ben and Rob by any chance?'

'How on earth do you know that, are you a witch or something?' he replied, obviously a little disappointed that she had got there before he could do the big reveal.

'No, but I spoke to Mum who said Rob had gone to the railway station to pick him up, and she presumed they'd called in for a drink as they were late getting back, so other than having a superpower, I just put two and two together. It wasn't rocket science.'

'Well does she know why he's here?' trying again to win the little game he was enjoying playing.

'No, but I've got the distinct impression you're about to tell me,' she laughed, as Damian started to slur his words a little, 'Why don't you come into the bathroom; I'm just about to take a bath. You can sit over there and tell me while I soak.'

Watching as his wife climbed into the hot bubbly water, he said, trying to remove his socks whilst balancing on the toilet, 'move over, I've got a better idea.'

Chapter 47

'So, hang on, what you're saying is he just turned up out of the blue, with his suitcases; no advance warning to anyone, saying he's moving to London to live, and he's already sorted a job out?' asked Clara, astounded when Amanda phoned her cousin early the following morning. She had waited until the children had left for school, Rachel had gone to the café to do one of her shifts and Damian had set off to do something or other in town before Theo arrived. She could not quite remember where he said he was going, but he said he'd be home by four o'clock at the latest, so not to worry. Clara was just exiting the lift on the sixth floor of her office building when her phone had rung, after popping out to the coffee shop across the road for her morning fix. Around ten o'clock, without a double espresso inside her, she was not worth knowing.

'Yep, that's about the long and short of it. According to Damian's drunken ramble last night, Ben decided a couple of months ago that it was time for a change and started to look around for another role. I remember Mum saying something about him mentioning moving closer to everyone, but they'd all assumed, obviously incorrectly as it transpires, that he was looking at another hospital nearer Boston. No one ever queried him, and I suppose everyone's been so preoccupied with their own problems recently, that no one ever gave it a moment's thought.

In fact, if I remember rightly, that weekend when he came to visit me at Rob's, I got so caught up in what Will had just told me about Maria, that I fell apart. I feel awful now that he probably wanted to talk, and instead had me crying on his shoulder, being anything but the supportive sister!'

'You're not to blame, so don't beat yourself up. There're enough of us around that if he really wanted to speak to anyone, he only needed to ask. Anyway, so where's he working?' asked Clara, obviously anxious to hear the whole story, but at the same time looking at her watch. She had noticed the senior editor prowling the corridors just before she went out for her coffee, successfully managing to avoid her, but seeing her loitering in the doorway of her office, she knew her luck had run out. 'The dragon', or Felicity to give her the correct title, was hounding for an article that supposedly needed a re-write before it would pass legal scrutiny, but Clara wanted to stand by what she had written, and just needed a corroborative statement from one of her contributors to back up the facts, so was stalling for time. She knew the magazine needed to be squeaky clean, but on days like today, she worried she worked with too many jobsworths, stifling her creativity whenever they sensed an opportunity to censor her.

'He's apparently landed a plumb job at the Great Ormond Street Hospital…' started Amanda, before Clara interrupted, 'Look sorry, but I'm going to have to hang up, something's just come up, but as soon as I get a minute, I'll ring you back,' before quickly ending the call, pasting a smile on her face, and preparing herself to face the music as Felicity headed in her direction.

Looking at her own watch, Amanda realised she needed to get a move on herself. Her mum had invited her over for lunch with her, Rob and Ben; her opportunity to find out what was going on. As Damian and Lucas had already spoken to him in the pub the previous evening, she needed to play catch-up and find out for herself what the story was. For Ben to suddenly up sticks and cross the Atlantic, without anyone being aware of it, she suspected it went deeper, and just hoped there was nothing to cause any concern. Today was going to be a stressful enough day telling Maisie and Alice about Theo moving in, without Ben's arrival throwing even more drama into the mix, and coupled with that she still needed to finish sorting out the spare bedroom, otherwise when the furniture arrived on Saturday morning the delivery men would have nowhere to put it. She could feel a headache coming on already!

'Mum, how is he?' she whispered as Monica opened the apartment door just over an hour later to see her daughter standing there, obviously fresh from the shower as her hair was still damp and she could smell her signature shower gel. Amanda had quickly thrown on some clean jeans and an Aran jumper; comfortable, but perhaps a couple of sizes too big for her, and other than running a comb through her hair, had rushed straight over.

'He's fine, they're both in the lounge having a beer before lunch, do you want me to bring you one through, or join me for one while I finish off?' she replied, kissing her daughter, before turning back towards the kitchen where the radio could be heard in the background, obviously tuned to one of the news or features channels as Amanda could hear voices talking quite vociferously about the role of the Monarchy. Monica had always been a royalist, so was obviously interested in the discussion, but it was not a topic that held much interest for Amanda.

'No thanks, I'm driving, but I'll go through and say hello then come and help you if you want,' she offered. Lunch, by the smell of it, was not too far off.

'No need, I'm fine. Everything's nearly ready anyway. I've just made a steak and kidney pie and put some potatoes in the oven. Rob had never had a steak and kidney pie before he married me, and now it's one of his favourite meals when we're over here.'

'It was always Dad's too, if I remember rightly,' reminisced Amanda, 'especially when you made it with suet on top, rather than pastry. He loved most of what you cooked though, rarely did a plate get returned with any waste on, and he was always up for seconds,' she laughed.

'Yes, you're right,' smiled Monica, 'your dad had a healthy appetite that's for sure, must have been all that fresh air and exercise he got gardening.'

The two loved to talk about Ken, always eager to keep him alive in their memories, and no matter how happy Rob being in their lives made either of them feel, those memories would never be diminished or replaced.

'Right, let me go and see Ben before we both get all maudlin, and then I'll come back and help you dish up that lunch. It smells delicious and suddenly I feel very hungry.'

Ben and Rob were sitting in the lounge, happily chatting away when Amanda walked over to them, giving them both a hug before perching on the arm of the settee next to Ben.

'So, to what do we owe this honour?' she asked, keen to hear the full story.

Monica was just carrying the lunch through, so they began making their way to the table ready to sit down to eat.

'Well, it's quite simple really,' he started, looking Rob and Amanda directly in the eyes, 'I've met the woman I'm going to marry, and it just so happens she's British.'

If Rob had not been close enough to catch the steak and kidney pie as it slipped from Monica's hands, then who knows what they would have had for their lunch.

Chapter 48

Reaching for his credit card to book his return flight from Boston, after what had effectively been a wasted weekend at home visiting Amanda, Ben had been feeling particularly low. Rather than spending a few days away from the hospital having a good time, catching-up with his sister and meeting some of his friends at the sailing club, he had found himself being an emotional crutch, providing support and solace, when all he was really looking for was a distraction from work, a bit of fun, with potentially some beers and good food thrown in. In reality, he had wandered around an empty house, whilst Amanda either locked herself away in the office, or cried herself to sleep in her bedroom worrying about Maria. None of his friends were around either at such short notice, and even Mrs Reilly was not at home to feed him or spoil him as she used to. So, deciding to pull stumps earlier than planned, he changed his flight for an earlier one, packed his rucksack and booked an Uber to the airport.

The internal flight between Boston Logan International airport and Chicago O'Hare International airport was only three hours, so leaving early-afternoon with the one-hour time difference would see him home just before rush hour traffic hit. Tomorrow was still technically a day's leave, so unless he had any urgent calls, he could message one of the lads from the squash club to see if anyone was free for a game. After all, he had nothing else planned, and staying around in his one-bedroom apartment moping was not a great option, so taking it out on a squash ball was probably good therapy.

The flight was oversubscribed, which was not unusual, the announcer politely asking if anyone was willing to change their ticket, offering a compensation package and a confirmed booking on the next flight for anyone prepared to step forward. Ben did not need the money, but equally had not need to rush home, so feeling more magnanimous than his mood would suggest, offered his seat up. After all, what was an hour's wait to him in the scheme of things?

Grabbing a coffee and a double-chocolate-chip muffin, that he knew was not good for him, but who cares anyway, he went to sit near the boarding gate; finding a seat that at least he'd be comfortable in whilst he waited, next to a socket, allowing him to charge his phone whilst listening to his music on his ear plugs.

No sooner had the other travellers boarded and the gate closed, but a young woman came and dumped her bags a few metres away from him, obviously travelling alone by the look of her carry-on luggage. From her demeanour, Ben could see that she was upset, and from the way she was frantically searching in her bags, panicking over having lost or misplaced something important.

The way she was hovering around, unable to settle, mesmerised him. He sat for around ten minutes simply staring, unable to take his eyes off her, the coffee and muffin abandoned on the table besides him, oblivious to the music blaring in his ears. Eventually she gave up looking and slumped into the chair next to Ben's.

'Are you okay?' he asked, taking his ear plugs out, tentatively, so as not to upset her further, 'it's just you look like you've lost something.'

'I think the only thing I've lost is my sanity, but thanks for asking,' she replied, with a clipped English accent and a smile that lit up the departure lounge. 'I thought I'd packed my charger in my hand luggage, but obviously not, and now my phone is about to die and I can't remember where I'm supposed to be staying when I arrive. One of my friends booked the hotel for me, and she just messaged me the details, and now I can't get to them. First world problems I know, but welcome to my life!'

Looking over at her phone, Ben soon realised it was the same model as his, so feeling like a knight in shining armour, immediately came to the rescue.

'Oh, you're a life saver, thank you,' she beamed as Ben handed her his charger, 'I'm Jessica, Jessica Hammond by the way,' she added offering a well-manicured hand to Ben.

'Hi, I'm Ben, Ben Mason. Pleased to meet you Jessica,' offering his hand quite formally to her in return.

For the next hour they just chatted, and chatted; about everything, but nothing all at the same time. Jessica was flying into Chicago for a friend's wedding, someone she had gone to primary school with, and then reconnected again with at university, who was now living close to Chicago and working for a local radio station. It was an odd job she thought given they had both studied mathematics, but then again who was she to judge, given she was working for a marketing agency in the centre of London, a short train journey away from where she still lived at home with her parents in Windsor; but at least some of her statistical knowledge was being put to good use, she argued.

Ben listened without really hearing a thing. He was too busy concentrating on her accent and the way her lips moved, revealing a perfect set of white teeth; the way her elegant hands and arms moved, animating everything she described, and the way her icy blue eyes shone whenever she emphasised something she was talking about. There was a real passion in her voice, and a real honesty in what she said.

She was dressed relatively plainly, in black straight-legged jeans and a grey scooped-neck cotton top, with a red ski jacket, unzipped but worn over the top. Her trousers were tucked into a pair of flat black leather boots, that not only looked comfortable, but were well worn. Her fair hair was casually clipped up, but looked as if released, it would be both long and wavy, with the faint freckles on her nose suggesting her clear skin may have recently had a little exposure to the winter sun, skiing perhaps given the jacket, Ben presumed? For all the plainness of her outfit though, he could sense her clothes were quality, and the discreet labels, evident on both her jeans and the sleeves and pockets of the coat, were obviously designer. Plus, the way she spoke clearly indicated she had been well educated and came from a close family; a family where there appeared to be a healthy balance of love and laughter, particularly as Jessica recalled the antics of her younger brother Sebastian, who seemed to get into all sorts of japes.

By the time their flight was called, they had not only exchanged mobile numbers but agreed to meet up in Chicago the following morning for a bit of sightseeing, a few drinks and something to eat, unless when she arrived her friends had made alternative plans for her stay. When Ben checked, Jessica's hotel was within easy reach of his hospital, and only a couple of stops on the subway from his apartment, so he offered to meet her outside the hotel at ten o'clock the following morning, with the obvious caveat, 'unless you get a better offer in the meantime, that is,' his fingers remaining tightly crossed that this would not be the case. Jessica was staying for three days after the wedding, so even if tomorrow did not work out, he was hopeful another day would. He reassured her, he knew the city like the back of his hand; she could have no better tour guide, so no need to worry, because after all, he was a doctor!

The following day, they met as planned, Jessica having received no better offers, but even if she had, she would have turned them down. Something about Ben had intrigued her and she was keen to spend more time with him; looking forward to getting to know him better. She had done most of the talking in the airport she recalled, rarely giving Ben a chance to talk about his own life or family. Other than knowing he was a doctor living in Chicago, with family in New England, she had not learnt too much else.

Jessica had not long since finished with a guy who she had been seeing for over eighteen months, but it had not worked out. Every time he met her parents, or got involved with her family in any shape or form, it was obvious that their relationship was not destined to last. He was an independent spirit, but someone who placed no value in family; in fact, the more she thought about it, their values were polar opposites. What she had originally seen in him, she shuddered to think.

With Ben though, they just seemed to click. Even though they had such different upbringings, their values were similar. He made her laugh, he respected her opinions, and although it was not the key factor, it was fair to say 'he'd not been at the back of the queue when they were dishing out good looks', as her grandma would have pointed out had she still been alive.

'Why don't you come as my plus one tomorrow evening for the reception?' asked Jessica as Ben was walking her back to her hotel later that evening, after a day that neither of them wanted to end. 'I'm sure no one would mind, and at least I'd have someone interesting to talk to. Other than the bride and one of her bridesmaids who was at uni with us, I don't know anyone. I'm apparently sitting between the groom's widowed uncle to my right, and a guy the groom works with on my left, who he plays football with. My dad's a big Burnley supporter, as he came from Lancashire originally, so I know all about football, and if pushed could even explain the offside rule, but I know nothing about the American rules. Conversation is going to be scintillating, I'm sure!' she added wryly.

Hearing the desperation in her voice, Ben replied laughing, 'I'd love to, but I'm on call until ten tomorrow night, and then back on duty at eight the following morning, so by the sounds of it we're both in for a tough day. At least you'll get some decent food and a glass or two of champagne, and a chance to put on your ballgown, whilst I'll have to be content with a plastic sandwich, a bottle of water, and my not too sexy scrubs, if I'm lucky.'

'Oh, I'd love to see you in those scrubs, doctor!' she said, Ben unsure initially whether she was being sarcastic, or flirting, 'I bet you have the nurses' heartbeats racing constantly.'

'I'm not sure that's happened so far, but I can always live in hope, but as most of the nurses on my ward are either matronly or gay, it's a bit of a challenge,' he laughed in reply.

'Okay, but let me know when you're free anytime between now and my flight home and I'll be right over. This hotel is dire, and I certainly don't fancy plodding the streets all alone,' she said looking up at the hotel's entrance. It had been given a four-star rating, but someone must have been very generous on the day of the assessment. She slowly started to climb the two steps to the revolving door. Turning to wave, she called out, 'Just remember, I'm a fully paid-up member of Uber, so just text me your address and I'll be right there. I'll even have your dinner ready if you want for when you roll in, although my cooking skills leave a lot to be desired!' she added, with a cheeky grin, blowing a kiss in Ben's direction as she finally entered the hotel.

As Ben walked home, with a massive grin on his face, he pondered what fate had done to him. Just think, 'if I hadn't changed my flight, or if I hadn't decided to come home a day earlier, I'd have never met Jessica.'

Leading up to that weekend, he had known that something in his life was missing, but until then, had no idea what that was. He had realised that his life needed a change, a new dynamic, and that he needed to affect that change if he wanted something different for himself, but under no circumstances had he ever expected to be hit by a bolt of lightning while simply sitting and minding his own business in the airport. Seeing Jessica had been like an epiphany, a life changing moment, one he felt powerless to fight against, even if he'd wanted to. He knew he would move heaven and earth to switch his shifts around to create some time off over the coming days to spend with her, because more than anything else he knew that this woman was going to play an important part in his life, and nothing, or no one was going to stop that.

Chapter 49

By mid-March, although there was no set routine, the Reynolds household was gradually settling down after the dramas of the previous two weeks. The girls were back at school after their half-term holidays, Rachel was helping Amanda with Theo, and Damian and Lucas were once again drawn back into the business, relieved at least that the pressure was now off and a level of normality had returned. Damian had found a renewed interest in his company; something he had struggled to take any pleasure from, or pay real attention to, over recent months, but with the help of Lucas' ideas and the fresh approach he had brought, he was both excited and optimistic about the future.

Amanda and Damian had sat down as planned and spoken to Maisie and Alice the Friday evening before Theo's arrival the following Monday. The concept of him coming to live with them, rather than being a shock or a disappointment, was met with the much more innocent questions of where would he sleep, would he go to school, and probably most importantly, would they need to share their dolls with him, or would he bring his own toys? None of the questions about why was he Daddy's son and not Mummy's, or where had he been for the last three years, or even wondering why they had never met him before were asked. No doubt these questions would come over time as all three children matured and their curiosity was sparked, with the experts cautioning that although they might appear accepting for the time being, they needed to be watchful for any behaviour changes in either girl, or in fact in Theo, over the coming weeks, months or even years. No one could put a definitive timescale on the settling-in process, or predict an outcome, positive or otherwise. No two situations were the same, and although not unique, the characteristics of their case were far from the norm.

Over the first few days, Theo clung to Damian like his own comfort blanket. He was the only one he knew or recognised; but all the time his eyes remained peeled to Amanda whenever she walked into the room or wandered around the house. He also watched Rachel as she dealt with the girls, taking them to and from school, or sitting at the kitchen table with them doing their homework, all the time observing, but never joining in. The adults all spoke to him in encouraging tones, whether it was to try to get him to eat, join in with a game or simply to check he was feeling okay, but for those first few days, there was no response. It was almost as if Theo was there in body, but not spirit.

On the Friday afternoon, Ben arrived for a short visit, having caught the lunchtime train out of Paddington Station, with nothing other than his backpack containing a change of clothes and a toothbrush. He had planned to stay over for the evening and catch up with Lucas, but was undecided where to stay. He had still not met Rachel, so was keen to see the girl who had stolen his twin's heart, but could not presume she would be happy for him to bunk down at her cottage for the night, so was hoping Amanda would offer him a bed. Staying with his dad and Monica was an option, but their apartment was too far away to stagger home from the pub. He was getting quite used to British beer and the atmosphere of a traditional pub, both of which had been difficult to find in Chicago.

He had been in London all week sorting out his new flat and completing the paperwork, before starting his role on Monday as a senior resident doctor, specialising in paediatrics at the renowned Great Ormond Street Hospital. Thankfully, the process had been made simpler due to the new post being one he was being seconded into from his Chicago hospital. The hospital Ben had been working at had a series of special arrangements with GOSH and other specialist and training hospitals around the world, that allowed for transfers of doctors and other disciplines under certain circumstances, principally where sharing of best practice or development of key skills were concerned.

When Ben had made it known he was looking for a change, and specifically an opportunity to work in England after having met Jessica, the exchange programme had been suggested, as the hospital was loathe to lose one of their shining stars without putting up a fight. In the short time Ben had been working for them since his graduation, he had done nothing but impress with his skills, his bedside manner and his overall thirst for medicine. For Ben, the role ticked all the boxes, so after a phone call between the right hospital directors, plus an interview on Skype and a cursory review of his CV, the deal was sealed and a date set for his transfer.

Jessica had been delighted. From the moment Ben had left her at the hotel door the evening before her friend's wedding, she had done nothing but think about him, fearing she might never see him again, or worse still that it had been a passing flirtation on his part and once he got back to the hospital, he would forget all about her, falling straight into the arms of a passing nurse. Although they hardly knew each other, it felt, to Jessica at least, they had made a real connection, and she could not envisage him not being part of her life, but she was unsure whether those feelings were reciprocated, or not. The relief the following day when Ben messaged to say he had managed to move some of his shifts around, meaning they could spend at least a few hours together during her last couple of days, was palpable, and by the time he accompanied her to the airport for her flight home, neither of them was left in any doubt that this was not just a holiday romance.

When Ben had phoned a matter of days after she had arrived home, letting her know he was moving to London to live and work, she could not believe her ears, or her luck. Although they had never really spoken about a long-distance relationship, as other things had occupied the limited time they had together in Chicago, Jessica had realised as soon as she got home to her parent's house just outside Windsor, that it would be difficult, if not impossible, to sustain any type of relationship. Ben, given the number of hours he worked, often through the night, or on-call should an urgent case require his support would be too busy to want to get involved. Plus, the sheer distance between them, including the small matter of an ocean, not to mention a six-hour time difference, made it even more difficult. It would mean as she was getting home after more than an hour's commute each way into the city centre, he would no doubt be in the middle of his shift, and as he finished work, she would be tucked up in bed. It was doomed from the start she had concluded sadly, before his call meant all her prayers had been answered. Not only was his role less than a mile from the agency where she worked, he would have a flat that she could visit, which would be much more accommodating than the squeaky bed in her bedroom, and even if he had to flat-share, that would be preferable to her parents listening in to their every move. Although Jessica was almost twenty-six, and had a first-class degree and a full-time job, to her parents, she would always be their little princess.

'Uncle Ben!' the girls squealed when they saw him walk through the door, running straight into his arms for a cuddle, 'come and meet Theo, he's our new brother,' added Maisie, as the oldest taking the lead as usual.

'Okay, but let me take my coat off first, please. You two nearly knocked me over,' he laughed as Amanda came into the hall to greet him, immediately seeing his rucksack by the front door, her eyes questioning what was going on.

'Hi Sis, do you have a bed free for a weary traveller,' he asked, smiling up at his sister, with those hypnotic blue eyes that must have worked miracles with his patients over the years, his blonde hair ruffled as he took off his beanie. Looking at Ben was like looking in a mirror for Amanda, they shared the same colouring and a lot of the Mason features inherited from their father, Rob. There was no doubt that both of the twins were handsome and of similar height, but Lucas' darker, moody looks and more muscular build were the direct opposites to Ben's fairer complexion, his innocent smile and slighter frame; presumably qualities inherited from his mother, Carrie, Amanda imagined.

'Of course, do you need feeding as well?' she questioned, giving her brother a hug, 'the kids are just about to sit down for their tea, but Damian and I will be eating later if you want to join us. It's nothing much, but it does involve a bottle of wine!'

'Thanks, but I'm eating with Lucas and Rachel, we're meeting up at the pub in a couple of hours, so we'll probably get something there. I've heard so much about her, but can't wait to meet her, and finally hear what on earth she sees in Lucas!' he added, laughing. Over the years, neither twin had ever struggled to get a girlfriend, but equally none had stayed around too long, with usually Lucas or Ben losing interest, or finding being in a relationship simply not worth the effort, so for both of them to have found their significant others, so close together, Amanda wondered if there was something in the water she needed to know about.

'Right, let's go and meet Theo before Maisie comes back and drags me through by my hair, she's a little minx that one.'

As Ben walked into the lounge and saw the children playing, Maisie and Alice in one corner surrounded by their dolls, and Theo on the rug in front of the fire, quietly playing by himself with his cars, it was almost as if magic-dust had been thrown into the air. Ben got down onto the floor and started to roll a car around, instantly drawing Theo's attention to him. And, as if a spell had suddenly been broken, Theo responded and started to talk to him, telling him which were his favourite cars, the ones that would go fastest, and the ones his mum had bought him before she went away. With the skill of a professional that knows intuitively how children's minds work, before long Theo was engaging with Ben as if they had known each other a lifetime. The girls, intrigued to hear Theo talk, came over and sat with them on the rug, and with the innocence that only children have, joined in their game; together creating an atmosphere that soon had them all laughing and chatting away like old friends.

Amanda had watched from the doorway, coming through to announce tea was ready, but on seeing them playing had decided not to interrupt them. Their tea could wait, what was important was finding a way to break through Theo's barriers, and smiling to herself, she thought Ben may just have found it.

Chapter 50

The week leading up to Easter had been particularly tough for Amanda, as she and Nick continued to manage to run the business with more than four thousand miles separating them. The number of orders was increasing, more than anyone had anticipated, the success obviously not only in the growth in the adult range they had designed the previous year, adding accessories into their portfolio, but further growing the kids and teenage wear ranges. They had eventually been forced into taking on additional seasonal staff in the packing and distribution departments to get critical orders shipped, but the rest of the management and design teams were still working to the tight parameters they had established when they first set off down this route, following Will stepping-back from the business over four months previously. Profitability was up, but so were stress levels.

Feeling a need to download over a couple of drinks, she had called into see her mum and Rob, after one of her visits to see Grandad Tom. She had taken his latest box of provisions, including another box of chocolates, soft centres he'd stressed, and a bunch of daffodils for his lady friend, who she had eventually been introduced to and quite liked. Mrs Judy Seymour was a bit of a character, a rather rotund lady in her late seventies, with a cheeky smile and bright red lipstick. By the looks of it, she had the measure of Tom, and was putting up with none of his nonsense, she stressed when Amanda had first met her one afternoon in his room. They had been sitting side-by-side on the settee, his hand resting comfortably on her knee, watching Countdown together, both partial to the odd custard creams it seemed, from the empty packet on the table in front of them.

'And as well as the business being manic, last night Rachel and Lucas came to see me and Damian. Have you heard they're planning on going travelling at the end of next month?' she asked, noticing from the look Rob was giving this was not news to them. 'Apparently, Lucas is keen to start up where he left off, but presumably without Sonia in tow this time, and Rachel having never travelled is excited at the idea, but I get the impression, more worried at the prospect of Lucas going off without her.'

'Yes, he mentioned it last weekend to us. They both came over for dinner on Saturday and it was brought up there. I'm only surprised he's stayed in one place for so long, I'd expected him to pack up long ago, never thought he'd stick it out the way he has,' remarked Rob. 'Must be what love does to you,' he added patting Monica's arm and smiling lovingly in her direction.

'Well, he has been a godsend and I don't mean that lightly. How Damian and I would have coped these last few months without his support I wouldn't like to hazard a guess. And Rachel has become like family, she's rallied around and been a fantastic help, not just with Maisie and Alice, but with Theo too. We're all going to miss her, which brings me to the problem of either getting another au pair or some extra help. With everything else to balance, I can't cope, and with Damian now back running the business, I can't expect him to either.'

'I know dear, and we've been thinking about nothing else since Lucas and Rachel mentioned they were going,' said Monica looking at Rob, almost questioning whether she should continue or leave it to him to follow up with their suggestion.

'What your mum and I have been looking into, well your mum mainly, is whether we could find a professional nanny to come and live full time with you to help you out. Someone who could give you the full support you need, and importantly have the right qualifications or experience should the children need further support once this honeymoon period has ended,' Rob suggested carefully, adding 'Theo has settled in wonderfully well, and we both think he's a treasure, but no one knows what's down the line, do we? Having two children at school, plus a pre-school toddler around the house will be hard work, and none of that is going to get any easier, what with after-school clubs, and everything else they get involved in these days.'

'Well, that's all well and good, but I couldn't afford to employ Mary Poppins, even if I could find her, and even then, I wouldn't need someone full time surely. Rachel worked a few hours, mornings and after school, but had most of the day and her weekends free,' replied Amanda, mildly put out that her parents had been scheming behind her back, but at the same time seeing the wisdom in what they were suggesting.

'Oh, don't worry about that darling, I've had a look in The Lady magazine, and there are various agencies that can help, and in terms of the cost, then Rob and I have already agreed we will cover that. It's the least we can do under the circumstances,' replied Monica, smiling over at her husband.

'And in terms of getting someone full time, that brings me nicely onto something else I wanted to raise with you if you have the time. Can you just hang on a minute while I give Will a ring as I said I'd call him when we started to discuss this with you.' Unsure what was happening, or why Will needed to listen in to a discussion about 'nannies', Amanda just sat quietly, staring out of the window pondering her options.

Sitting in the kitchen two hours later, with a glass of wine in her hand, and a completely bemused look on her face, she explained to Damian what Rob and Will, when he came on the video link had suggested, watching his face as he absorbed the enormity of what she was saying.

'So, let me get this right. Rob and Will have been in discussions, unbeknown to either you or Nick, about setting up Will's business in the UK, transferring the whole operation out of Boston, to some premises near here, and they want you to run it full-time,' Damian said, summarising what he believed he had heard.

'Well, not quite. They don't just want me to just run it, they want me to own it, with the two of them as my financial backers, sleeping partners as Rob called them. Will wants to step back and enjoy life, but he isn't ready to sell up just yet. This way, he can still get a return on his investment, without taking any day-to-day interest, leaving him free to spend his time enjoying life with Maria, or playing more golf. Rob invests in new businesses all the time, and has quite a big property portfolio already, so it's apparently right up his street too. He's had a team of people searching for premises locally, similar to what Will has in Boston, but slightly bigger, for the last few weeks and they think they've found somewhere that would be ideal. They believe that with the right IT capability and structure, all the design work could be managed from the UK, with a team of designers that I would need to employ locally. The manufacture could be done either in the US, where they suggest I keep a satellite facility and a small workforce to oversee it, to meet the US orders, and perhaps manufacture some of the items that sell best over there. The new purpose-built facility here would then be the HQ as well as dealing with all the UK and European orders.'

'Wow. And what do you think, and do you have to contribute anything financially to the set-up costs?' Damian asked, but seeing the smile on her face knew it was a rhetorical question.

'I think it's a brilliant idea, but said I wanted to talk to you first, and no, I'm not being asked to fund anything. Rob is backing me, and he assures me its peanuts in the scheme of things, so not to worry. I'm not sure what Will is getting out of it financially, but no doubt that will become clearer if I agree, as the lawyers would need to draw everything up properly.' Seeing the concern on Damian's face she added, 'It will mean me taking on a lot, and it will impact both of us as I'll probably be on the road more, but with the nanny that I've not even told you about yet, I think it could work.'

'What nanny? Where's that idea come from? We've never discussed a nanny,' questioned Damian, a bemused look on his face.

'Oh, I'll tell you about that in a minute, that's another part of their scheming,' she replied quickly, not wanting to veer off her current train of thought. 'But going back to the factory, I even think Nick would be on board, because from what he said last time we spoke, he's ready to head back home. His parents aren't getting any younger and his guilt streak is starting to bite. I think with his business nouse, my absolute genius when it comes to the design side, and two sleeping partners that not only have my back financially, but believe in me professionally, I can't fail!' she replied with an excitement Damian had not seen or heard in years from his wife. 'Once I've spoken to Nick and got my head around it all, and hopefully got his agreement to relocate back to England, because I don't think I can do this without his help, then the only question left will be, where do I sign!' she said, reaching for the bottle and pouring herself another glass of wine. 'Perhaps we should have opened the champagne!' she winked to Damian, 'we've certainly got something to celebrate tonight!'

Chapter 51

'Now are you sure you've got the tickets and the passports?' Rachel asked for perhaps the fourth time that morning, 'your dad will be here shortly to collect us, and I don't want to be on the last minute, or keep him waiting, or miss the train.'

'Will you please stop panicking, Rachel, this isn't the first time I've travelled you know. Relax. Everything's sorted, the passports, the chargers, the credit cards, they're all here, and in terms of your luggage, I'm not sure you could fit much more in that rucksack even if you tried, not to mention those other bags you've left by the door! You do know we're supposed to be travelling light.'

'Ha, ha, very funny. You do know I've got some things in those bags that need to be dropped off with Ben, don't you? I think Monica has bought him new bedding and a few towels for his flat that she wants us to give him when we call in later.'

'Yeah, okay, I'd forgotten,' he conceded, smiling over at her.

Rob was driving them to the railway station to catch the train into London Paddington, and Ben and Jessica were meeting them at the station and taking them back to Ben's flat for the evening before they caught the Eurostar over to Paris the following day. They had decided that they would start their travelling with the European leg that Lucas had intended doing before he returned home, travelling by train between countries until they decided it was time to move on. Being June, it was the best time to see Europe, as the weather was warm, and the schools had not broken up, so it was more reasonable when compared with the price hikes in July and August.

It was also Lucas' opportunity to meet the girl who had stolen his brother's heart. He had seen photos of Jessica and heard Ben waxing lyrically about her, but today would be the first chance for them to meet properly before Lucas and Rachel started travelling. It was funny Lucas thought how he had arrived in England and fallen in love with an American, whilst Ben had lost his heart to a British woman who had travelled to America. Funny how things worked out, but he was pleased the Mason men were doing their bit to support the Anglo-American strong relationship the two countries' leaders always insisted existed.

Since they had made the decision almost two months ago to go travelling, after a drunken night in the pub, with Lucas reminiscing about some of the places he had been to, the adventures he had experienced, it had been a roller coaster of emotions, for Rachel particularly. Coming to the UK nearly twelve months ago had been her adventure of a lifetime, so now to be off again, travelling to more remote places than she had ever imagined, she could not believe her luck. It was not just the fact she was travelling though; it was the fact that she was doing it with Lucas, someone who over such a short period of time, she could no longer imagine ever being without.

Over Thanksgiving, whilst back in Boston for a few days, Rachel had spent most of her time at home with her mum and siblings, enjoying some quality family time or catching up with the friends she had missed whilst living in England, leaving Lucas to spend his time with his dad and Monica. But the more time she spent with her family, almost picking up where she had left off, the more she realised she could not allow her life to fall back into that same routine. As much as she loved her mum and siblings, her life had moved on, even if theirs had not; she was no longer that same innocent girl who had flown into Heathrow, wondering if she had landed on another planet, but now a young woman with her eyes opened, not just to a different sort of life, but importantly to love.

As she had sat cradling a glass of wine that had long since gone warm, listening to Lucas talk, almost dreamily about his travels, describing some of the scrapes he had got into with a passion and excitement that she had never really heard before, she realised that in his mind he was already thinking it was time for a change, his itchy feet were calling out to him. He had been in the same place for almost nine months, working with Damian to protect the business, and whilst he had enjoyed every minute, in his heart he felt that it was perhaps time to move on. The more he spoke, Rachel began to feel nervous, sensing he was building up to the big 'it's not you, it's me' type discussion, with him deciding to pack-up and move on; leaving her behind to mourn the break-up of their relationship. So, when he finished his monologue, after taking a big swig of his beer and said, 'So, what do you think, are you up for it?' you could have almost picked her up off the beer-stained carpet.

'Are you serious? I'd love to travel, but I'm not sure I can afford what you've got in mind. I've got a few savings from working over here, perhaps enough for some flights, but other than that I'd struggle.'

'Don't worry about that. If you're up for it, then I can sort out the rest. What's the point of having a trust fund and not being able to spend it on the woman I love!'

She looked over at him, with her eyes wide open. 'Did you just say what I think you said?' she asked, conscious that although she knew how she felt about him, he had never before said he loved her, and rather than repeat it, he pulled her into his arms, giving her the type of kiss that confirmed everything.

Having made their decision, Rachel was left with the worry about leaving Amanda, especially now there was the extra responsibility with Theo around the house, but having worked for her for nearly a year, she knew that as much as she loved children, a career in childcare was not her destiny. Theo was a lovely little boy, and the girls could be a delight at times, but running around after them, picking up the pieces and filling in the gaps whenever Amanda or Damian needed it, often at short notice, was extremely stressful. No, she would certainly miss them, and would be forever thankful for the opportunity she had been given, but would not be applying for another au pair role in the near future.

Lucas had been less worried about leaving Damian, because although he'd had the time of his life stepping up and running the business, he'd recognised a few weeks previously that now that it was back on a reasonably even keel, the challenges that had attracted him so much in the early days were now behind them. Damian was taking more day-to-day responsibility, as was right, leaving Lucas on occasion twiddling his thumbs and contemplating his future. The whole experience had done nothing to dilute his desire to be an entrepreneur, and if anything had reinforced the concept of running his own business at some stage, but now was not the time for him. He still had some living to do before settling down, but saying all that, it had been a great interlude, and without it who knows where he would be, up some tower or other iconic meeting place with Sonia, living out one of her romantic fantasies? No, he had dodged a bullet there.

'Right, my dad's here,' shouted Lucas as he saw Rob's BMW pull up outside the cottage.

'Okay, I'll be right down,' replied Rachel, 'I'm just checking I've switched everything off and locked all the windows.' 'For the tenth time,' thought Lucas to himself, smiling as Rachel eventually came down the stairs, her denim jacket draped over her arm, and her small tote bag in her hand, but with a faraway look as she scanned the sitting area of the cottage for the last time, capturing the scene before her, tears starting to build in her eyes. This cottage had been her first real home, a place where she not only felt safe, but happy, but more importantly a place where she had found the confidence to live her own life, and most of all, true love. No matter where she travelled in the world, this place would always hold memories she would cherish a lifetime.

'Are you two ready?' asked Rob as he started to carry the bags out to the car. 'I hope you don't mind, but there's a couple of little stowaways in the back seat, who wouldn't let me go without coming too,' he smiled, as Lucas and Rachel noticed Maisie and Alice excitedly waving over at them.

'No, we don't mind. It's great to have a proper send off, and we're going to miss you guys, but as they say, we'll be back!' replied Lucas, locking the front door behind them, handing the keys to Rob, and taking Rachel's hand as he led her to the car and the waiting arms of his nieces.

Their next adventure had started.

Chapter 52

'Come on, guys we've got a show to get on the road, and we're quickly running out of runway,' shouted Nick to the delivery men who were slowly transporting the last of the specialist cutting equipment onto the factory floor, ready for the engineers to install and commission it the following morning. This was the final stage before the machinists would be all set to go. They had installed state of the art equipment, that was streets ahead of some of the old machines Will had been operating with for the last decade or two, with today's hi-tech solution being computer driven to improve quality, but also reduce labour costs.

The IT had all been installed over the previous couple of weeks, managed primarily by Damian, who was throwing himself wholeheartedly behind this new venture his wife was undertaking. With Lucas' help, before he and Rachel had ridden off into the sunset, they had scoped out what would be needed to make the company fit for the twenty first century in terms of technology and communications equipment, to ensure Amanda and her team would have systems that would not only communicate with the States, where a base would remain, and was in fact still operating in parallel under Nick and Amanda's watchful gaze, but with her growing customer and supply base. Over the last twelve months, although their key suppliers were predominantly in the Far East, many more artisan and niche suppliers were emerging from other parts of the world, people that could offer something a little different that would help set their brand apart.

'Good morning, Nick. How we doing?' asked Amanda, carefully carrying two coffees as she walked into the building around nine o'clock on Thursday morning, deftly managing to avoid the delivery drivers and all the packaging they had discarded on the forecourt. She had dropped Maisie and Alice off at school on her way in for their last day before the summer holidays started, each taking a present in for their form teacher as a small thank you for putting up with them all year, after ensuring Theo was settled at home with the new nanny, a nice enough lady the agency had sent on trial three weeks ago, who seemed a little formal; but it was early days, Amanda reassured herself each time she failed to receive a smile from Rose whenever she spoke to her.

'Do you think we'll be ready in time for the opening on Monday, or should I look to postpone it? I could always ring round and delay things, the caterers and the press are the main ones I presume,' she asked seeing the mayhem all around her.

'No, we've still got a couple of days, and we're not planning on starting manufacturing from here until mid-August, so I think we'll be alright. The rest of the building is almost ready, and what's still to be sorted should be done by close of play tomorrow anyway, so I think we're alright,' he replied, smiling over at his new boss as she handed him a coffee.

Nick had been almost as surprised as Amanda when she had contacted him to relay the discussion she'd had with both Will and Rob about the future direction they wanted the business to take. Nick had sensed for some time that Will was grooming Amanda as his successor, but had not assumed any decision would be taken so soon, or whilst Maria was ill, but the more he considered the position Will now found himself in, and the more he realised how much Amanda had proved herself over recent months, without even realising she was being tested, then it all seemed to fit into place.

Whilst he was pleased for her, for a while he considered his own position; where this left his life and his career. He quite liked Boston, but like Canada before it, he had no roots there, so nothing to hold him. He knew that getting another similar role would not be difficult, head-hunters were regularly circling, but he liked working with her, and although fashion was not his first passion, over the last twelve months he had developed a real appreciation for it. Working under the pressures of the last few months particularly, where all hands were on-deck and everyone was forced to multi-task, he had developed skills that he did not know he had. The camaraderie among the team, all pulling together for the greater good of the business, was a quality he had not seen previously, and if nothing else that would be something he would sorely miss when he moved on.

So, when Amanda had made it clear that she wanted him to work alongside her, and preferably relocate to England to be at the heart of the operation, it took him no time to say yes. He had been fretting for some time that his parents were becoming more vulnerable, rattling around in their four-bedroom house in an isolated part of the countryside now that he and his two brothers had moved away, and although he had no intention of moving back in with them, or providing them with the grandchildren they so dearly yearned for, he did want to be closer by to offer support. He might even try to persuade them to move into a similar type of complex to the one Amanda's grandad had moved to, because by all accounts he was having a whale of a time.

'Has Loretta arrived yet? It's just her hire car isn't on the forecourt and I thought she said she'd be in before now,' enquired Amanda as she headed towards the flight of metal stairs to the small office that she had created for herself on the first-floor mezzanine, alongside one for Nick and an adjoining one for Loretta, who had also jumped at the chance to transfer to England for a few months whilst they got everything established. There was nothing and no one keeping her in the States, so why not have a bit of an adventure of her own, was her view.

'Erm, yes, she's here,' said Nick a little sheepishly, avoiding catching Amanda's eye. He was dressed today in an old pair of work jeans, trainers and a faded T-Shirt that was sticking to him given the heat of the sun, that was slowly making its way to the front of the building; but even though he was dressed down, Amanda had to admit he still looked good. 'I gave her a lift in this morning as I was passing hers on my way,' he added, without providing any more detail, or the fact it had put an extra ten miles onto his journey. He did not want to arouse any suspicions in Amanda, or the rest of the team for that matter, keeping whatever was happening between them strictly professional.

Over the last few weeks, before he had left Boston, he and Loretta had become quite close, and although he would not go as far as describing it as a relationship, they had gone out for dinner or a drink on a couple of occasions after work. Nick had always steered clear of having a relationship with a colleague, or in fact anyone within his work environment, customers or clients included, and frankly since the disastrous episode with his wife and her Pilates teacher, had been wary of committing to seeing another woman under any circumstances. His feelings and his male ego had been hurt more than he was prepared to admit, but there was something about Loretta that he found quite appealing, and possibly worth the risk of trying again.

She had flown into Heathrow five days earlier, in plenty of time to ensure the opening event ran smoothly, and was staying in a local B&B five miles away until a flat could be found for her; on the assumption she would be staying for a few months, she needed more space than a bedroom at a B&B could provide. He enjoyed her company and her friendship, she was smart and funny, with a wicked sense of humour when you got to know her; and if in time something developed from that, then so be it, but for the time he was playing his cards close to his chest.

'Good morning, Boss,' Loretta almost sang affectionately at Amanda as she entered the outer office, the boxes of papers couriered over from Boston already neatly stacked against the dividing wall awaiting filing; the desks clear of all rubbish and packaging that had been left there the previous evening when they had unpacked the office furniture; the kettle plugged in, with a row of bright yellow mugs and matching tea, coffee and sugar caddies ready should anyone need a drink, and a pretty vase containing pink carnations sitting proudly on the window ledge.

'Wow, this looks very organised. I'm sure it's not the same office I left yesterday evening. Were you working through the night, or have the fairies paid us a visit?' replied Amanda, astounded at the transformation she'd made. She knew how efficient and organised Loretta could be, but she had truly excelled herself on this occasion. Since joining Will's organisation around nine months ago, she had become an invaluable cog in the system, her ear always to the ground, so someone both Nick and she could rely on to keep them informed whenever the workforce got twitchy for whatever reason.

'Oh, it was nothing. I got Nick to carry the packaging downstairs and out of sight, and the rest just needed a bit of sorting and a quick wipe over. We'll be up and running in no time. I bet you're so excited for Sunday, I know I am,' she assured her with a smile on her face.

As Amanda surveyed the office and looked out of the window to the workshop below, she felt an immense amount of pride, as well as excitement, at what they had all achieved in such a short period of time. It was only three months since Rob and Will had first floated the idea of her running the business, and here they now were, on the cusp of a grand opening, well perhaps not grand, but an opening nevertheless.

Rob and Will had been true to their word in terms of all the financial and legal paperwork, signing everything over to Amanda to enable her to have full control of the decisions at every step of the way. Rob offered to fund the lease of the building for the first two years, or until she felt confident to cover it herself, as well as gifting her a substantial sum of money to kit the factory out with whatever equipment was necessary, using Will's business as a blueprint, but recognising that the world, and more importantly technology had moved on since Will had first set himself up. He had also engaged a business consultant to sit with her and Nick to work through the numbers, getting them comfortable with not only what Will had predicted his turnover and margins to be, but understanding the stock valuations they were taking on from the old premises and the order book they already had. To Nick this was old news and very much his territory, but for Amanda it was important that she fully understood what she was taking on, even if she was going to continue delegating the business side to Nick.

Finally, he had engaged a legal team to ensure the business was established correctly, with the right licences, permits and governance in place, satisfying the reams of red tape that comes with setting up any business, regardless of which side of the Atlantic it was on. He knew the British system was not his forte, so paying for a legal team to be on a retainer for the first two years should anything untoward happen was his way of covering this risk off. In time, Amanda knew she would have to either employ those specialists herself or learn fast, for the last thing she wanted was to fall short on some bureaucratic technicality; but for now, she was just grateful for Rob's support, and guidance, but above all his backing and the immense amount of confidence he had placed in her.

As well as all the logistical challenges associated with the new premises, sourcing the equipment and the IT, along with all the fabrics and accessories they would need once the manufacturing started, recruiting a number of staff across a wide range of skillsets had been a real challenge. Amanda knew what made a good team work, particularly when it came to designers who needed to feel comfortable being able to bounce their ideas off each other, so had deliberately chosen a mix of people with experience and vision, even contacting a couple of the students she had taught who she knew had gone on to graduate in design, believing they could provide the extra spark or element of originality she was looking for.

Finally, the stage was set for her to run her empire, an empire that she would never have dreamed possible only four years ago when she had sat in the classroom teaching her sixth-form pupils the technicalities of art and design. Never in her wildest dreams would she have imagined running her own business, or doing it with such style.

Chapter 53

Monday morning arrived, and with it the forecast of a perfectly warm sunny day, after a weekend that had brought an electric storm, displaying spectacular thunder and lightning, lighting up the skies overhead, followed by a downpouring of rain so heavy, that whilst the gardeners might have been pleased after a summer of drought, was not what everyone wanted. Amanda had lain in bed in the early hours of Sunday morning, unable to sleep as the rain beat against the window frames. She pondered whether the gods were trying to tell her something; forewarning stormy days ahead, perhaps? She had visions of the forecourt of her new factory, that she, Nick and Loretta had finally cleared the day before, now being littered by falling trees, overhead cables and at least six inches underwater after the drains had blocked trying to clear the incessant rain. Her grand opening was clearly going to be a washout in the true meaning of the word.

Before breakfast on Sunday, and unable to settle, she sent Damian over to do an inspection, scared to go herself, too anxious about what she might find, so when he had still not returned over an hour later, she feared the worst. Hearing the car pull into the driveway, she ran to the door.

'So, what's the damage?' she asked. 'You've been ages,' she added, panicking a little as she watched him reach back into the car.

'No damage at all, everything's fine. I just called into the Coffee Pot on the way back and picked up some of your favourite pastries for breakfast, and I got chatting to Gloria. You know how she can talk! She was asking how Rachel was getting on, it seems some of the customers are missing her nearly as much as we are.'

'Oh, thank God for that, I had a vision of it being a complete disaster, and the longer you took the worst my nightmares became,' she sighed, finally relaxing as she took the pastries from him and carried them back into the kitchen where all three children were sitting at the table still in their pyjamas, eating their cereals, completely oblivious to the catastrophe that had just been averted. Theo was comfortably sitting between Maisie and Alice, his eyes going from one to the other as they chattered away, saying little, but taking in every word.

Since the breakthrough they had seen when Ben had first arrived, Theo had very gradually, day-by-day opened up a little more; showing sides of his personality that previously he had kept hidden. Subtle changes in his behaviour became noticeable, and instead of keeping himself separate from the girls, he now followed them around, being rewarded when they included him in whatever game they were playing. He had started to eat a little more, again copying Maisie and Alice, asking for whatever they were having when he was questioned on what he wanted to eat or drink. Bed times were still a challenge as he struggled to be in a room by himself, especially if the lights were switched off, so night lights had been fitted to help keep him calm. Many a morning though, Amanda would find him snuggled-up in bed alongside Alice, very reminiscent of when she was little and had done the same with Maisie. The two girls still shared a bedroom, and no amount of tempting them with new furniture, decorations or anything else would get them to consider having their own rooms. Amanda was reluctant to move a third bed into their room, but was beginning to wonder if that might be a short-term fix, although she was sure there would be pushback from both Damian and Rose to her idea.

Rose, the middle aged and spinster nanny Monica had found through an advert in The Lady magazine was a little stricter with the children than Rachel had been, trying to introduce more discipline and structure into the children's lives, and indirectly Amanda noticed, hers and Damian's too. She had been nannying to twin boys in central London for over ten years, but they had grown to the age where she was no longer required, so had been encouraged by her previous employers to seek another position. One of the attractions of working for Mr and Mrs Reynolds, Rose had thought after having her interview and meeting the children, was the attractive cottage that came with the role, and the chance to move into the quaint Cotswolds village. After living in central London, a quieter life was something she looked forwards to in her late forties, and the prospect of buying a small car and pootling around the countryside, visiting teashops and garden centres on her weekends off, really appealed. It was very much early days, with everyone being perhaps overly polite during the honeymoon period, but Amanda was quietly optimistic it might work out. She certainly needed it to work for the sake of her business, because of all the things that could go wrong, childcare was not the element she was prepared to fail on.

Standing now, in front of her mirror applying the final touches to her make-up and an extra spray of perfume for luck, she started to get a little nervous about the day ahead. She had dressed in a smart pale blue trouser suit, worn over a cream blouse, with a silk scarf loosely tied around her neck, her hair neatly pulled into a stylish clip, allowing small blonde curls to escape of their own accord, softening the look. Her outfit was not quite business attire, but suited the image she was trying to create. After all, their business was leisurewear, so being too formal was not the look she was aiming for, but by the same standard, her trusty jeans and sweat top would not cut it today either.

Clara had arranged for a features editor from her magazine to come to the opening to take some pictures, so looking her best was essential if her photo was to be published for all to see. The interview that would accompany the photos had already been done, at least that was one thing less to worry about, she thought, so other than a few words when she cut the ceremonial ribbon, what could go wrong?

'Right, Damian, kids. I'm off, wish me well,' she announced as she got to the bottom of the stairs. 'I'll see you all in a couple of hours, don't be late, and remember to behave yourselves when you get there as lots of people will be looking at you.' She added kissing each of them in turn.

'Good luck Mummy, we will,' said Maisie speaking on behalf of them all, adding 'you look and smell amazing by the way,' emphasising one of the new words she had picked up recently.

'Yes, mummy you do. And I like that scarf too, can I please borrow it for my dolls?' chirped in Alice.

'Bye-Bye Ammy,' added Theo, waving with the others, using the name he had coined for her. She was unsure if it was his nod to Mummy, or to Amanda, but either way she was happy to go with it.

'Good luck, darling. You'll smash it. We're all behind you, and I for one am very proud of you today,' her husband added, joining the children waving her off as she made her way to the car.

Chapter 54

The grand opening had been scheduled for two thirty in the afternoon, with champagne and canapes being served from one forty-five. A local catering company was supplying all the food and drinks, along with a few waiters and waitresses to work the room and help clear up afterwards, taking all the dirty glasses and plates away with them. Loretta had organised everything to run almost like a military operation, arriving early before nine o'clock that morning to get ahead of the day, with her clip board in hand, ticking off each task as it was completed.

They had invited around a hundred or so guests for the event, including a mixture of friends and family, but also some of their locally based suppliers, the odd UK based stockist, with media representatives from two of the local newspapers, the local radio station, as well as the national fashion magazine that Clara had arranged. It was a good news story, a new start-up offering employment in an area that traditionally struggled for hi-tech jobs, as well as investment that would see knock-on benefits to the surrounding localities.

As it was the summer holidays, Amanda had expected about half of those invited to either not turn up, or cry-off at the last minute, but provided those that mattered were there, then she would be okay. Standing by the door though just after one thirty, her knees began to tremble; what if no-one turns up, she thought to herself, allowing herself a moment's panic?

'All set,' remarked Nick coming to join her by the door, two glasses of champagne in his hand. 'Here, take this, it'll settle your nerves if nothing else,' he said to her smiling, 'Cheers!'

'Cheers to you too, and in case I forget to mention it later, none of this would have been possible without you, so thank-you from the bottom of my heart,' a slight quiver in her voice as she suddenly started to feel emotional.

'Don't start that now; look, your first guests are arriving,' he observed, seeing Clara and Lisa walking across the forecourt, both looking stunning in colourful summer dresses, in Lisa's case teamed with high heels to bring her up to Clara's height.

'Welcome, I might have guessed you two would be first given there's free champagne,' laughed Amanda hugging her two closest friends, and as Lisa took the glass that was being offered to her, Amanda's eyes were drawn to the ring on the third finger of her left hand. 'OMG, what's that! Is it what I think it is?' she asked looking at the two of them, quizzically.

'Yes, and I've got one to match,' added Clara showing Amanda her ring, an identical replica of Lisa's not insignificantly sized diamond solitaire, set in platinum.

'Well, you dark horses. I wasn't expecting that today,' laughed Amanda, suddenly relaxed. 'Congratulations, that's definitely something to celebrate.'

'Well, we weren't expecting it either, come to think of it,' started Lisa, before Clara added, 'No, we'd only popped into Bristol to get a few bits. Lisa wanted some new earrings, to go with an outfit she'd bought, so we called into the jewellers on the high street.'

'Yes,' continued Lisa, happily finishing each other's sentences, 'but when we got in the shop, there was a tray of rings immediately in front of us, all shining brightly. The shop assistant, a polite looking young man, came over and seeing our attention was drawn to the rings, enquired if we were looking for an engagement ring.'

'We both exchanged a glance, and before we knew what was happening, we'd both said yes.'

'Well, as far as romantic gestures and proposals go, that has to be up there with the best,' laughed Amanda, 'no getting down on one knee for either of you then!'

'What are you all laughing at, I hope it's a bit of good gossip,' the dulcet tones of Grandad Tom could be heard behind them. He had ordered a taxi to bring him and Judy to the 'do', not wishing to inconvenience anyone, he said. Amanda had mentioned the event to him a couple of weeks ago in passing, never assuming he would want to attend, but he had jumped at the chance. 'Oh no, I'm not missing out on champagne, or a chance to take my young lady for a flashy day out. Judy would love the chance to get all dolled up and meet the family, and it will give me something to tell the lads all about when we meet up.'

Whilst she had been talking, a couple of suppliers she recognised had come through, so she excused herself and wandered over to talk to them, leaving Lisa and Clara to fill Tom in with their news. They were followed by some of the locals from the village who had been intrigued enough to come along to wish her well, including Gloria from the Coffee Pot who had made a celebration cake for the occasion. By two o'clock more people than Amanda had ever expected were milling around, sipping champagne and nibbling away at the canapes that looked to be going down well, but her nerves had not let her taste yet. Nick, Loretta and she continued circulating, keeping energy levels high and the conversations flowed.

'Ah, don't they look adorable, what beautiful children, and what lovely outfits,' Amanda overheard someone saying behind her, turning to see Maisie, Alice and Theo as they walked in, all holding hands and looking angelic; their faces scrubbed to within an inch of their lives, and wearing the best of next year's children's collection. Amanda had asked for the team over in Boston to run up the clothes as samples for the event. The package containing these, and a few other pieces that Loretta had already placed on tables around the room, had arrived a few days ago, and although she said it herself, they looked amazing.

'Don't you all look beautiful,' said Amanda bending down to receive hugs, 'and you've not scrubbed up too badly either,' she added to Damian, standing proudly behind them.

'Thank you, is everyone here yet?' he asked, noticing there was only about fifteen minutes before the ribbon cutting ceremony was planned to take place.

'There's just Rob and Mum to arrive. I thought they'd be here by now. I hope nothing's held them up,' she replied, starting to get a little concerned, but no sooner had she said that, than a smile from ear-to-ear replaced her frown, and tears came to her eyes as she saw not only Rob and Monica walking through the door, but Ben walking alongside them, holding hands with a very attractive young lady, who could best be described as an English Rose, who she presumed must be Jessica, but best of all, Will walking slowly with Maria on his arm, wearing a smile the size of which matched Amanda's.

Chapter 55

The stage was finally set, the glasses topped up, the cake sitting proudly on the table and the golden ribbon now in position in the doorway, Loretta having quickly fastened it into place once Amanda had given the nod that everyone was there and they could get on with the formalities.

As Amanda cast her eyes around the assembled throng, she allowed herself a quiet moment to reflect on what had brought her to this position, the next phase of the adventure that had become her life. To be here, standing in front of not only her family and friends, but some of the people who had supported her and her family through both the good and bad times over the last four years, was incredible. They had witnessed the highs and lows, and stood firmly besides her throughout, willing her on at every juncture to succeed; never giving up on her, even though sometimes they may have questioned her decisions, or had their doubts about what she intended doing.

She thought back to that awful time when she had received the letter from her dad, still mourning his loss and crying as she read his words, imploring her to seek out her biological father, and follow her heart. He had told her to deal with whatever consequences life threw at her along the way, sensing she was strong enough to do that. Well, she had certainly come a long way since then and weathered some storms. Who could have predicted where that letter would have taken her, or how many lives her actions had affected since then? Ken had been a very wise man indeed.

No one knew what the future held for anyone, the last six months paid testament to that, but looking around the room now, it certainly looked promising. The factory was all ready to go, the enthusiasm to get started evident not only to Amanda, Nick and Loretta, but to the rest of the team, who sensed they were taking the business in a new and exciting direction. Everyone at the facility in Boston had been spoken to, all being given the opportunity to continue with the company if they wanted, and whilst a few had taken the opportunity to find an alternative role, or in fact follow Will's lead and retire, several had opted to stay, ensuring an experienced team was left in the States to deal with that leg of the operation.

Will, since making the decision to properly step back and hand the reins over to her, and in doing so enjoy the benefits of being a sleeping partner, seemed to have had a massive weight lifted off his shoulders. No longer was he juggling the responsibilities of running a successful business, with the demands of caring for Maria, but he was getting on with enjoying his own life. He now had the time and the money to sit back and relax, improving his golf handicap, or spending quality time with Maria, planning holidays and more travel as soon as she received her final clearance from the consultants. The doctors had apparently approved the short trip to England when she had made it clear she had no intention of missing out, on the proviso she did not over-exert herself, and seeing the way Will was constantly checking over at her, pandering to her every need like an attentive servant, there was certainly no risk of that.

Her mum and Rob looked equally happy, having just celebrated their third wedding anniversary; still very much in love, and whilst they would probably always have minor disagreements about where home was for them, they seemed content to split their time between their two bases, always eager to be involved and supportive of whatever their family was doing. Although, Rob had secretly acknowledged to her, forbidding her to tell her mum, that with more of the family now living this side of the Atlantic, the pull back to New England was lessening each year. Ben had not made that position any easier since declaring London as his home for the foreseeable future, and looking at the way he was with Jessica, obviously the pair of them still in the first flushes of their romance, made Amanda smile. She remembered Rob telling her only last week about his own youth, recalling the first time he had set eyes on Carrie, the twins' mum, at a costume party organised by his sister Lily. He knew then that she was the one for him, so had every confidence that if Ben had decided Jessica was his soul mate, then no one had the right to question him otherwise.

Damian was standing just to her left, with the three children, Maisie, Alice and Theo by his side. They were the real stars of the show; their new family unit, the family they were obviously destined to have. To think only twelve months ago, she had been oblivious to Theo's existence, or even the fact her husband had fathered another child by his ex-mistress. The sheer gamut of feelings she had experienced since then. Not only having to deal with Theo's existence, but so soon after the loss of her own son. Her feelings, ranging from anger, to panic, to hurt and despair, even confusion, to eventual acceptance had all been exhausting; not only taking their toll on her, but on her and Damian's relationship. So now, to have come out of the other side not only happy, but virtually unscathed, was nothing short of a miracle.

She smiled as she fingered the heart-shaped gold locket she wore around her neck, presented to her the previous evening by her husband after the children had gone to bed. When she had opened it, she had seen it contained small pictures of each of them.

'We completely missed celebrating our tenth wedding anniversary last year, so I've bought you a small present,' he had said as he had fastened it carefully around her neck, 'I hope you like it.'

'I love it, I love you, and above all I love our little family,' she had replied with tears in her eyes. 'Thank you. It's perfect.'

'Right,' Nick said bringing her out of her reverie, and handing her a pair of scissors, 'I think we had better get this ribbon cut before we run out of champagne. I've just seen your grandad and his lady friend eyeing up another bottle,' he laughed.

'Sounds like a sensible idea, I think I'm ready,' and with more confidence than she really felt, she moved towards the podium, and took a deep breath.

'Ladies and Gentlemen, welcome to our grand opening…' but before she had time to continue with the short speech she had prepared, the assembled group burst into applause and the cameras started to flash.

At that point, Amanda knew everything was going to be alright, she had finally found her happy place, her forever home, right here just where she was, among the people who loved her.

Looking skywards she offered a silent prayer. 'Hope you're proud of me today Dad.'

The End

Printed in Great Britain
by Amazon

12849382R00174